THE LESSONS WE LEARN

BALANCE OF POWER

BOOK 4

BERLIN WICK

A NOTE TO THE READER

Our beautiful FMC is nonverbal. I talked to many different people and tried different ways to represent her external dialogue in a way that best represents ASL speakers. I found that the CMOS recommendation of American Sign Language best acknowledged this. In this book you'll find her external dialogue shown in quotations <u>and</u> Italics. If another character is signing with her, you'll see their external dialogue also in quotations and Italics.

My goal was to do my best to represent a voice for ASL speakers, as well as allow the reader to easily understand the flow and avoid getting taken away from the story.

Dane, Ethan and Hannah's story is a fun, spicy and emotional ride. There is no SA between the MC's or externally between other characters. However, there are some triggers that you may need to be aware of. To avoid spoilers I post them **here on my website.** If you don't have any triggers, read on and enjoy my friend!

PLAYLIST

• Cooped Up/Return of the Mack
Post Malone, Mark Morrison & Sickick

• Drip Off
Austin Giorgio

• Lonely Together
Sickick, Vikkstar & Aloe Blacc

• Symmetry (feat. Karen Aujla)
Ed Sheeran

• Get Down Saturday Night
Oliver Cheatham

• Poison Ivy
Hemi Moore

• Mystical Magical
Benson Boone

• 12 to 12
Sombr

• I Am Not Okay
Jellyroll

• Bad Dreams
Teddy Swims

• Regrets
Stevie Howie

• Hot Blooded
New Constellations

• Secrets
OneRepublic

• Savage
Alexiane

• Latch (feat. Sam Smith)
Disclosure

• Don't You Worry Child
Swedish House Mafia

• Dandelions
Ruth B.

LISTEN HERE ON SPOTIFY

DEDICATION

*For the free spirits that crave adventure and the Type-A personalities
they drive crazy.*

*And to the dandelion dreamers
May all your wishes come true.*

1

DANE

Ralph Waldo Emerson once said *"Happiness is not a destination, it's a journey."* But I doubt his destination was the best glory hole in Paris.

Although my journey here wasn't bad either.

Three weeks ago, I flew to Rome and backpacked my way north to Florence, then Milan before stopping in Switzerland for a few days.

I performed a quick game of eeny, meeny, miny, moe when deciding if I was going to head here or Munich but cheated when 'moe' landed on Munich because I've been anxious to come back to Paris to visit *Avec Plaisir*. A full service sex club equipped with the best glory holes a man can find.

As they say, Paris *is* the city of love.

So I packed my bag, got on a train, and here I am enjoying a late night stroll from my hostel to the club.

It's the perfect warm summer night in good ole' Paree. I've been here more times than I can count. Hell, I travel more days out of the year than I am home, but this is exactly how I've lived my life for the last ten years and I've loved every second of it.

After graduating college—Summa Cum Laude—with a

double masters and nine figures in my bank account, I set off to see the world and still have yet to settle down. I guess that was the biggest benefit of licensing the AI code that I created to the biggest tech company in the world.

Some people do drugs because they're bored in their dorm. I got bored enough to create a program that no one in the world had ever seen.

It was the first smart code of its kind and it's the base of multiple artificial intelligence platforms that I'm paid more royalties on than I could ever need. I'm not complaining, but if I would have known what AI would develop into I probably never would have created it.

Even though someone else would have.

My idea behind it was to help people so it can be utilized as a tool. However, modern day use of it is replacing real life experience, understanding, common sense, and most importantly human interaction.

Nowadays, it's used more for fraud than a tool to help guide humans.

I may have not created the code to help people defraud others, but my AI platform surely started a revolution, knowing people could do a lot more with basic code than we ever imagined.

Guilt blankets me daily, even with the Foundations I've created to help build awareness and help others. As each year passes, the technology gets better, outsmarting the most logical people.

In any case, I ended up with more money than I know what to do with, a piece of paper affording me any job I wanted, and a desperate desire to live simply while traveling the world with no obligations.

Since money was of no concern, I chose the latter. I've been to every continent, including Antarctica on a boat that rivaled the size of some hostels I've stayed in. I can say with profound veraciousness, I thought I was going to die on that tiny boat.

How did I end up on the most remote continent with miles of glaciers and nothing but penguins, you ask? Because someone I once met said, *a true world traveler will be able to claim they have been to Antarctica.* Well, naturally I took that as a challenge and my always-up-for-anything character trait clearly had a death wish to die of seasickness and hypothermia with a hefty side of boredom.

Needless to say, it was an *adventure* all right. Not one I'll ever repeat, thank you very much.

So now, I travel to my most beloved places as often as I can. Europe, Japan, and back *home*, which I consider to be wherever my friends are.

Recently, they have all moved to the Pacific Northwest, in or around the Seattle area. Well, Jake, Hudson and Seamus have because they have all settled down with their significant others. Kobi and I are still galavanting around the world. Except mine is for pleasure and Kobi's is for business.

Although, I think Kobi is getting tired of all of the travel.

I can't say I blame him. Lately, I've felt the need for stability and routine—something I've never needed or wanted—and I have no idea why. I suppose my ripe old age of twenty-eight is catching up with me, or maybe it's watching my closest friends settle down or *maybe* I'm going through a midlife crisis, which would be fucking terrible.

There hasn't been a moment in my life that I've been stagnant or forced to stay in one place for an extended period of time. As odd as it may be, I think the excessive freedom has put me in a slump.

Which is why when a good friend of mine, the Dean of Polytech University in Seattle—the same city all my friends currently reside in—asked me to teach an MBA course in the fall, I took it. I'm far from qualified, but he was looking for someone who had a name and fresh energy with life experience to motivate the students in more ways than just academically in a classroom.

I figured I'll teach there for the semester, maybe two, get this strange desire to be grounded out of my system, then throw a dart at a map and get back on the road.

I round the corner where the club is located and scan the parking lot. It's full, which is great for me tonight and I'm blanketed with anticipation.

As I take a step toward the building my cell phone pings.

Kobi: I'll be in Paris tomorrow. Will you still be there or are you heading to Antarctica to spend time with George?

I knew it.

I knew I never should have told my so-called friends about my Antarctica experience.

Emperor penguins are not aggressive, they said. *It'll be fun*, they said.

Yeah, it's fun until a baby penguin of the pack gets curious about the six foot human in their territory and waddles at your feet. Then said human picks up and pets the cute, adorable baby penguin—that I lovingly named George—and proceeds to get the wrath of hundreds of angry penguins.

Of course, a video of me running from a herd of penguins, pecking and flapping their ungodly sized wings at me, spread like wildfire and I haven't heard the end of it since.

Dane: Did you know emperor penguins are like three fucking feet tall? Literally half my size! It was the most terrifying moment of my life.

Kobi: More terrifying than when that WWE wrestler threw you over her shoulder and tried to take you back to her hotel room?

Dane: …

Kobi: That's what I thought. Where are you staying?

Dane: A hostel in Left Bank.

Kobi: You and those damn hostels. You can literally afford to buy the Ritz. Why do you always stay in those? 😬

Dane: Hotels are borrrrringg. Hostels are wild and unpredictable. You should try it sometime.

Kobi: Not a chance in hell. See you tomorrow.

"You have no idea what you're missing," I singsong outloud to myself as I pocket my cell phone and walk into *Avec Plaisir*.

2

DANE

The old century French Gothic building is just as stunning inside as it is on the outside. The grand entrance is tall as it is wide. The skeletal framework of the arches in the ceiling are highlighted by dramatic uplighting from the corners of vertical pillars.

The moment you walk in, you instantly feel transported to a completely different era. One of classic elegance and timeless beauty. But I know the truth of what lies behind those hidden lobby doors.

"Dane?" I glance over to where I heard my name.

"Juliette!" I say with a bit too much excitement and my words echo off the cement pillars and granite floor. Stepping toward her, she smiles as I lean down pecking her with a kiss on each cheek.

Juliette has been the manager of *Avec Plaisir* since it opened four years ago. I came for their opening night celebration, but so did half of the LGBTQ+ community in Paris. Needless to say it was wild and a tad out of control. Parisian police couldn't control the crowd and a man with more threats than wit came barging through the doors, grabbed Juliette and held her at gunpoint.

With more adrenaline coursing through my body than logic, I tackled him and held him to the ground until the police could restrain him.

Don't dig too much into my heroic actions. I am no hero.

I just act first and think of the consequences later.

I have a genius level IQ, with the instinctual behavior of a jellyfish, and the emotional intelligence of a baby panda.

But, from that point on, Juliette has always given me a bit of special treatment.

"It's been a long time. How have you been?" she asks.

"I've been good. Traveling, causing trouble," I wiggle my eyebrows, "you know, the usual. How about you? How's Tom?"

She holds up her left hand, the diamond on her ring finger shining just as bright as her beaming smile.

"Oh no, not you too." I roll my eyes with a smile and she smacks my chest. "I'm kidding! Congratulations, I'm so happy for you guys."

She's giddy with excitement as she tells me how he proposed and a foreign sensation forms around my chest that feels like a vise around my ribcage.

This is the third, or maybe fourth, time this has happened in the past couple of months. The sheer panic that blankets me when someone I know gets married, engaged, or announces they're having a baby. A brief feeling of sadness and jealousy rakes through me before an overwhelming feeling of anxiety comes barging in like a fucking bull in a china shop.

I place the palm of my hand over my chest and rub at the breastbone.

What. The. Fuck.

I don't want to settle down. So, why does my mind reel straight in that direction while my body completely malfunctions?

Naturally my lungs expand attempting to pull in air and I force myself to breath out slowly and heavily.

"Oh gosh, you don't want to hear all this. I'm so sorry—"

"No, no, that's not it at all," I reply urgently, "I just walked here and it was a long trip today." I plaster a wide smile on my face and lie, because I have no idea how to explain the foreign feelings coursing through my body.

She appraises me deeply before a closed-mouth smile graces her lips. I know she suspects something but, thankfully, she doesn't show it nor does she push.

"Well then, let's get you relaxed, shall we?" She rounds the lobby barrier to the computer that sits in the middle of a high table, punching a few keys before continuing. "We were at capacity earlier but I know some other patrons have already left." Immediately transitioning from my friend to the erotica concierge she is. "So, what's your pleasure tonight, good sir?"

3

DANE

The dim, ambient lighting instantly relaxes me as I make my way down the hallway toward the glory holes. The smell of sex and arousal is in the air but not in the grotesque seep-into-your-nostrils way. It's clean and subtle. Just enough to look forward to the anticipation of what's to come.

I've been to *Avec Plaisir* many times before. As vast as the options are for what you're seeking, I always end up here because the prospect of the unknown is unlike any adrenaline rush I've experienced.

Glory holes get a bad rap. In most cases they are run down *arcades* in cheap buildings, located in crappy areas. But this one is far from that.

Not only do all the members need to present updated test results prior to playing here, but the club is exceptionally clean as well.

There are five rooms that line each side of the wall. I typically choose one of the rooms on the end as opposed to the ones in the middle. The center rooms have a hole on both sides, the end rooms only have one. As much as I enjoy three-somes—especially with a male-female dynamic—when it comes to this, I like to hyperfocus on only one dick, along with my own of course.

I glance above the doors looking for the signature green light for a vacant room. I rub my palms together with a smirk on my face when I see the green light inviting me to the corner cube. The room next to it is lit up in stoplight red, noting it's taken, so hopefully I don't have to wait long.

Gripping the brass handle, I open the door and step through, locking it behind me. The light above transitions from vacant to occupied and the reddish hue blankets the small room creating a sexy ambiance that's an instant turn on for me. There's just something about the color red and dim lighting.

With one hand, I unbuckle my belt and pull on the button, splaying open my denim jeans as my right hand presses on the LED screen to search for a video to watch. I can already feel my pulse begin to race with excitement as I glance down at the hole and see flickers of light coming through from the movie he's put on.

The distant sounds of high pitched moans tell me he's chosen a video with a woman in it, so he's either bisexual or lying to himself that he's gay. That makes my pulse race even more. There's nothing sexier, or more exhilarating, than experimenting with a bi-curious man who wants to explore his sexuality.

To be relatable, I click on an orgy video so the audio is a mix of female moans and males groaning, along with the signature slapping of skin on skin and that sexy slurping that happens with messy blowjobs.

Blood rushes between my legs with the sight and sounds, making my cock grow dense and hard.

Kicking off my shoes, I pull down my pants and move the chair closer to the hole in the wall. As I sit down and lean back I side-eye a glance inside the hole. A silhouette of a man sits tense and rigid, unlike my slouched, comfortable posture and I can tell, this is probably his first time here.

I can't help the smirk that crosses my lips because fucking hell, bi-curious men just do something to me. I love watching them come undone for the first time with a man after holding back for so long. My cock hardens even further at the thought and I wrap two fingers around the rim of the hole in the wall between us, telling him I'm interested.

His head makes a sharp turn in my direction then he stands abruptly, his chair falling back making a loud thud against the back wall.

Jesus, my fingers might as well have been a goddamn scorpion tail by his reaction.

Okay, this is going to be interesting.

I don't want to intimidate him and I definitely don't want to scare him off. So, instead of dipping my hand further into the hole, I pull it back and place my chair closer to the opening, in a position where I think he can see me stroking myself.

The TV screen is bright enough with the red undertones to see me wrap my fingers around my stiff cock. I squeeze at the base and begin to stroke it slowly, and to give him a little more encouragement, I moan, "Mmmmm, fuck."

I tip my head back, sneaking a side-eye view through the hole again, seeing his shadow appear in front of it.

Internally, I high five myself, but keep stroking my cock in the same painfully, pleasurable rhythm so I don't do anything that might make him change his mind.

"Fuck, this feels good," I say, loud enough that I know he can hear.

His body shifts, shining more light into my side and I fear that he's stepping away. A moment later I hear the dragging of the chair legs against the ground as his body blocks the excess light and I know he's back watching me again, giving me the adrenaline boost I love from this.

I smile at the thought because I haven't felt this excited in a long time.

I'm jealous of the high he must be riding. Battling the arousal and anticipation, the anxiety and excitement.

I tug a little harder, fisting the tip of my cock that glistens with pre-cum and use it to coat my shaft, moaning even more.

Closing my eyes and continuing my pace, I imagine all the things he's probably dreaming of doing to me. Everything that he's held himself back from and the internal battle of finally letting go.

"Umpf, fuck," an unintelligible grunt falls from my lips as my eyes burst open to see his hand gripping the base of my cock. His arm is pushed all the way through my side and his fingers are curling into my bare skin, holding me, frozen in place.

My hands still as my mouth falls open and I steady my breath.

Letting go of my cock, it falls forward, and the pre-cum laced tip bounces against my abs throbbing with its own powerful pulse.

His hand is tight and tense at the base. A deep scar in the shape of a checkmark crosses over the top of it. It starts from the base of his thumb, to the corner of his wrist, then drags all the way up to the middle of his pinky.

The olive tone of his skin contrasts harshly against the alabaster scarring. Scars like that have a story. I want to reach out and touch it, trace it with my fingers but my body is stalled, still shocked that he's touching me.

Instead I inspect the scar and stare at his hand, it's trembling but firm. The anxiety of his internal battle is palpable before he finally gives in, wrapping his thick figures around the shaft and tugs upward.

"Oh, fuuccck," I hiss through my teeth.

My hands fly to the sides of the chair as I grip on for dear life.

Jesus Christ, the man's got a kung fu grasp on my cock. I'm unsure if that's how he likes it or if his nerves are really taking over.

I'm all for getting roughed up a bit. I tend to be a switch with both males and females, taking control when I need it and giving it up when I want, but the way he's treating my cock is coming from a place of anger, like he's hating himself for wanting it.

Clenching my teeth as I suck in some much needed air, I shift my hips and place my hand on his forearm. He stiffens instantly and attempts to pull back but I wrap my fingers around his wrist, gently holding him in place and use my other hand to reach forward and grab the bottle of lube from the shelving next to the TV.

Flipping it open, I drip the cool liquid over my cock before pulling his wrist closer to me. There's a brief pause in his shaky hand before his fingers wrap back around my slick shaft and I guide his wrist up and down at a medium pace. He's a quick study and easily takes that in, so when I let go he's moving at the pace of perfection with a flawless grip on my cock.

"Oh, fuck, that's good," my voice echoes between us. My body pushes forward with his jerking and it's been too long, because I'm already too close, but I don't want him to stop.

Squeezing my eyes shut, I think of being chased by hundreds of emperor penguins, my fifth grade science teacher Mrs. Dankworth, who always had something stuck in her teeth with breath that smelled like dead rats and hair that looked like a two-hundred-year-old bird's nest.

Even with those frightening thoughts, I'm ripped away and thrown back into this moment as his palm circles around the tip, rotating over the thinned crown of my achingly hard cock, then back down the length. Pressing his palm at the base, his fingers wrap around my balls, giving them a gentle nudge. They begin to tighten at the attention and tingles build at the base of my spine.

"Oh, Fuck," I spit out with worry laced in my tone. "That's gonna make me come," I confess. I attempt to sit up and change my position to take back some power, but his hand flies to my chest, pushing me back further so I'm leaning in the chair, then his exquisite, scarred hand returns to my cock giving it the exact attention it needs.

His fingers squeeze hard at the base, stroking up, circling over the tip then back down as his fingers wrap around my tight sack. He repeats that motion, over and over and over. My leg trembles as I try to hold back. My eyes bounce from his hand to the wall, wishing for a glance of the man who's making my entire body ride a high like I've never felt from just a fucking handjob.

I move my hand, wanting to place it over his so I can fall over the edge with some control but hold back and dig my fingers into the flesh of my thighs, gritting my teeth together to hold back my unruly groans.

But it's fucking useless.

"Let go if you don't want me to come all over your hand," I manage to spit out, impressed with my level of consideration in giving him a warning.

A very clear, deep moan is heard from his side of the wall before he lets out a drawn out, measured breath. Unexpectedly, he keeps pumping that perfect goddamn hand over my rock hard cock and I lose all control.

My abs clench and toes curl as my balls pull up, tightening almost painfully before I groan. "Fuck, I'm coming."

I explode with a roar, pumping my hips into his hand, keeping the perfect rhythm through my climax. Ropes of my white, hot cum pulse out of my cock, dripping over his hand and down my shaft.

"Goddamn, that was good," I admit, as my entire body melts into the chair.

Every nerve ending in my body is alive and I feel like I'm floating. I chuckle out a euphoric breath as I come back from whatever dimension he sent me to. I glance down, reaching for his hand but it's gone.

There's a moment of panic as I fall to my knees peering into the hole. The light from his TV is gone, just a faint deep red hue remains. It's hard to see his silhouette until his arm crosses my line of sight and his hand wraps around the door handle to leave.

"Wait," I spit out. "Don't go."

There's a long pause, both of us stalled in our spots.

Please don't leave.

I realize I may have said that out loud, but at this point I don't care if I sound like I'm begging. I audibly swallow because for some unknown reason I feel nervous. For him? For myself? I have no idea.

"I want to make this good for you," I confess because that much I know is true.

My breath is held hostage in my throat as his body remains completely still. Finally, his chest lifts and he takes in a commanding breath before slowly exhaling.

His body visibly relaxes. His shoulders slouch and his hand falls from the door handle.

Fuck. Yes.

His shadow stands completely still as his trembling hands fumble with his belt buckle. He lets out another heavy breath and if I were to guess, he's scolding himself right now, and I hate that for him. I want to say something, comfort him, make him feel better about this but I also don't want that to send him running.

Instead, he surprises me when his pants fall to his ankles and he turns, facing the hole.

He palms his engorged cock, stroking it in front of me, sans all nerves, and the confidence is so fucking sexy.

That's a beautiful cock.

He chuckles and I realize I spoke out loud again.

But I care less about that and more about him. I want to make him feel good. My body hums with excitement and I find myself desperate for him.

With another shocking move, he steps forward, pushing his cock through the hole, forcing me to lean back to accommodate the size. It's just inches from my face and it's just as gorgeous close up.

On instinct my eyes glance up as if I can see his face, because fuck I wish I could. Instead, all I see are the metal bars that cross the top of the wooden panel and a rhythmic thud against the wall and I realize he's hitting his forehead against it.

This man is literally beating himself up for this.

I have no idea what internal battle he's facing, but I have every intention of sucking every ounce of those self-deprecating thoughts from every corner of his body through this beautiful appendage of his.

"Grip onto the handle bars. You're going to need them," I tell him, as I wrap my fingers around the length of his cock, pulling him gently so he's flush against his side of the wall.

I lick the salty liquid bead at the tip before I wrap my lips around the crown and push forward, taking him all the way down my throat.

His body shutters and I hold him there before pulling back and repeating.

"Oh, fucccckkk!" Another thud sounds, as his head bangs against the wall with a long hiss and more moaning, and goddamn, it's everything.

I moan around his cock, the vibration granting me another shutter and more profanities on the other side of the wall.

"Fuck. Goddamn it," he moans more and, Jesus, this man is

so verbal. I love every bit of it. "Mmmm, so good. Fuck, that's good," he whispers as he repeats in different variations, and I have to admit, it's giving my ego a massive boost.

I keep going at this pace, stopping urgently to edge him, then continue before he can pull away. He groans in both need and frustration and I can't help but smile around his gorgeous cock as I press it further down my throat.

The sounds he's making are like a drug and all I can think about is making sure I catch him before he leaves so we can do this in person, in a room, all fucking night long.

"Oh, Fuck. Fuck, I'm close," I hear him spit out as he frantically taps the wall. I smile even wider at the fact that he's done his homework and knows the etiquette, but I don't give a fuck about getting a warning.

I. Want. Everything.

Curling my hand around his shaft, I wrap my lips over the crown, flatten my tongue behind the length, and push my head forward until the tip breaches the back of my throat again. Breathing through my nose, I swallow, tightening around the thick crown and he moans, still frantically tapping on the wall.

"Mmmm, fuck, fuccccck." His tone is dripping with so much lust and anger. "I'm...I'm coming," he stutters through a heavy breath.

A hot burst of salty liquid blankets my mouth and I moan with every pulse.

Pulling out, I lick and suck, cleaning every ounce of what he gave me with so much pride. Not because I pleased him but because I love this experience for him and I hope it was good enough to stop hating himself.

Pulling further away, I throw my head back and smile, satiated and happy.

That was unbelievable.

Glancing down at myself, I'm still naked and dirty from my

orgasm earlier and chuckle. I reach over, grabbing a towel from the shelf to wipe myself off.

"Well, I can honestly tell you that was the best handjob I've ever had in my life." You can hear the smile in my words with my confession. There's no response, not that I expected one, but it's eerily silent so I look up and glance through the hole to make sure he's not berating himself.

A burst of cool air hits my skin as I peer through and my face falls. His door is wide open, a green hue now lighting the empty space.

4

DANE

I've never hated the color green more than I do now. Seeing that color drenching the room after feeling so high makes me see red. And not the red I wanted.

I raced out of the building, frantically looked around the parking lot and found it to be empty and desolate. I poked around a bit, peered into some of the cars and finally left feeling pissed and frustrated.

I know exactly what a glory hole is for. Anonymity at its finest—to literally and physically hold the skeletons in your closet, but for whatever stupid reason I didn't want to stop with him.

As I walk back to the hostel, I scold myself. I should have withheld an orgasm from him, forced him to give me his name and number. He probably would have just left, but fuck I hate how I feel right now.

I've never left feeling unsatisfied or wanting more. That's not what the club is for. The purpose is to get off, enjoy yourself, and leave. Something I've always wanted and reveled in, so why can't I get over this?

Entering through the hostel lobby I wave at Sally, who

graciously checked me in earlier. She glances in my direction and I smile, contradicting my current frustration, then turn toward the hallway and take the stairs two at a time to the second floor where the rooms are.

This hostel has two large rooms with eight beds each and two separate bathrooms. There was a group of four checking out earlier when I got here but no one else had checked in yet.

Using my room key, I scan it over the reader and it buzzes with a green light, unlocking the door.

Every hostel is completely different. I love this one specifically because of the square footage they provide in the bedrooms. A majority of them have very minimal space since most of the people renting them are just looking for a place to sleep for a night. So, when I found this one I was pleasantly surprised and immediately in love.

Bunk beds line the brick walls that are evenly placed between the windows. The beds are immaculate every time I've been here and the soft linen scent gives you a sense of comfort that most of the overnight rooms don't have.

Along with all of that, there's a table in the middle of the room surrounded by bean bag chairs and a small kitchenette in the corner where you can heat up your food.

I glance around the room as I walk into it, completely empty and eerily quiet. It's the first time I think I've ever been inside one without anyone else in it.

My heart does that weird thing it's been doing, sinking to the bottom of my stomach and I expand my chest as I take in a deep breath.

I've always enjoyed and wanted—hell, admittedly needed —the company of others. I meet new people every time I travel and most often end up traveling with them until our time runs out and I meet another person or group to spend time with. It's how I've spent my adult life traveling. Hell, my entire adult life in general has been spent this way.

This is one of the reasons why I love hostels so much, I'm never alone and there's always something new and exciting.

So, being here in the silence of a mammoth room with no one else overwhelms me with a loneliness that I don't often feel, something that's never bothered me until recently.

I can't believe I'm saying this to myself, but I'm actually looking forward to spending an extended amount of time in Seattle, near my friends. But for now, I have a month of free time to explore and go anywhere I want. I need to get my head on straight and enjoy my nomad lifestyle while I have it.

Taking my backpack out of my locker, I toss it onto a bottom bunk I chose for myself and unzip the top.

Pulling out a loose tank top and cotton grey sweatpants, I glance around the room again. I tilt my head at the door, as if looking at it harder would help me hear better, and it's still remarkably quiet. It's close to midnight so the chances of someone coming are possible since people land in hostels at all hours of the day and night, but rare.

I grab my clothes and put my bag back in my locker, then head to the bathroom down the hall. There's nothing elegant about showering in a shared bathroom and typically you have to be so quick you hardly feel like you're clean.

I take a few extra minutes and allow the warm water to snake over my body, lathering myself up as I think about the events from tonight.

Normally, it wouldn't bother me, but thinking about him leaving so suddenly grates on my nerves.

I have a quick thought to ask Juliette, see if I can dig further and get some information on him, but think better of it.

That's called stalking, psycho.

I palm my face, giving myself a disappointed chuckle, then slam down on the faucet turning off the water.

Kobi will be here tomorrow and at least my mind and time will be preoccupied.

The steam bellows around me as I wrap a thin towel around my waist. The mirror is completely fogged up, signaling I probably stayed in here longer than I thought and still no one knocked so the place must really be vacant tonight.

I swipe my hand across the mirror, wiping away the thin layer of condensation. I run a small hand towel along my chest and arms, wiping the excess droplets, while shaking out my damp hair. It's still drenched and with the dim lighting in the bathroom it appears to be a deep shade of chestnut brown when really it's more like caramel colored champagne.

Running my hand through my short beard, it's a little bit more wild than usual, but I enjoy letting it naturally do its thing rather than grooming it nonstop. When I start teaching in the fall I plan to either shave it or at least trim it daily. Maybe.

Normally I would dress and not walk out in just a towel, but fuck it.

I scoop my clothes up into my arms and open the door. The crisp air hits my skin as I pad my damp feet down the hallway to my room. Walking into the room, I toss my clothes back on the bed and rip the terry cloth from my body, feeling that cool air hit everywhere.

I exhale deeply as I round my neck in circles and twist my body from side to side. I love air drying, but hardly ever get to do it so this is a bit of a treat.

Wrapping the towel around my shoulders I dip my head to the side, rubbing the damp cotton into my hair to prevent the drippage coming from the tips.

"Ahem," someone clears their throat and I startle, jumping around as I rip the towel off my neckline and hold it in front of me.

A man, maybe in his mid-twenties, sits on the bed across from me. His dark eyes appear lighter than they are with as wide as they are. The sides of his head are neatly trimmed, matching the floppy but styled hair that lays in symmetrical waves on the top.

His jeans look the perfect shade of organized and his shirt doesn't appear to have a wrinkle in it.

He's clean cut, put together, and not naked like me.

"Holy shit. I am so fucking sorry." My voice is genuine, as I hold the towel in front of my body, discreetly wrapping it around myself. "I really thought no one was here and I was taking full advantage of the privacy."

His eyes are trained directly at my now covered dick as if he was staring at my ass before I turned around. He quickly blinks, turning away. "It's no problem, I would have probably done the same thing." Then an awkward but kind smile crosses his face as he shifts his eyes toward me and...wow.

Do they make jaw implants for men?

A sharp jawline peppered with mouthwatering facial hair, a thousand-watt smile, and a tan pigment decorates his skin, making me wonder if that's due to days of backpacking or his natural lickable tone. His eyes are dark, with a tough exterior like he's been through more than he should have for his age yet there's a kindness in the slight squint of them.

Subjectively, he's *exactly* my type.

I run a hand through my damp, messy hair, taken aback for a moment before I compose myself.

What has gotten into me lately? My normally fun, playful, wild self who's usually the life of the party is totally... completely...entirely... *Fuck.* I stutter through trying to describe myself inside my own brain.

"Hey." I step forward using my left hand to grip the hem of my towel, returning my own million-dollar smile as I reach my other hand out. "I'm Dane."

He stands, sliding his hand into mine. "Ethan." He squeezes my palm with the perfect mix of dom-sub energy and I wonder if he's a switch like me.

I'm usually quite good at judging people, except I can't even trust my own actions or feelings right now.

My eyes peer down to where our hands meet and my smile falls as all the blood drains from my body.

A scar.

The scar.

The exact same bumpy scar crosses along the top of his hand forming a distinct checkmark from the base of his thumb all the way to his pinky finger.

Some people see scars and view them as a disfigurement. They're unable to hide the disgust in their face when they see someone with flawed skin. But I love tracing the lines, inspecting each and every rope and divot. It's like they all have their own personal story and whatever this one is, must have been pretty intense.

I tilt our palms as my eyes trail along the ridges of the marred skin, reconfirming my discovery then my eyes immediately bounce back up to his.

There's a slight squint in his eyes as he returns a confused gaze and I realize he's suspicious of my reaction and not of me.

I impress myself for ignoring the reaction to immediately pull this man into my body and kiss the hell out of him. Instead, I'm going to play this so goddamn cool, like I didn't just hit the fucking serendipity jackpot.

Impressing myself further by filtering my usually unfiltered responses, I bite my tongue and reply coolly with, "Awesome to meet you, man."

"You too," he replies as he drops my hand and I hate it. Instead, he runs that gorgeous hand through his hair and I salivate as I conjure up all the ways I want it to run over my body.

"American?" I ask, because he has no accent and I have an uncanny ability to pretty much guess where someone is from just based on their voice and fashion alone.

A side effect of being a nomad, I guess.

"Yeah, we started in Portugal, then Spain, now here," he replies, using the word 'we' like he didn't just jab me with a hot poker with his words.

"We?" I turn away to hide my expression and grab the T-shirt off my bed.

We can mean so many things. We, my friend. We, my mom. We, my brother.

"Oh hey," he says, so I turn around but I realize immediately he was addressing another person.

Jesus, they're both like stealthy little ninjas.

A jaw-dropping gorgeous woman steps up next to him. She's only a couple inches shorter than him with luscious, dark chocolate brown hair and eyes the color of the Caribbean. As she turns my way, my eyes immediately flicker down to her neckline seeing a scar about twice as long as the one on Ethan's hand. It crosses over her jawline and down the column of her throat, landing at the tip of her collarbone. It's deep and bumpy, but she doesn't try to cover it up.

"Hannah, this is Dane. Dane, this is my girlfriend, Hannah," he introduces us as she quietly reaches out her hand with a smile that shines through those gorgeous ocean eyes.

My eyes flit between her and Ethan, then back down at the scar on his hand.

There's no way this *isn't* the same guy from the club. But, where was she tonight if he was at the club? The idea he left her wandering the streets of Paris alone bothers me. Did she know where he was?

A cargo train full of thoughts runs through my mind as I stare at his hand.

His fingers twitch, pulling me out of my trance. Avoiding his eye contact, I reach out my hand and clasp it in hers mirroring her smile.

"She's nonverbal," he adds, and my eyes flicker between the both of them again, then their scars and back to his face. "She can hear you, but you'll want to try and ask close-ended questions to make it easier, or she can respond with her notes app or pad."

I pause for a minute as I release her hand, taking in the information. Still curious as to where both of their scars came from and why he was at the club tonight.

It's not my business.

I try to remind myself over and over again but I'm suddenly feeling pissed and really fucking irritated. Did he send her off somewhere so he can get his rocks off at a glory hole? Does he do that often? Is he a cheater?

My dad was a serial cheater and I hate what it did to my mother.

Okay, I'm jumping to conclusions. Maybe he didn't cheat, maybe she knows. But...maybe...I shake my thoughts away. It doesn't matter. It's not my business.

But it is.

I had his cock in my mouth tonight, his cum down my throat and I wanted more. I was dying for more.

Fuck it.

I'm going to dig. Starting with their scars.

Giving her my friendliest smile, I say, "It must be a blessing not to have to talk to some people, huh?" She smiles back, returning an adorable nod. I wink at her before glancing back at him.

"So...what happened?"

5

ETHAN

Dane's question comes out harsh and a little aggressive compared to the way he talked to Hannah.

In fact, his body language toward me changed completely the moment she walked in. Earlier, he was completely naked, nothing but a paper-thin terrycloth towel and lingering water droplets decorated his body.

Oh, and that tattoo that wrapped around his shoulder blade.

A dandelion with a curved stem and a sphere of delicate fluff, half of the puffy florets were blowing off, as if currently floating in the wind. It was easy to spot because he had no other tattoos, leading me to believe it was more meaningful than it was for a love for inked skin.

He was singing under his breath as he dried himself off. His whole energy was easy going and carefree, while he was making fun of himself and smiling. Now his jawline is clenched and that exquisite body, I couldn't help but stare at, is tense and rigid.

His eyes are bouncing between my hand and face and I can't say I'm surprised by his question, but I'm taken aback by its intensity and prematurity. He's asking what most people avoid altogether. They ignore them because it's easier to pretend like our scars don't exist than ask the awkward, uncomfortable question.

But that's the thing, we can't ignore them. We never could. We couldn't ignore the outcome, the repercussions of the accident, and we sure as hell haven't been able to get over the lasting effects of the scars, physically or mentally.

I peer over at Hannah and the natural smile she wears is still there, it always is. She doesn't mind if I share our story, she was an open book before the accident and even more so after. I'm just the one always having to answer for it, in more ways than one.

She points her index finger to her chin pushing it forward, signing for me to tell him.

He watches Hannah sign the words, a little tip in his brow, before his eyes land back on mine. "We were in a car accident," I respond with nothing more because I'm unsure of how much more I want to say.

Especially when Mister GQ model of the year over here is looking at me with intensity and concerned curiosity.

He gives me a slow, lengthy nod then turns around toward his bed sensing my irritation.

Hannah gives me an annoyed *you know better* look before stepping back, grabbing her bag and tossing it on the top bunk. She signs to me that she's going to the bathroom, kisses me on the cheek, then heads out of the room.

I watch her in awe, so proud of everything she's done to rebuild herself and keep that bubbly personality she's always had. She hasn't let the circumstances change her or the drive she's had. And scar or not, she's still the most beautiful woman I've ever laid my eyes on.

"Are you a bottom?" Dane asks and I whiplash my face in his direction.

"Excuse me?" I respond with an incredulous tone.

"Do you like the bottom?" He dips his chin in the direction of the bottom bunk.

"Oh." I laugh out a breath. "Yeah usually. I tend to move around a lot and she sleeps like the dead."

The corner of his lip quirks up. "I'm a top and a bottom. I like both, depending on my mood."

What the hell are we talking about right now?

Is this the encrypted language of sexual innuendos?

Did he just tell me he's bi?

My cock twitches at the thought and I have to avert my gaze away from his because it's lighting every cell in my body on fire.

I'm still riding the high from the glory hole earlier and I haven't had a moment to process anything. Desire. Shame. Need. Regret. It's like they're all battling each other and my mind can't settle on just accepting it for what I know it was.

One of the most erotic sexual experiences of my life.

Sex with Hannah is amazing. It always has been, but she knows about my curiosity.

She suggested a glory hole because of its anonymity. She thought maybe it would help me get past my own self doubts and insecurities about being with a man.

She was right. The moment I saw that guy in the other room and I knew he didn't know who I was, nothing else mattered.

I was in the moment and not in my head and all of it felt unbelievable.

The way he sucked the soul from my cock should have been illegal and probably is in certain countries.

I can't think of that now and sport a huge boner in front of my roommate for...I wonder how long he's here for?

"So, how long are you and Hannah staying here?" he asks, as if he was reading my thoughts.

"Five days. It's the final stop in our trip. You?" I ask.

"Same," he replies quickly, grabbing a baguette out of his backpack.

The harsh brown paper crinkles loudly in his hands as he tears off a piece of the crunchy bread and tosses it in his mouth.

"Plain bread as a snack?" My brows pinch together as I judge his food choice even though I like the way his mouth moves when he chews on it.

His eyes widen before he repeats my words. "Plain bread? Plain bread? There's no such thing as *plain bread* in Paris."

Just then, Hannah walks through the door, shutting it behind her and walks toward me.

"Hannah, come here," Dane says excitedly.

She stops, her eyes looking suspiciously between us then takes a step closer to him.

"Your boyfriend is judging my *snack* choice. You need to tell him how good it is."

She smiles and nods, giving him a look like her favorite thing to do is give me a hard time.

He takes a step toward her. "Close your eyes."

6

HANNAH

I look over my shoulder at Ethan, then back at Dane. I have no idea what I just walked into but I can feel the sexual tension swimming in the air.

"Just trust me," he says, like it's a natural, totally normal thing to just close your eyes in front of a guy you just met. "I don't bite, I swear," he adds, beaming that gorgeous smile of his.

I suck in a deep breath and close my eyes, then fold my hands into each other because I don't know what else to do with them.

My body naturally cranes back as I feel his body inch closer to mine. I hear the crackling of a paper wrapper and the sensation of something close to my face.

I flinch when his whispered voice is right next to my ear, "Inhale."

As if it's a reflex from his demand, my lungs expand taking a deep breath and the buttery aroma hits my nostrils. It's nutty and warm, and distinctly bread.

"Open," he says, and I swallow thickly. My brows pinch in a mediocre attempt to open my eyes, but I know he meant my mouth, and for some reason I listen without questioning anything.

My lips part as I stick out my tongue. I hear a pleased groan from somewhere deep in Dane's throat as he lightly presses something on my tongue. I close my mouth around it and my lips catch the tip of his finger.

He lets out a deep breath as I pull away, my tongue caressing along his sensitive skin.

Bergamot and something citrusy along with the crispy shell of the crust of what I assume is a french roll or baguette invades my taste buds.

I don't know if it's just the bread or perhaps the fact that one of my senses is now limited but it's undeniably delicious. It's got a thin crispy shell with a nutty and chewy inside that tastes like pure heaven.

I can't help but moan, opening my eyes, as I continue to chew through the crust and into the soft flesh of the bread.

"You moaned," Dane says, surprised.

I smile as I swallow then lick the corner of my mouth, savoring every last bit of it.

"She can still hum and moan and when she clears her throat or coughs her throat produces the noise. But they had to remove her larynx after the accident. No voicebox, no words," Ethan replies, answering Dane's question.

Dane nods, still looking straight at me, his bright blue eyes a shade darker than before. "I like that sound," he whispers as if he accidentally said it out loud.

My cheeks flush pink because it's been a long time since a man flirted with me and never has a man had the audacity to do it just feet away from my boyfriend.

Most people see my scar and run in the opposite direction. If they don't, they definitely don't look at me the way Dane is right now.

"So, go on now, tell your boyfriend how much you liked my

snack." Dane's flirt meter is overflowing as he wears a smirk like someone who knows he already won.

I turn around and dip my head to the side with a small agreeable shrug and a tight-lipped smile.

"Traitor." Ethan rolls his eyes with a lopsided smile.

Dane holds out a fist in a mini celebration; I bump it as he beams a victorious smile in my direction.

"I don't want to say I told you so, but, I told you so." He pokes a bit more at Ethan, then tosses him a small pastry bag, giving him his own carb filled snack, then sits down on the bottom bunk. Tearing his loaf in half, he hands one side to me and I take it, then sit down on the bean bag chair next to his bed.

Biting into it on my own the second time around is still good, but there was something about being fed by this sexy man while Ethan watched that was far more exciting than I'd like to admit.

I'm no exhibitionist, far from it actually. I hate when I know that people are staring at me because they're never staring at ocean blue eyes or silky dark hair. I've always been told I had great bone structure with high cheekbones and a perfectly symmetrical nose. But no one sees any of that anymore, just my scar. In one instant moment, it was like everything about me faded and my life was defined by one scar.

It doesn't bother me, not like it used to at least. I don't care what other people think, I never really have. But no matter how confident I am, it's never easy when the staring becomes a grotesque, silent curiosity that turns into sympathy and sorrow.

Dane didn't look at me that way, though. Not once did a look of pity cross his face. He looked at me the same way he is now, with intent and genuine interest. The same way he's been looking at Ethan.

I take another bite of Dane's self proclaimed snack then turn my gaze, smiling at Ethan and sign, *"Yummy snack."*

"It's not a snack," he signs back.

"I mean him."

Then my gorgeous, grumpy man blushes.

I love that I can get him worked up so easily. Although, tonight was the first time I've seen him worked up for anyone but me. After the club he was quiet but he had the same look of desire that I saw when he finally admitted his curiosity.

It started when we were watching a video of a threesome, then the two men started stroking each other off. I couldn't explain it, something about it was just so alluring.

Two sexy men, exploring each other's bodies. The deep moans, the guttural groans.

It was the first time I'd ever seen two men together like that. When I glanced over at Ethan, he was just as mesmerized by them, and his face gave away everything.

We watched them pull their cocks together oiled with lube, stroking hard and fast. They're moans grew louder and louder and I could feel the tension of Ethan holding himself back. He looked down at me with so much need and desire but his confession was full of shame when he admitted how much he liked watching them. *"I think I want that,"* he said.

My orgasm came out of nowhere with his confession and the two men roared out their own intense climax. Ethan watched them, soaking everything in and came harder than ever.

I always suspected that was something he wanted but could never admit to, and I hate that he hid that desire for so long from me, even probably from himself. But after he finally admitted it, I wanted him to know how much I wanted it too, for both of us. So I've been encouraging him to explore. Which is why we ended up taking this trip.

We've been in Europe for a little over a week and tonight was the first time he acted on it.

The sex club was supposed to be a way for him to feel

anonymous, so that he wouldn't feel so ashamed of the things he wanted. Get past that hurdle. I encouraged the club specifically because when I researched this one, they had glory holes that I thought would be a good first step.

He didn't like the idea at first because he felt like I wasn't part of it, but I think part of his shame comes from worrying that I won't like it or that I'll see him in a different light.

That couldn't be further from the truth but I knew it would be easier for him to do this without me watching and as anonymous as possible.

Hence the club tonight.

He didn't say much after, he just wrapped his arms around me, tucked his head into my neck, and held me.

I gave him a few minutes and finally pulled away, signing the question I'd been dying to know.

"Did you like it?"

He just nodded and whispered shamefully. "But I don't want to do anything like that again without you." He cupped my cheeks, looking at me with a serious stare.

"But, you do want to do it again?"

His eyes fluttered closed as he took in a deep breath, like the memory of his experience was too much to handle.

"Yes, but only with you."

"Okay."

"Come on, let's get to the hostel and I'll tell you all about it."

We haven't had a chance to talk about the details, but I'm dying to know. I want to know every dirty detail of what happened in that room.

"So, what are your plans in Paris?" Dane asks, bringing my thoughts back to the present.

"Sightseeing mostly. Standard Paris stuff," Ethan answers for us as he shrugs, sounding terribly uninterested even though I know he's far from it.

Not only has he been looking forward to coming to Paris,

he's also crushing on our new roommate and my grumpy man hates it.

"*Stop brooding,*" I sign.

"*I'm not,*" he signs back.

"*Then be nicer.*"

My movements are slow and deliberate because just like when you speak in a more serious tone, I do the same when I sign and he knows it.

And since I like poking at him, I continue.

"*I will tell him our plans to go back to that club...and invite him.*"

I give him a snarky smirk.

His eyes widen and he leans forward looking as if he wants to kill me. I meet him with the same reverence, not backing down because this is what we do.

"*You will not.*"

"*Try me.*"

"*I will tie up those gorgeous hands if you don't stop.*"

"*Don't threaten me with a good time.*"

Just then Dane starts choking on his water, and a mist of liquid sprays out on the floor as he leans forward beating on his chest.

Ethan pushes himself off his bed and steps over to Dane, patting him on the back as he leans down in front of him.

"Are you okay?" he asks, as he continues to pat.

"Wrong tube," Dane chokes out as he glances back and forth between the two of us.

He uses his bath towel, tossing it on the floor in front of him to clean up the water and apologizes again.

"No worries, you good?" Ethan asks again.

"Totally, all good." He pats his chest like he's invincible. "I have far too much to live for than to die from water bottle asphyxiation." He looks over at me and winks and I can't help but blush.

"I just remembered, Sally needed some extra details from

me and I forgot to go back down there." He stands and grabs his wallet from his backpack.

"Who's Sally?" Ethan asks.

"The lady at the front desk. Well, technically she's the owner. I've stayed here before so I know her. She let me check in but I forgot to give her my credit card details. I'll be right back."

Dane pats Ethan on the back then turns toward the exit and winks again. That damn wink of his.

Right as he passes through the door, Ethan steps toward me, placing his hands into the bean bag chair and hovers over me.

"You flirting in front of me is doing unexplainable things to my cock."

"*Is that right?*" I sign with a smirk.

He nods as he nuzzles into my neck, kissing my jawline until his lips land on mine.

I know we don't have much time, but I want to hear how he felt, what he thought, and every detail of what happened.

"*Tell me about the club.*"

7

DANE

I step outside the door, leaving it slightly cracked, then lean against the wall craning my ear closer to the opening.

"You flirting in front of me is doing unexplainable things to my cock."

Me too, man, me too.

There's a long pause between what sounds like a wet kiss and I'm irritated that I can't see what she's saying.

At what point do I tell them ASL is the only other language I speak fluently? I ponder that for a minute.

Uh, never. The devil on my shoulder speaks for me and I can't say I disagree. I don't know what their normal conversations are like, but if they're anything like this I'll secretly eavesdrop on them for eternity.

When she mentioned the club I was immediately relieved, realizing they do this together.

"He'll be back soon, we don't have much time."

Another brief pause, then what sounds like him sitting on the bean bag chair with her.

"I was nervous at first but the guy was...I can't explain it. He made me feel at ease. He...he gave me a blow job. Fuck, it was so good."

So, it's confirmed, she does know. They do this together. But it sounds like it was his first time or something new to them.

I have a mile wide smile at his confession. People like them are exactly why I love staying in places like this.

I don't really have to give Sally anything, but I need to find out how many bunks are rented out. So, reluctantly I step away and head down the stairs to the front desk. Sally is sitting behind it, with her hand over her mouth completely focused on her kindle.

"Hey, Sally." I rap my knuckles on the desk to get her attention.

She glances up at me, then at the clock showing it's well after midnight, then back at me. "Dane, is everything okay?"

"Of course, it always is." I beam back a smile as I lean in closer. "I just wanted to ask if all the bunks were reserved already for the week?" I pause, realizing I'm tiptoeing the line of crazy right now.

"Tonight and tomorrow, it's just you and the other couple that checked in just a short while ago. Although, that could change since we offer walk-ins." She taps on her keyboard, then moves the mouse. "After that all the beds are booked out for the rest of the week," she adds, and I can't help but screw up my face and cringe.

I suck in a deep breath.

"So, Sally. I'm really not feeling a crowd this time around. I'd like to pay you double what the others are paying for all the beds for the rest of the week..." I pause. "If you would be so kind to block it out for walk-ins and cancel anyone else that's coming."

Her brows pinch together as if trying to absorb the information and understand my psychosis.

"Why don't you just go to a hotel and get a room with that money?" she asks, and not in a rude, nefarious way. In more of a, *are you out of your mind*, way.

"I love this place, the location is perfect. And you know Paris hotels, all the good rooms are almost always taken," I spit out easily because both are very true.

She pauses for a moment, taps on her computer, then slides her eyes my way

"What are you up to Mr. Campbell?" she asks in a playful suspicion.

I relent because she's totally on to me.

"I have the rest of the week until I fly home before I start my new job and I really don't want to deal with the plethora of random personalities that are checking in this week. I'll pay you double for every bed, for the rest of the week, *and* I'll pay for a hotel room for anyone that you have to cancel." I pull out my credit card, laying it on her desk as I one finger push it toward her. "Whatever that total is, double it again and pay yourself...for your discretion."

Her eyes widen as she peers up at me, then around the room, as if she wonders if my request is some kind of test.

"So, let me understand," she says in what I imagine is her mom voice. "You want me to cancel on everyone that has a reservation through the remainder of your stay, block out any further rentals, and not tell anyone about it?"

I really have lost my mind.

Giving her my most charming smile. "Can I cover your quarterly bonus, too?"

She huffs out a long breath, shaking her head with a tiny little smirk as she returns to clicking on her mouse, then taps her keyboard a couple times.

"I'll block it out for the next four days. You're last night here though, I can't do anything about, there's a large group coming and it's—"

"Deal," I spit out, interrupting her. I'll take four days over nothing.

"Oh, Dane, I think you might be a little crazy." She grabs my credit card, tapping a few more strokes on her keyboard, then swipes it through.

If this is what crazy feels like, I'm all in.

8

ETHAN

It was surprisingly easy to share what happened at the club with Hannah. I mean, I've always been able to talk about everything with her, but this is different. The deep desire I've been craving. The questionable thoughts I've had about my sexuality.

I never want her to think it has anything to do with her or something that she's not providing me. She's perfect. More than I deserve. The fact that she's now encouraging this is beyond my wildest dreams.

Now, I just need to get past my own mental hurdles.

Tonight was definitely a start. My mind flashes back to the moment I wrapped my hand around his length. The desperate whimper that played on his lips as I stroked him up and down. The pulsing of his cock as he came and his begging to please me.

Fuck.

I know I want more of whatever happened and I can't help but wonder about the guy behind the wall. Was it the action of what I was doing that turned me on or was it him?

Hannah and I were both virgins before we met and I've only

ever had the emotional and sexual connection with her. But the way he talked to me, the way he helped me through tonight. It made me feel like he understood me. Like he knew it was my first time.

I'm not normally a sentimental person. In fact, I'm most often skeptical and annoyed by an over-saturation of feelings. Which is why I adore Hannah so much. She's level-headed, straight to the point, honest, and doesn't care what others think of her. She leads with more passion than emotion and it shows in how she supports me. How she supports us.

I hate the fact that I'm attracted to men. But she's encouraging and confident in our wants and desires. I'm still questioning every thought and fantasy I've ever wanted. But that's normal, right?

It really doesn't matter though, we're just exploring on this trip. Nothing more than that, and nothing more will happen when we're back home.

Once school starts, Hannah will dive head first into being the star student she is and I'll continue to chase her tail-feathers, as they say, like I normally do, struggling to reignite the passion I lost after the accident. I'll never get it back, because I'll never play baseball again.

Four years later and the trauma is still as apparent as these scars. The only thing I can focus on is the one good thing, Hannah. So, I'll follow her wherever she needs me, supporting her and doing what I need to do to be good for her.

If I can't be what I want to be in baseball, at least I can be what I want to be for her.

I crane my neck up over the top bunk and see her curled up on her side, her signature sleeping position. I have no idea how she falls asleep so fast. I mean, we had a long day but it's not due to exhaustion. She just has this amazing ability to sleep anywhere, anytime, any place.

I still suffer from random bouts of insomnia and dream of the nights I can fall asleep like that.

I don't know if those will ever come back for me. Peaceful nights.

The moment I close my eyes I still see the flash of jagged headlights mixed with the sounds of screeching tires and metal crunching together. I feel the weight of the medical bills because the drunk driver that hit us had no insurance and the heaviness of the debt my dad holds over my head sits like an elephant on my chest.

I will never tell her all that though. She thinks the surgeries she had were covered, and I'll never tell her the promises I made to my father to make sure what she needed was provided.

I hate that he has that kind of hold on me, but she made it through one of the worst injuries a person can make it through, and I'll never regret indebting myself to him for her.

Brushing her hair behind her ear, I place a kiss on her temple and step back, bending over to pull the covers down on the bottom bunk.

The door clicks closed behind me and I turn to see Dane coming through the door, walking a tad lighter than when he left. He points as he tilts his chin at the top bunk and I nod, putting my finger up to my lips with a quiet shushing noise.

We've stayed in hostels our entire trip, if they weren't completely packed they were close to it. Dane is the first roommate we've had that has been respectful of our space and noise.

Well, except the fact that he was buck naked after he showered. Although, I can't say that bothered me much. I couldn't pull my gaze away from his body and it took everything in my power to clear my throat so I didn't look like a complete creep watching him for longer than I should have.

He remains quiet as he steps closer to me. The strands of his golden hair are still damp but lighter now that the tips are dry. He still smells like he's freshly showered with a hint of some spicy undertone as he leans in closer to whisper in my ear.

"I come to Paris a lot. Let me show you guys around tomorrow. You can see all the standard Paris stuff," he air quotes copying what I said earlier, "and I can show you all the cool stuff you normally wouldn't see."

Pulling back, I feel the distance immediately.

We're roughly the same height and weight. But his presence is commanding. It's fun, friendly, and it's easy to be drawn to him.

I glance up at the top bunk then back at him and nod. His smile grows in an instant and I can't help but smile at how happy he is that I agreed to his invite. He pauses for a minute and I swear his eyes flicker down to my lips then back up to my face.

Something passes between us and for a moment I feel like he knows my secret. Like I don't need to tell him with words that I'm bi-curious and unsure. That I find him attractive, that both Hannah and I do. I never really thought about my type in a guy. But if I did, I'm certain Dane would be it.

I don't catch myself staring at his soft lips until a tiny lopsided smirk ticks up on the corner of his mouth; I quickly blink away and step back toward my bed, attempting to ignore the inferno of emotions running through every cell in my body. Even though my entire body feels like it's on fire, I crawl into the bottom bunk leaving everything on as some form of armor from the sexy-as-sin gorgeous man sleeping in the bed directly across from me.

"Tomorrow then," I say, ending the night and abruptly stopping any other silent moments to pass between us.

"Tomorrow," he repeats. "Night, Ethan."

And, as usual, I lay awake for hours, recapping the events of the day and overthinking on what the future looks like, before finally falling asleep.

9

DANE

"This is all really great, Dane, but I don't think we can afford this," Ethan tells me as he glances over Hannah's shoulder at the menu for *Le Jules Verne*.

Hannah is nibbling on the corner of her lip as her eyes bounce all over the menu, assuming she's trying to find something in their price range.

They don't list prices and it's a prix fixe menu, so there aren't many options to modify your meal. As there shouldn't be. The chef creates each course to pair with the appetizer, entrée, and dessert down to the drink choice. It's an entire culinary experience.

This is one of the areas I splurge on whenever I'm traveling. Visiting the world's best restaurants and diving headfirst into the culture's cuisine.

"I know the manager and he owes me a favor so don't worry about the price," I lie as I respond back to Ethan without looking at him, because I hate lying. I do know the manager, but Hugo doesn't owe me anything. I'll just have him charge me without them knowing about it.

Speaking of, I see the tall, lean Frenchman in the corner of the restaurant talking to one of his servers. He side-eyes in my direction and tips his chin in acknowledgment, then holds up one finger in my direction. I smile and nod then turn back to Ethan and Hannah.

Hannah gave the menu back to the hostess and Ethan is standing next to her, holding her hand.

The thin strap of her floral sundress has fallen over her shoulder and the peak of her breast is holding her dress up with immaculate precision. Her sun-touched skin is glowing from our touring around Paris today, pairing perfectly with the bright yellow fabric of her dress.

Reaching out, I take the strap between my fingers and trail it back up her arm and over her shoulder. Goosebumps scale over her skin as I touch her, and there's an audible hitch in her breath.

Her eyes meet mine and my cock stirs behind my pants and I peer over at Ethan who watches both of us with the same intensity he has been all day. There have been moments between each one of us throughout the day, lingering gazes, playful touches, flirty banter, and the best part, light-hearted and witty conversation.

I thought it would be a challenge to communicate with Hannah, but I've just been asking her questions she can easily answer and it's been effortless to read her body language and facial expressions.

I suppose since I secretly understand the conversations they have when they sign to each other that makes me part of their conversation, too. But, I haven't let them in on that little bit of knowledge yet.

Regardless, nothing they've done has made me feel like an odd man out. In fact, they both seem as interested in me as I am in them.

Other than Ethan, practicing his roadrunner skills the

moment the sexual tension between us gets too high, then acting angry about it.

Neither one has mentioned the club again from last night. But, I've decided I want to take them there.

I have no idea how I'll bring it up or what I'll do to convince them, but we *are* going. Even if I have to give up a kidney or some other decently useful organ, I'm getting them there.

Today I took them all around the standard places you see when you go to Paris. The Louvre, Notre-Dame, the Palace of Versailles and now here, at the Eiffel Tower.

I originally wanted to take them off the beaten path. But now I have an excuse to hang out with them another day, since I have more places to show them that they won't easily be able to find themselves.

Glancing at my watch, we have about two hours until Kobi gets here. We're meeting him after dinner at Vortex, one of Paris' most popular dance clubs, and I'm more than excited about the fact that they want to keep the night going. Apparently, Ethan hates dancing but Hannah loves it. He agreed to go because she's clearly a weakness for him and I can totally see why.

I've gotten to know a little more about both of them today. They're both likeable, in dramatically different ways, but I find myself so easily drawn to them.

It feels magnetic. One side of me is easily attracted to Hannah and the collision is unavoidable. While, it's the opposite with Ethan and he repels the moment we get too close.

I glance over at Hannah again and she's absolutely stunning. Her ocean blue eyes and dark hair give her a sultry look not many women can pull off, yet the bright color of her canary yellow dress paired with that universal smile she gives everyone makes her the easiest person to open up to.

My eyes trail over to Ethan as he glances around, taking in his surroundings. He's so goddamn sexy and perfectly groomed. Everything on him is put together. His hair, his outfit, even his five o'clock shadow seems to behave perfectly. All of that strict disposition trails over to his personality, too. Unlike Hannah, it took him a long while to warm up to me today, but the moments he did were full of laughter and fun. Then when the flirty tension got too high, he backed off, fighting that magnetic pull even though I wish he'd just give into it.

There were multiple times I felt it, I know they both did. Hannah would smile and flirt back. Ethan would shut down completely.

So, pretty much, he's the exact opposite of me in *all* the ways.

In any case, everything about today has been perfect with them and I just don't want it to end.

"Dane!" Hugo walks up to me with his arms held out. He places his palms on the outside of my arms, kissing me on one cheek, then switching and kissing me on the other.

"I'm delighted to see you, it's been too long. To what do I owe this pleasure?" His french accent is more apparent than ever, or maybe I've just been away too long.

"These are my friends, Ethan and Hannah," I smile as I hold out one arm, gesturing toward them. "It's their first time in Paris and I was hoping to give them the best dining experience the city has to offer."

There's one thing to know about the French when it comes to food or fashion. They love a good compliment.

"Ah, Oui, Oui!" He snaps his fingers, getting the attention of the hostess who immediately steps to his side. He quickly whispers something in her ear.

The moment he turns his attention back toward us, she turns on her heel, snaps her fingers at two others, then rounds the corner out of sight.

That was a whole lot of snapping that just happened.

"Hannah, Ethan. Welcome." Holding out his arms again, he

leans in kissing Hannah's cheeks, then steps to the side doing the same to Ethan. Hannah is all smiles while Ethan remains skeptical. But most Americans aren't quite prepared for the affection granted by strangers in France.

"I owe this man everything," Hugo tells them as he points to me.

They glance at each other then back to me and I shake my head as I wave my hand. I was hoping he wouldn't share our story. He's grateful and I'm happy about that but I don't deserve any credit.

I met Hugo a few years ago at one of the hostels I stayed at. He was down on his luck, homeless, and only able to afford a bed to stay in once or twice a week. I could tell he was kind and had a passion that you don't see often. So, I introduced him to my friend who was the manager here at the time. When he got a job as a host, I paid for him to stay in that hostel for three months. Enough time for him to save while he worked there so he could get a place of his own.

"I simply introduced you to the right person at the right time, you put in all the work to get where you are now, Hugo."

"You believed in me when no one else did. I am forever grateful for you, my friend. Forever grateful," he says, as he places his hand on my shoulder with a thankful smile.

"Let's get you and your friends fed, yes?" The hostess comes back and waves us in her direction. Hannah and Ethan follow first and I stay a few steps behind with Hugo.

"No mention of who I am and they pay nothing," I lean in telling Hugo. He knows my background, we've become friends over the years and I'm not frugal when spending my money on food or experiences. He realized this over time, Googled me, then brought it up. Which is why I never tell people my last name. I've been burned and taken advantage of far too many times. Hugo is the exception.

He's never asked me for anything or told anyone that we've

met about my background and I've always appreciated his loyalty and discretion.

He looks at me skeptically as he takes in what I just asked him. He's used to seeing me a bit more carefree and not so rigid but Ethan and Hannah bring out something in me that makes me want to be better, more responsible and more accountable to myself and others.

"Have you fallen in love in Paris, my old friend?" he asks with ease.

I snap my eyes up to his. I run my hands through my hair as if there's a neon sign hanging from my head that I need to remove.

"No. God, no. Nothing like that," I respond quickly, as if I need to convince both him and myself.

I'm just infatuated. Obsessively infatuated.

Nothing more than that.

There's a slight tick in his brow as the corner of his mouth lifts up.

"Ah, okay. I understand," he says cryptically as a big-ass smile creeps up on his face.

I squint, giving him an incredulous look.

Yeahhhhh, I don't think he does.

And the French are hopeless romantics so I'm highly skeptical of his tone.

Before I can say anything more, he takes two large strides forward catching up to them and pulls out Hannah's chair. She smiles and sits as he places the napkin over her lap. Two of the other servers pull out our chairs as we sit down at the table that has the best view of Paris.

It's a four-person square table. Ethan and I are on either side of Hannah and her unobstructed view is directly out the window of the tallest level on the tower.

"Bon Appétit," they all say in unison as they hand us menus and retreat.

Wow, Hannah mouths and Ethan remains quiet but his face says the same thing.

"What do you eat when you come here?" Ethan asks, as his eyes peruse the menu, unsure of where to begin.

I never pick up the menu, so I honestly never have any idea what's on it. I know the meals are seasonal and there are a few different options to pick from for each course.

"I've never chosen. I always just tell them, *chef's choice,* and I've never been disappointed."

"Seriously?" Ethan says with a bit of concern behind his tone. "What if you get frog liver or duck feet or something equally questionable?"

I chuckle.

"Then I'm eating frog liver and duck feet for dinner. You gotta learn to let go, not be so in control all the time," I say with factuality, leaning forward and lowering my voice because I'm referring to more than just our food choices. "You'll be amazed at the things you discover about yourself. The things you like that you never thought you would. The loss of control is liberating."

10

ETHAN

Fucking Christ. Dane is a walking sex billboard that talks. I hate it.

My body physically reacts to him when he does that deep, low voice thing. Hell, who am I kidding. It reacts with everything he does and Hannah can see it. I think he can, too.

He's talking about food right now, right? Or am I just conjuring up every syllable of his words to mean something more.

I quickly avert my gaze from his to look at Hannah. She's flushed, just like I am.

Nothing sexual has happened between us today but I'm riding a high like I've never felt just being in his presence.

Hannah signs to me, *"The view is gorgeous."*

Turning my head I look out the window and Hannah's right. It's stunning.

Strips of lights line the streets of Paris, shining bright amongst the contrast of the dark skyline. The city lights have a dark orange glow making the city look like it's purposely on fire. You can see everything but gorgeous still doesn't seem to cover it.

I turn back toward her.

"It's not as beautiful as you."

No matter how often I compliment her, she still blushes and I love that shy smile she returns. It's the only time I see that more timid side of her.

When I finish signing I place my hand over hers on the table, giving it a gentle squeeze as I caress my thumb over her knuckles. I glance up to look at Dane, his eyes are fixed on where our hands meet, and I can see he's deep in thought.

I'm curious about him. We happened to run into a few people that he knows in Paris today. He only introduced us to them by first name but they all looked like they belonged in a corner office overlooking the city or on a billboard running for the next prime minister of France. They all seemed powerful in some way or another.

Actually, they reminded me of my father. They gave off a snooty confidence that I felt instantly uncomfortable with. All ego and no heart. The french accents didn't help either.

The fact that Dane, dressed in cargo pants, a basic white tee, and flip flops who appears untroubled in all things in life knew these business men, was...weird.

Now we're at the most prestigious restaurant in Paris, where we walked in without a reservation, landed a table with the best view of the city, and the price doesn't seem to be an issue.

The waitress comes back to our table, bringing champagne none of us asked for. "Compliments of the manager." she says, placing a flute in front of all of us. "Have you decided what you'd like for dinner?"

Dane sits back in his chair, his hands folding into each other as he gives me an assured and pointed look.

I've learned to be mindful of my decisions and always think of the consequences of the choices I make, especially after the accident. But the challenge in his eyes, brings something careless out in me.

"Chef's choice." My gaze never leaves his and his lip quirks up.

"Same," he replies, eyes boring into mine.

He stares at me like if he were the chef, his choice would be me.

I shift in my seat, finally breaking the connection, and turn to look at Hannah.

"And you, my dear?" the waitress asks.

"Me too."

"She'll have the same," I tell the waitress for her.

"Très bien," she replies with a curd nod and retreats. Leaving us in the wake of our decision of what chef's choice really means for me.

11

HANNAH

I've never had such attentive service at a restaurant before or so many meals. There's been a tiny appetizer dish before each course. Hugo said it was meant to be a palate cleanser from the previous that will help pair well with the next.

So, this final dessert dish will be the eighth plate pushed in front of us.

We all selected the *chef's choice* option at Dane's recommendation so all our entrees were the exact same, however we were asked what our preference was for dessert. Sweet or tart?

Both Ethan and I said tart and were given a lemon lavender fruit cup. I've never consumed any form of lavender before, but as I take my first bite, my eyes flutter and my jaw drops.

The taste actually brings out a smile from me, it's so good.

"Oh my god," Ethan mutters as he finishes swallowing.

This is probably the best dessert I've ever had in my entire life.

"Oh man, this *one* is good. Here, try this," Dane says as he dips his tiny spoon into his creme brûlée dish. There's a glassy crunch as he presses through the top shiny layer, scooping up the custard and lifts it toward me.

Instead of handing me the spoon, he leans forward, holding it a few inches from my mouth as his eyes bounce between my eyes and lips.

My tongue darts over my bottom lip, as my teeth rake over the surface, before I lean in, slowly opening my mouth. Dane presses the spoon on my tongue and I wrap my lips around the stem as he inches it back out.

Oh my god. There's an explosion of heavy flavors on my tastebuds. It's decadent and sweet. So soft and creamy. I've had creme brûlée before but nothing like this.

My eyes widen as I peer over at Ethan. He's gripping the table, looking between the two of us then clears his throat.

"That good, huh?" Ethan asks.

"You have to try it," I sign to him, but Dane's already refilled the spoon and is holding it in his direction. There's a brief pause as he looks down at the spoon, up at Dane, then back at me.

He's always been so reluctant to try new things, so I'm shocked when he reaches his hand out and takes the offering from Dane.

Dane smiles as his hand retracts, then says, "You won't regret it." There's a sensuality behind his tone, but I've come to realize with him that he lives in the flirt zone. I swear everything he says is either ridiculously funny, over the top sweet and serious, or so sexy it lights my core on fire. I have no idea how he balances it all so well.

It's not just me either. He speaks to Ethan the same way and I love how easily it affects him. Ethan is so high strung all the time, yet I've seen him let loose more times today than ever before.

After only one day of hanging out with Dane, I know if we could explore with anyone I could be comfortable doing that with him. I'm not a hundred percent certain he's into guys, he hasn't flat out said it, but if I were to guess, he likes us both.

Ethan and I have been talking for what feels like forever about his bisexual curiosity. I know he's embarrassed by it, or maybe just shy to explore it. But, I feel anxious about it. To see him get pleased by another man, for me to please a man in front of him. The thought of all the possibilities excites me like nothing else has.

Meeting Dane in Paris, the way we did, feels like a bit of kismet, and I want to take full advantage of the opportunity. Ethan is a lot of things, but assertive in his sexual desires—especially the one he's been suppressing—is not one of them. I know I'm going to need to step in and make the first move if anything is ever going to happen. And, god, do I want it to.

Lifting the dessert toward his mouth, he takes a bite, then returns the utensil to Dane.

Dane smiles and without dipping it back into the brûlée, he takes the spoon in his mouth, wraps his lips around it and pulls it back out, licking off the excess completely.

"Mmmm, delicious," he says.

Annnnd Ethan is speechless. From the sexual way Dane devoured the spoon that my boyfriend just had in his mouth or from the actual dessert, I'm not sure. But I'm here for it.

I've been drowning in the tension growing between us, lost in our own little world, but the chatter I hear coming from the table next to us feels like getting dunked in a cold plunge.

"What do you think that's from? It looks so bad." Whispered words grab my attention.

I look down and freeze, shifting just my eyes to the table on my left to see two women sitting across from each other. I can see in my periphery that one is leaning forward with her hand over her neck and the other looks in the direction of our table.

"I don't know, but I wouldn't wear what she's wearing, especially at dinner. Talk about losing your appetite." Her tone is both disgusted and humorous, like she was delivering a punchline.

"Those guys are hot, too. I mean she's kinda pretty, I *guess*," one girl says.

Then the other adds, "But that scar," a long hiss leaves her lips, "her date needed to bring his wingman to get him through this one." They giggle.

Do they actually think they're whispering?

Dane's eyes blink over my shoulder as the pinch in his brow gets deeper.

Reaching out, I place my hand over his, because I can tell he wants to say something and I don't need to create any more negative attention. That always makes everything worse.

He shifts his gaze to our connected hands, up to Ethan, then back to mine and the fury that was there a few minutes ago is replaced with something different now. It's still dark but full of lust, need, and some sort of delighted curiosity.

I know this is all new to him, but not to me. I'm used to people staring, used to their eyes unavoidably appraising my scar then quickly turning away. Some go as far as whispering to whoever they are with, but most often there's just a quick look of disgust or pity, before covering it up and attempting to ignore the fact that it's there.

If I were just with Ethan, it would be easy to disregard their lingering looks and whispered comments. But now with Dane here, it's staggering my usual confidence.

I tilt up my chin and sit a little taller, going through all the steps I do to build myself up when I'm feeling emotionally compromised and decide, fuck it.

I shift my gaze over to Ethan.

"Trust me?"

He squints, granting me a curious look, then signs back, as we usually do when our conversations are private.

"Always."

I slide one hand over Ethan's forearm, while my other hand slips over the top of Dane's hand, connecting the three of us.

Keeping my eyes on my gorgeous boyfriend—who might want to kill me after this—I lean in, bringing my lips to his. It's soft and sensual as our tongues collide and he moans in pleasure. I can feel Dane's gaze searing into us, his hand tightening in my grasp.

I pull away slowly and lean over toward Dane.

Dane visibly sits taller, peering between the two of us, uncertain of my next move. But I know exactly what I'm doing.

I turn my gaze directly at the girls, smile, give them a wink, then turn back to Dane. That's all it takes for him to read me like a book and before I can even begin to fall into him, he cups his hand around the nape of my neck and pulls me in for a passionate kiss.

It's soft at first, curious. Like he's testing the flavors.

His hand disappears from under mine and I'm suddenly pulled closer to him. The legs of my chair screech along the floor, before he cups both of his hands over my cheeks and kisses me deeper.

My heart races. My pulse goes crazy and a groan from somewhere in the back of my throat makes a rare appearance.

I pull back, feeling overwhelmed by sensory overload but Dane holds me close, pressing his forehead to mine.

"Oh yeah, I love that sound," he admits again, like it's a new life goal to do things to pull that small moan from me.

"Now, give these girls no doubt how badly we both want you and go kiss your boyfriend again. Let him taste me on you."

12

DANE

E than's shocked eyes stare me down as I push Hannah's chair back in place. He's clenching his jaw, and as Hannah leans toward him, I can tell he's stuck somewhere between anger and unrelenting desire.

I think—at least I hope—the anger is for what those girls were saying and not the fact that I just devoured Hannah like she was the grande finale at this Michelin star restaurant.

Hannah gets closer to him but this time, he dives in. Pulling her off her chair and onto his lap. As if my kiss sparked a bit of competition and he needs to outdo me.

Fine by me. Because I have every intention of doing whatever I need to spoil them both with the utmost pleasure.

I shift my gaze over to the two plastic Barbie dolls at the table next to us. I had a feeling that they were going to be a problem when I watched them arrange their silverware and criticize everything as they sat down. I've seen and met girls just like them before. They've probably had more surgeries than Elizabeth Taylor had husbands, and if you removed the layers of make up they would resemble something closer to a used-metal vintage lunchbox than an actual face.

They spend as much time cutting people down as they do complimenting themselves and I despise people like that.

But, the way Hannah handled that? Shoving her scar, and us, in their faces like she owned both? Fuck, it was hot. And she can own me all day, any day because I'm diving head first, taking full advantage of whatever is happening right now.

Hannah and Ethan stop kissing but she remains in his lap and I can't help my shit-eating grin as I look at the girls, mouths agape, with offended looks on their faces.

I peer around the room and catch eyes with Hugo, quickly passing him an incredulous look for the dinner he fed us. Oysters, cold pomegranate and fig soup, hot honey watermelon salad, cocoa crusted filet. I swear not one dish was missing a sexual heightening aphrodisiac and I know he did that on purpose.

Not that I'm really complaining about it.

Waving my finger in the air in a small circle, I tell him we're finishing up and heading out. He nods, and since he has my card on file we can leave anytime.

Which is now.

Kobi messaged that he landed a few minutes ago and now, not only am I looking forward to seeing him, but also where this night is headed.

Standing, I hold my hand out to Hannah to help her up. My eyes meet Ethan's and a look of understanding passes between us. Fuck, I want to devour this man too. If I could bend down and kiss him with certainty that he wouldn't punch me in the face, I would do it.

Ethan places his napkin on his plate and stands, rising to meet me face-to-face. His eyes dip to my lips as his tongue pokes out and licks the corner of his mouth, like he's still tasting me from that three-way kiss.

Or maybe he's trying to establish his dominance over me for kissing his girl.

You can alpha me into submission, anytime, big boy. You have no idea the things I'm willing to do for you.

I hold my arm out toward the front of the restaurant letting him trail behind Hannah first.

Before following, I turn to the girls at the table.

"Barbie. Skipper." They both look confused at my nicknames for them. But, their eyes light up and a tight smile crosses their stiff botoxed faces as I toss a stack of hundred dollar bills on their table. "I'd love to buy your dinner so you can afford some manners in the future." Their mouths fall in perfectly timed, jaw dropping shock. I internally fist bump myself.

"Have a good night ladies. I know I am." Wiggling my eyebrows, I turn and head out of the restaurant, meeting Hannah and Ethan in front of the elevators.

"Ready for Vortex?" I ask nonchalantly, fighting to hide every ounce of excitement that wants to bubble out of me.

Hannah presses the down button and nods with the most radiant smile.

"You better dance with me or Dane will," she signs to Ethan and he playfully smacks her ass.

I don't know what it is, but I feel more connected to them than I have with anyone and it's only been one day.

Hugo might be on to something.

Three more days of this and I might actually fall in love.

13

ETHAN

The club was loud before we walked into it. As we trail through the dance floor to the booth that Kobi, Dane's friend, reserved for us, it's absurdly loud.

I've never been a so-called *clubber* or lover of loud music and tight spaces. It's chaotic and you can't even hold a conversation with people, not that I enjoy talking to anyone but Hannah. Still, I find the whole experience overwhelming and irritating.

But for whatever crazy reason, she loves it. We don't go often because we're always too busy or too tired from our rigorous schedule, but when we do, she dances until her feet can't hold herself up anymore.

"You guys are very different!" Dane screams at me from over the thumping bass that I feel vibrate through my chest.

He tips his chin over my shoulder and when I turn around, Hannah is already deep in her element—arms up, waving her hands to the beat, her face beaming with a bright smile.

A huff out a chuckle. "Yeah, she loves this," I agree as we round the DJ table to a booth tucked just behind the speakers making the music a few decibels lower. It's still loud, but at least now I won't lose my voice trying to have a conversation.

Hannah is still standing, moving her hips to the beat, as Kobi speaks fluent French to the hostess that just led us to our table.

I was surprised when Dane introduced us to Kobi. I don't know what I expected a friend of Dane's to be like. But it wasn't a six-foot something half-asian guy with piercing green eyes that speaks five different languages, working as a translator for the Japanese prime minister. *That* was definitely not it.

"I'd rather you check me out, instead of my friend," Dane says as he steps up behind me.

I jump-turn, startled by his close proximity but also offended that he thinks I'd be checking out his friend.

I open my mouth to defend myself but as I look into his bright blue eyes, they're a tad bit more vulnerable than I expected. I feel the need to thank him for what he did for Hannah earlier.

"I—I like what you did back at the restaurant...for Hannah. That was nice of you." I invisibly roll my eyes at myself.—*That was nice of you?* God, I'm a fumbling idiot.

"Devouring your girlfriend's mouth was nice of me?" he asks, the playful smirk that maintains permanent residence on his face gets a little deeper, causing a small dimple to appear at the top corner of his mouth.

"No, I m-meant—" I stutter through a few words before he saves me with a question.

"So, she likes this..." He tips his chin at Hannah, still in her own world dancing and lip-syncing to the music in front of our table. "What do you like?"

I pause thinking about that question. It's not that I don't know what I like, it's that I hate opening up to people.

But, there's something that makes opening up to him easy.

"A quiet night in. That's more my style. She's always been a bit more of the party animal and risk taker. I'm safe, reliable."

Boring.

To this day, I have no idea how Hannah and I connected so well; we're opposites in almost everything, yet somehow, we match each other perfectly.

She's a bookworm and was always a straight A student but she still knows how to let loose and have fun. She's also easily liked by so many. All of which is the exact opposite of myself. I got by in school, but I've always had more athletic ability than anything—which means nothing now—so, I'm forced to rely on my mediocre degree to get a mediocre job that I feel mediocre about. And no one really finds me likable.

I suppose I wasn't always like this, but this way feels better than letting people in who I don't care to get to know.

Since I met Hannah, she's been the most important thing in my life and I have every intention of keeping it that way.

"How about you?" I flinch at my own question, internally scolding myself for asking. I don't really care. Why did I even ask? And by the look on Dane's face, he's just as shocked by my question as well. Hannah's been actively acting as a buffer between us. She's been purposely signing me questions to ask him all day. This is the first one I think I've asked on my own.

Plus, I've been attempting to ignore him since he made that comment at the restaurant earlier.

Let him taste me on you.

I still don't know if I'm pissed, irrevocably turned on, or all in at this point.

Whatever it is that we're doing is leading in some direction that I'm unsure of. I want it more than I'm willing to admit, but frankly, it scares the shit out of me.

"I'm sort of a free spirit, I guess. I go with the flow, live day by day. Life's too short, you know?"

"Dane's a 'shoot first, ask questions later' kind of guy. He's the most exciting, but impulsive guy you'll ever meet. Insanely honest, loyal, and kindhearted, too," Kobi chimes into our conversation as he sits down next to Dane, "oh, and he's willing to try anything once." His slight European accent gives that last statement more sensuality than it should.

Dane shrugs, raising his eyebrows, clearly unable to contest what he said.

"Just ask him about George. Oh, and Sarina, that's a good story. Oh, Oh, did you tell him about—"

"Kobi," Dane elongates his name in a threat.

Kobi's hands shoot up in surrender and a surge of jealousy rolls through me.

Who the fuck is George?

At least now I know for certain he swings both ways. I can't imagine any woman's name is George. I mean, you never know but still. I suspected he likes both, it's been clear by all his actions today and especially tonight.

My dick begins to stir behind my pants and I need to get the fuck out of here. This booth feels tiny all of a sudden.

I stand, ignoring this conversation about *George,* and the foreign mixture of bitterness and lust building inside me.

"I'm going to check on Hannah." It's a lame excuse since she's only a few steps in front of our table but I still need to get away. Stepping up behind her, I wrap my arms around her waist and begin to move my body with hers. I hate dancing, but it's better than sitting there listening to his crazy escapades with a past lover. Lovers, in his case.

The waitress comes in between our table and where Hannah and I are dancing. She hands each of us a martini glass full of dark brown liquid and a creamy foam top with a small bean placed elegantly in the middle.

"What is this?" I yell over the music at Dane.

"Espresso martini." He tips his glass up in a silent toast, then takes a sip.

Great. Alcohol *and* caffeine. Neither one I drink much of. It's going to be a long night.

14

DANE

"Did I offend him?" Kobi asks, as I watch Ethan sway behind Hannah.

"No, that's just how he is. He's pretty closed off. It's ironic really. She's nonverbal, yet I've communicated with her more than him."

"Irony is the fact that you know ASL when less than one percent of the population does," Kobi replies, and of course he would know that fact. He's a professional linguist.

"Yeah, but they don't know that," I tell Kobi as Hannah turns around and signs to Ethan.

"*Are you okay?*"

"Wait, they don't know you know? So, you've just been spying on their conversation this entire time?" he asks with way too much judgment in his tone. But I nod confidently, continuing to read their conversation.

"*I'm good.*"

"*You don't seem good.*"

Her eyebrows lift in a questioning look and I love how expressive she is even without verbal words.

"*You like him,*" she signs, leaving out a question mark.

He runs his hands through that luscious, dark hair of his and I can tell he's nervous.

"I like him, too," she signs again, as if it would help him admit it as well.

Satisfaction fills in my chest as I attempt to smother my smile.

"You're going straight to hell," Kobi half chuckles. "I don't know what they're saying but I can guarantee they don't want you eavesdropping on the conversation," Kobi says, trying to be all noble.

"Oh, shut your face. How many conversations have you spied on, monitored, then used to your advantage." He opens his mouth to reply, but doesn't say anything. "That's what I thought."

I turn back to continue my how-to-get-these-two-in-bed secret spy mission.

"I'm just saying, she reminds me of a certain someone. You seem very smitten, with both of them, and it's only been one day."

I pause, taking in his words because I know what he's trying to say without saying it.

"She doesn't look anything like Celeste," I reply, looking down and avoiding his gaze.

"No, physically they are very different. But, her smile," he pauses as we both glance over to her, beaming a radiant smile that instantly sent me back to the moment I met Celeste when I saw Hannah, "and...her energy. Same fierce energy."

I sigh, turning my gaze away because he's right.

Admittedly, it's been a long time since I've *really* thought about her. It took a long time for me to learn how to push aside the incessant thoughts of Celeste, especially when I used to drown myself in my memories of her.

The first day of kindergarten when the little girl with matching pale blonde hair to mine instantly became my best friend. In second grade when we didn't get the same teacher and cried for an entire day about it because we wouldn't get to spend everyday in the same classroom together. Fifth grade, when I saw her kissing scrawny Tyson Mellick and felt jealousy for the first time in my life. In seventh grade, when I finally confessed my undying love for my best friend and we became even more inseparable from that moment on.

Then in our freshman year of high school, when she was diagnosed with Acute Lympocytic Leukemia and started treatment almost immediately, missing months of school. Day after day of seeing her get weaker and weaker. Losing her hair, dynamic energy and, on some days, the will to keep going.

When she made it through all the IV drips and chemotherapy, kicking cancer's ass, we celebrated for days on end—and continued to—by living a life of spontaneity and fun, because *life is too fucking short*, she would say.

The first time I backpacked through Europe was with her the summer after we graduated high school. Healthy and happy, and cancer free.

We moved from hostel to hostel, seeing every country we could, exploring everything together. We learned so much about ourselves that summer. Our likes and dislikes. Sexuality and desires. That was the summer of discovery for both of us and it was so enlightening.

After that, we moved to Houston where we went into our freshman year of college with so much happiness and hope. We met new people and became close with Kobi, Hudson, and Jake, building an unbreakable friendship with them that year. Until finals in our freshman year when she got really ill.

At first she brushed it off as stress, ignored all the symptoms until she fainted while we were getting ready for our summer backpacking trip.

The cancer had come back.

She died a few weeks later.

Taking my soul with her.

I run my palm over my mouth, as if to stop myself from replying to Kobi so he won't hear the unavoidable crack behind it.

"You don't need to read between the lines here, Dane. I'm not suggesting anything. I've just never seen you so invested, so quickly. I think it's a good thing. I just want you to be careful. They're already in a relationship and things can get very messy."

Clearing my throat, "Yeah, I know. I'm just having fun." I reply with a fake smile and a half truth. "He's bi-curious. You know how I love having fun with guys like him," I admit because that one is more than true.

Kobi raises a brow. "Did he tell you that?"

"No...but she has."

I smirk as I continue to read Hannah's hand cues.

"Let's be open minded and just see where this goes. He's perfect to explore with, even if it's just once."

Ethan tips back his head, pulling Hannah flush against him, as if he's thankful for her saying what he can't.

She presses her cheek against his chest and as Ethan kisses the crown of her head, our blue eyes connect and I give her an assuring smile. She's studying me, appraising me as if she needs to be sure I'm a safe bet for them.

Kobi's right. It might have just been her smile at first but throughout today I've seen so much of Celeste in her. Her supportive, caring nature. How encouraging she is with Ethan about his sexuality—just like Celeste was with me. The way she sucker punched those girls at the table without saying a word. Her wild energy and the way she smiles when she's happy.

Her lips lift up in a soft, tender smile, as if she can read my thoughts as easily as I can read her words and I wonder how much of the real me she can really see.

Giving me the lifeline I need to get out of my own head, she reaches out her hand in a come here motion and gestures her chin to the dance floor.

My eyes flick over to Ethan who watches her as she invites me over. His chest lifts in a heavy breath and in perfect timing we both shoot back the rest of our martini. Kobi calls for a second round as I stand up and join them on the floor.

15

HANNAH

I have no idea what time it is as we stumble through the doorway of the hostel.

"Shhhhh—" Dane hisses so loud there's nothing quiet about it. Ethan laughs at him as one foot slips off the first step and he falls into the staircase. Now it's Dane's turn to laugh while Ethan shushes him.

Ethan doesn't drink much, so to see him like this, laughing and care-free, makes my heart soar. It's not that I would like to see him drunk all the time but he always runs himself on such a tight rope in our day-to-day schedule. Especially since he started working for his father. *This* is exactly what we needed this summer.

He was hard on himself before the accident. Adhering to a rigorous workout and training schedule. All his focus was on baseball and getting the grades he needed to get his scholarship. After the accident, when he was told he would never play college or professional baseball, he kept the same schedule. Waking up early to go for a run and the gym, but the hole that baseball left in his life has changed him. Like a part of his heart died.

His focus shifted to supporting me in all the classes I was taking to make up for the healing time with all the surgeries I needed, and I think that made him feel like he had purpose. But now that we're both working toward our future, I know he feels lost.

To see him let loose like this is a treat that I'll be taking full advantage of. Especially because Dane brings out this playful side to him that I rarely see.

I climb up the stairs first, finally making it through the doorway of our room. I fully expect a crowd of other travelers so I'm shocked how dark the room is, as I trip over my own feet, plopping down in the bean bag chair.

"Hannah, where are you?" Ethan's voice carries through the room. I can barely see the outline of his shadow, his arms are out in front of him, trying to feel his way around the darkness.

He trips over something and falls forward, just as a loud bang echoes through the room.

"Ouch. Shit."

The lights flash on and Dane stands in the doorway, his eyes glancing over the room to see me, giggling on a bean bag chair, and Ethan on the floor in front of his bunk holding a hand over the top of his forehead.

"I was only a second behind you guys. What the hell just happened?" Dane walks over to Ethan, helping him sit on the edge of the bed, inspecting the area just above his eye.

I sit back, attempting to make myself invisible as Ethan's intense gaze bounces between Dane's lips and eyes. Dane is wholly invested in making sure Ethan is okay, pressing the pad of his finger gently over the reddened area of his skin.

As usual, the room is swimming in sexual tension just like every time those two are next to each other and I love the sensation it brings.

There's a wave of anxiety that rolls off Ethan but as uncomfortable as he is, there's a high behind his eyes that I can feel, even from a distance.

"You didn't break the skin but you'll probably have a gnarly bruise," Dane tells him as he drops his eyes meeting Ethan's gaze.

Dane's finger trails over the side of Ethan's temple, circles around his jaw, then slowly dips down the column of his neck. Ethan's throat bobs as he swallows thickly, shifting in his seat.

There's a long pause and a heaviness in the air. It weighs on all of us like an anchor, holding us in place.

Ethan peers out of the corner of his eyes in my direction. I squeeze my hands together, holding myself back from saying anything because I want him to act on his own free will based on how he's feeling.

His eyes shift back over to Dane, who's nervous and tense, unlike his normal casual demeanor. His finger is still hovering over Ethan's skin, in the sensitive spot where his neck meets his collarbone.

Finally, Dane breaks the silence.

"Are you done pretending that you don't want me?"

"What?" Ethan's brows pinch together.

There's an eerie silence in the room, only the sound of Ethan's steady, but heavy breath before Dane finally speaks up again.

"I know it was you in the glory hole at *Avec Plaisir*."

16

ETHAN

"I—" My throat bobs as I swallow thickly. "I don't know what you're talking about," I manage to spit out even though I can't keep a straight face. It dropped, as did my stomach, the moment the words left his lips.

"Ask me how I know," he says with far too much fucking confidence, looking me dead in the eye.

Panic sears through every cell in my body and everything around me feels instantly smaller. I lean to the left but he follows, blocking me. Then shift to the right but it's the same.

"Get out of my way." I nudge him to the side and stand, stepping away from the isolation of the bunk and the man I can't stop thinking about doing unthinkable things with.

How does he know?

How could he know?

Hannah would have told me if she told him and as I glance in her direction, her wide-eyed, surprised expression is exactly what I would expect. So, how does he fucking know?

I turn around, unable to face him and place my hands on the wall between our bunks. I hang my head as I go through every moment of today. Every conversation, every touch, all the flirting. I knew it was aimed toward both of us, but when he would feel my discomfort he would be extra flirty with Hannah, playing it off.

Not now, though. Now he's calling out all the silent moments that passed between the two of us today and he knows I went to the sex club, specifically the glory hole.

"Ask me how I know," he says again. This time it's a whisper in my ear as his body steps up behind mine, getting closer than he ever has.

I flip around and my back presses up against the wall, creating the space I need from him and his alluring scent. That same masculine scent from last night when he was wrapped in just a towel and his golden skin was still glistening from the shower.

My cock stirs behind my pants at the thought, and at his proximity, but the worry still laces through me.

I'm slightly taller but slouched back, so we're eye-to-eye and it feels like he towers over me as he steps closer. His eyes are dark and burning with a fire I've never seen. They're lustful, determined, and begging for an answer that I can't seem to pull out of myself.

I'm angry and embarrassed and rage fills my chest. I want to push him away but my arms are heavy and my feet stay planted as I press my body harder into the wall.

"You're mistaken," I'm able to finally breathe out a shaken answer. It's a lie, but it's something.

A self-assured smirk tugs at the corner of his lip.

His knowing eyes don't leave mine as he presses his right palm into the brick wall behind me, caging me in. My breath grows heavy as his left hand grabs my right and he peers down, appraising it, tracing his thumb gently over the line of my scar.

I want to move. I want to pull back, but my body is frozen. The sensitive touch sends a bolt of electricity through me and an unknown excitement spirals through my body.

"I know because this gorgeous, scarred hand slid through that hole giving me the best fucking handjob I've ever had in my life."

"Oh, fuck," I spit out with his confession and swallow hard. "Fuck."

Pulling away, I run my hand down my face, attempting to wash away the words.

It was him? *It was him.*

My mind reels through every second of every moment that happened in that room. How comfortable he made me feel. How much he wanted to please me. How loud he moaned when I kept jerking him off after he told me he was close. How determined I was to please him.

Against my will, my cock hardens behind my pants and I can't help but flex my hips forward. The movement is small but enough for him to notice.

"Your cock tasted so good coming down my throat." He leans his body into mine, our cocks flush against each other as he rolls his clothed hips into mine and my breath catches in my throat. "I want to hear you moan again, but this time I want your eyes on me while you scream out my name."

I shake my head. Not believing that this man was the same man in the room next to mine, as I fed my cock unknowingly through that hole. It throbs again at the thought and I hate how fucking turned on I am by just the memory of him.

"No?" His lips form a tight line as he nods slowly. One foot lifts as he starts to take a step back, respecting my space, but that's not what I want.

I need him to conquer it, take it over and not allow me the chance to think about it.

I need him to destroy all the negative thoughts I've had about this moment.

I need him to shatter all the things holding me back.

But I can't form any words.

My arm rockets out to his chest, gripping onto his shirt and he freezes. Dane peers down at his chest, staring at my clenched, shaking hand, then his eyes trail down my body. I'm cemented into the wall, stiff everywhere except the nervous tremble in my hands, yet the bulge in my pants screams for attention. He notices and blinks as his eyes rise back up to meet mine.

Tucking his fingers into the waistband of my pants, he yanks me forward, rubbing our dicks together, but harder this time.

Both of his hands hover over my belt as he expertly removes it, ripping it out of the loops.

I feel exposed even though I'm still fully clothed. I have no idea what to do. I grip the other side of his shirt and yank it apart, the buttons fly off as the front of his shirt tears open. He needs to feel as naked and vulnerable as I do. But that easily fed his desire instead of halting it.

He glances down, and that stupid contagious smile of his appears on his face, as he shifts his gaze between his torn button down shirt, Hannah, then me.

"I loved this fucking shirt." His tone is playful as he grips the open lines of his torn shirt and slips it off his shoulders onto the floor.

His fingers circle my wrists, then he pulls them up over my head and pushes me against the wall, pinning me down.

I buck, in a weak attempt to fight back, but he presses the full weight of his body against mine and I can feel his hard length against my hip. I've never been in such a compromising position, especially with a man.

My eyes bounce between his now dark, determined pupils and lips and I can't help but press my head against the wall and squeeze mine shut to avoid drowning in them. It was easier when there was a wall between us. All the thoughts of why I shouldn't be doing this cycle through my mind, but my disloyal body feels otherwise.

I attempt to push away again, but Dane just presses into me harder, his cloth covered cock strokes mine and I let out a stunted moan.

His lips hover over my ear. "I want to make this good for you."

I stiffen at the memory of those words, the same ones he whispered through the wall as I had one foot out the door. He sounds as genuine as he did the first time and for some unknown annoying reason, my body listens to him. My shoulders relax, releasing the tension they were holding and my breath calms as if his seductive voice soothes me.

"Mmm," he hums, pleased with my submission. "Good. But, can I trust you not to push me away?"

I want to trust him. I do trust him. But, I can't trust myself. My mind will override everything and break away from this wall the first chance I get, even though I want to stay glued to his touch.

"Yes," I reply through a clenched jaw.

"That's what I thought." A slow, sexy smirk appears on his lips. "Hannah, can you please come over here and keep your boyfriend's hands busy so he doesn't rip my skin off while I suck his cock."

17

DANE

The soft pleather crinkles and the styrofoam beans rustle as Hannah pushes herself up and makes her way toward us.

It's as if she was waiting all day for me to do this exact thing and say those words to her because she treads our way with ease, pushing the thin straps of her gorgeous yellow sundress down her arms. By the time she reaches us, the top of her sundress hangs past her breasts, settling at the crevice of her waist.

The confidence she displays as she reaches up, trailing her fingertips on Ethan's arms and over my hands makes my cock twitch behind the denim of my thick jeans that I know Ethan can feel. Instead of replacing her grip with mine, she gently intertwines her fingers in his, then lifts up on her toes, pressing their lips together, providing him a comfort she probably thinks he needs.

She pulls back slowly, lowering his hands and places them over the peaks of her chest. Her lips part and eyes flutter as he caresses and pinches her nipples that harden at his touch.

Fuck, they're sexy together.

Their eyes are fixed on each other with nothing but silent knowledge moving between them.

With my hands free again, I grant her a lopsided grin, and unbutton his pants, pulling down his zipper. His pants hang loosely over his hips, his sexy-as-sin V-line peering under the denim, as I tug them down exposing his charcoal grey boxer briefs covering that massive bulge I've been dreaming about since he walked out of that room on me.

I sink down to my knees in front of him, his eyes shift down to me and I keep my gaze locked on those chocolate brown orbs the entire way down. This is exactly what I wanted, his slacked jaw and lust-filled eyes watching me as he filled my mouth with his cock.

Dipping my fingers into the elastic waistband, I pull down the front exposing that gorgeous cock and it springs out, bouncing just inches from my face with a bead of pre-cum already leaking from the slit.

"W-Wait," he says with a nervous stutter as he attempts to move but Hannah cups her hands around his face and pulls him down for a kiss. I take full advantage of the distraction, wrapping my lips around the tight crown of his cock and then push forward, taking him all the way to the back of my throat.

He moans loudly and a muffled *fuck* with a mixture of groans, and other profanities, fly out his mouth and into hers as I bob up and down.

Fuck, he tastes so goddamn good. Exactly like he did through that glory hole but this time I get an unobstructed view of the pinch between his brows and the subdued sounds of his moaning. It's slightly dulled by Hannah's mouth on his and not a barrier between us, which I fucking love so much more.

I hold the tip of his dick at the back of my throat and bob deeper as my eyes peer up at him, taking in everything as I sear it to my memory. The way their tongues slide over each other, his distressed expression that comes from pure pleasure fights its way out. His hands find purchase on her body as one grips her hip tightly and the other cups around her breast.

"Oh, fuck. Oh god," he confesses between kisses. Releasing her hip, he runs his fingers through my hair and latches onto the roots, using the hold to control my movements.

A bolt of electricity runs through me with his touch and I moan around his length at the excruciating pleasure. The vibration of my stifled sounds radiate over the velvet skin of his hard shaft and he hisses, whimpering a few words before swearing out loud again.

"Fuck. Fuck. Fuck." His head thuds against the brick behind him as he squeezes his eyes closed so tight that multiple lines bunch around the corner of his eyes.

I couldn't be fucking happier with my view. As much as I love the glory hole, I'm so visual that sometimes just the sight is all I need to get me there and Ethan's facial expressions are becoming a new favorite.

He's still angry with me. I can see it in the tightness of his jaw and feel it in the intensity of his grip and when he glances back down at me watching me with hooded eyes, his dark pupils tell me everything I need to know about how he's feeling. He's so fucking close to coming down my throat and I can't help but rut my hips into the air, dying for some friction.

"Oh, Jesus. I'm close. Please, stop." His words hold no meaning behind his desperate tone.

Like him telling me that is actually going to make me stop.

I manage to roll my eyes and shake my head while keeping this gorgeous hard cock lodged in my mouth. I moan around the tip as I pull all the way out, lick the crown then push back in, repeating twice more as his body tenses.

He cups Hannah's face, pulling her forehead to his, their eyes burning into each other in a way I'm jealous of. There's comfort between them. Trust. She looks at him with a silent understanding and acceptance and my heart stutters in my chest with the memory of Celeste gazing into mine that same way.

"Fuck, it feels so good," he tells her as his chest heaves, feeding my desire. He squeezes his eyes closed and his head falls back against the wall.

Hannah looks down at me, the same comfort she provided him she's giving to me as our eyes connect. My mouth is full of her boyfriend's cock, yet she looks at me like she's grateful for me, like she needs this as much as I do.

She bites her bottom lip and her hooded ocean eyes take me in as I continue my pace. She moves her hand in between her legs, lifting up her dress, as she dips her fingers into her panties.

Oh, fuck.

Unable to hold myself back, I lift my knee over Ethan's foot, pressing my cock into his shin and I rut, humping his fucking leg because I'm desperate, so fucking desperate.

I can see the outline of her knuckle underneath the fabric of her thong as she moves over her slit. Her chin tips up as her eyes flutter and she releases a long, choppy breath, circling her clit. She's inches from me and I wish I could manage to suck on both without stopping but I don't know how Ethan would react to that. So, I painfully watch as her hand moves faster, her panties dampen with moisture while the scent of the two of them mixed together has me rolling my hips harder into Ethan.

He glances down, seeing her hand caressing herself and me frotting against his leg, and groans.

Hannah removes her hand from between her thighs, reaches up, pushing that same finger past Ethan's lips and into his mouth.

"Fuck," I muffle around his cock as he moans around her fingers.

Electricity shoots through every vein in my body as the

tingling at the base of my spine grows. I'm going to come in my pants before he comes and that's going to be so fucking embarrassing.

My head bobs faster over his cock and his moans ascend around her fingers.

And, fuck it. I reach out, tucking my thumb into the side of her soaked panties and stroke it over her slick center.

"Jesus," he whispers, his hips push forward, forcing his cock further down my throat.

She presses into his chest, her pointer fingers gesture toward her frantically, then she grips onto him as she bites into his skin.

"You're coming?" he spits out, as he looks down at my hand caressing her clit and head bobbing over his cock. I peer up, our eyes connect and the desperate need behind his dark eyes is my undoing. I groan around his cock as I rut into him again, my cock pulses against his leg.

"Oh, fuck, Dane. I can't stop...it's...I'm coming," he says in a warning but I hear nothing other than the sound of his orgasm mixed with my name bouncing off his lips.

I. Come. In. My. Pants.

Cum spills into my underwear as I hum around his length. His release hits the back of my tongue and his rousing moans drown out the pulse pounding in my eardrums. I know that I'm loud in bed. I've always been incredibly verbal but this man rivals the thunderous groans I've been known to make and I fucking love it. By the satiated look on Hannah's face, she does too.

I sit back on my heels, using the back of my hand to wipe off the excess saliva on my lips, and glance up at the two of them with an unavoidable grin.

The unrelenting pull I've had toward them since the moment we met isn't one-sided and the idea that we have the entire room to ourselves for two more nights gives me the utmost gratification.

Hannah smiles back at me as she straightens out her dress, then kneels down to my level, reaching for my pants.

I shake my head and urgently put my hands out, stopping her from going any further.

She squints as if pained by rejection and I debate lying and not telling her about my premature mishap. Tonight was about them, but I was no match for what just happened between us, and I want them to know exactly what they do to me.

"I, uh—I came in my pants." I press my lips in a tight line and shrug shyly. That's not normally like me but I'm dying for them to like me as much as I like them.

Her eyes light up with an adorable curiosity, like she's impressed with my admission.

That's good because I'm embarrassed as hell.

She leans forward, kissing me softly over my cheek and smiles. I glance up to Ethan and the darkened pools have hardened into something cold and distant.

"I'm going to go clean myself up," he says, his words as detached as his eyes, then steps in between me and Hannah. The cold breeze he leaves in his wake might as well be a glacial whirlpool.

18

HANNAH

"So, is he going to be okay? I mean, should I go check on him?" Dane asks as he glances at the door for at the least the fifth time since Ethan left.

He's pulling back the covers on his bed after he paced around the room a bit. I could tell he was doing everything in his power to stop himself from following Ethan out of the room.

Dane is a fixer. He wants to help make anything better. It was crystal clear in the way he handled dinner with those two girls sitting next to us.

Grabbing my small white board from my bag, I write, *he just needs some time.* Then flip it around to show Dane. He looks back at the door and nods and it's truly endearing.

He's been so respectful of me and Ethan—to both of us individually and as a couple—I find myself glaring at the door as if Ethan could sense my irritation with how he's responding to such an amazing experience.

We all had a great time. I know Ethan did, even though he'll try to deny it or just completely ignore it for the time being. I've never heard him moan so loud or look so satiated after sex, and we didn't even have actual sex.

My god though, when we do, that'll probably be like experiencing a total solar eclipse. Rare, cosmic, unreal.

I peer over at Dane and he quickly turns his gaze away as if he were caught staring. He smiles but he has the same somber look he had when he was talking to his friend Kobi at the club today.

I haven't mastered reading lips yet, but I tried to eavesdrop on their conversation at the table when Ethan and I were dancing and all I got was that I reminded him of someone named Celeste.

I've never been one to shy away from open communication, even without my voice, and I want to know more about him.

I erase the words I previously wrote on my white board and write the question that's been on my mind. *Who's Celeste?*

Turning the board around, he glances up, reads it then quickly glances up at me.

"Where did you hear that name?" he asks; his tone is light, defeated.

I point at him, then my lips to signal I heard it from him.

"Ah, at the club." He nods slowly.

I nod back.

He veers his gaze back toward the ground, then sits on the corner of his bed. I mirror his movements on the bed opposite to him, giving him my undivided attention.

"Celeste," he says her name almost as a whisper. Like it's been too long since he's really said her name with the passion it deserves. A small smile tugs at his lips before he continues. "She was my girlfriend. My best friend. We met in grade school. She passed away almost ten years ago. Cancer."

He glances back up at me, giving me a foreign smile—one that doesn't reach his eyes, then continues, "That was a long time ago."

My hand is covering my heart, like a part of it is breaking for him. I can't imagine what he went through and at such a young age. He can't be more than thirty years old so this had to have happened during high school or college.

I hate that he's minimizing his feelings. I can tell there's more and I'm sure he doesn't want to talk about it but I know he wasn't expecting me to ask. I also hate when people feel like it's been a long time so they *shouldn't* feel it as deeply or strongly as they do.

I cross the space between us, erasing my board and write, *Time is relative.*

"Yeah," he agrees and nods robotically.

I write more as he watches me.

Singular.

He stares at the word for a moment before peering up to meet my gaze, huffing out a small breath.

"You're like a reincarnated Edgar Allen Poe." I squint, confused at his statement. " He was a master of words, known to speak with very little volume, intentionally low, so people were compelled to listen," he smiles at me, "and I'm very compelled to listen to you, Poe."

My cheeks flush at the nickname and my stomach backflips to my heart. Other than Ethan no one has ever really listened to me since the accident. But Dane, he's present paying attention to every tick, expression and written word, *hearing* me fully.

He sucks in a deep breath, looking at the door again. "I think your boyfriend is probably plotting my death," he says with a light chuckle but I know this is one of the times he's saying something as a playful joke but half-heartedly means it.

I point back at the first line on my board and he nods again, still smiling. "Ah, yes, thank you Mr. Miyagi."

Shoving his arm, I smile and he laughs. It seems as if a weight has been lifted off him. I don't know if it's from him telling me about Celeste or from the release of all the sexual tension but this softer side of Dane makes me even more confident in our decision of opening up to him the way we did. Even if Ethan will take longer to accept it.

Standing, I glance back at the door and see a shadow shift on the ground from the small crack and fight myself to hold back from stomping over there, ripping the door open, and forcing him to sit next to Dane and give themselves the post-orgasm attention they need, but, I take my own advice—giving him time, and climb up the ladder to the top bunk.

"Goodnight Hannah," Dane says as he crawls under his blanket and switches off the lamp.

I just hope that Ethan gets out of his own head before he misses out on the fun we could be having for the last two days of our trip.

19

ETHAN

I linger outside the door of our room for at least another thirty minutes before slowly creeping it open.

I know I'm a total idiot for waiting that long, especially because Hannah probably saw me out here before she went to bed, but I couldn't face them. I have no reason to feel that way. Hannah has done nothing but support me, and Dane...well Dane has been annoyingly perfect.

In fact, everything he does is perfect. He's so similar to Hannah, I find myself jealous of how light hearted everything is around him, when all I seem to cause is more stress.

And his fucking mouth. My cock stirs back to life at the thought and there's no way that thing should have any functionality after the orgasm they gave me.

Seeing her fall apart as he fingered her while he was on his knees taking the full length of my cock down his throat. I'll never forget it. I've still scolded myself since the moment I stepped out of the room but I needed to get away because his admission that he was the one on the other side of the glory hole was too much.

I've had passing thoughts of the stranger behind the wall,

but now knowing it's someone that I've grown to like as well. My emotional well-being couldn't handle that information.

I tip-toe past the bean bag chairs and kick my shoes off next to my bed. Sliding under the top cover, I freeze when I hear Dane's voice.

"Hey," he says with an ease I'm jealous of.

I roll over knowing I can't avoid him. "Hey."

There's a long pause, as if he's choosing his next words wisely. I can only see the outline of his face in the dark, so his thoughts and facial expression are a complete mystery. He's propped up on his elbow, his hand resting on the side of his face, like he was waiting for me the entire time and had no plans of sleeping until I came back.

"There's a theme park nearby. I have tickets to it. Want to go tomorrow?" His tone is soft, vulnerable.

This surprises me. That was the last thing I expected him to say. But, being a natural deflector of my bicurious status in the given moment, I'm all for this conversation.

"Hell yeah, that sounds like fun." There's an excitement to my tone that surprises even me, and even through the dark space between us I can see Dane grinning and something warm in my chest radiates through my body at the thought that I made him happy.

Dane's laugh travels through the hallway of the empty hostel yet again as if it's a reenactment of last night. Except this time we're not drunk. We had a couple of beers throughout the day at the theme park—which was by far the most fun I've ever had at one—but we're nowhere near as intoxicated as we were last night.

Hannah tosses the large stuffed animal in Dane's face then takes just a couple of strides in the direction of the door before he catches up to her and tosses her over his shoulder. They've been playful like this all day long. I shake my head and smile as I cut in front of them, using my card to open the door and let him walk through with her still draped over his body.

He nods with that goddamn smile of his and I smack her ass as they pass by.

Something about today just made everything easy. I don't know if it was what happened last night, which we have all ignored—more than likely because they knew that's what I was doing—the theme park, or just the fun energy that Dane brings to both of us. I really have no idea, but it's been a long time since I've felt this at ease.

Dane tosses Hannah down on the bean bag, bringing his hands to her sides and tickles her before he plops down on the bag next to her.

His hair is a mess, as it's been most of the day. In and out of a low man bun that I'm quite obsessed with. His hair doesn't go past his shoulders so when he pulls it back, a few of the strands fall forward and even though it's totally unintentional, it's like he purposely places them there to make him even more sexy.

"I think I need to kiss you." Dane's words to Hannah should surprise me, but don't. I've come to learn, he's just like that. Saying exactly what he wants when he wants it.

Hannah's face beams in an adorable smile at him before she glances over at me.

Nothing has happened between the three of us today, sexually at least, but I can't say the thought of watching them together hasn't crossed my mind. I can see how much Hannah is drawn to him and I want her to know that all of this isn't just about me. Even though it may have started that way with my curiosity.

I want her to feel the same type of pleasure and excitement and, if I'm being honest with myself, I'm dying to see them together.

I take a step back and sit down at the edge of the bottom bunk. Holding my slightly curved palms in front me, I push forward and sign to her, telling her to go ahead. Not that she needed my permission or that I'm trying to keep my words secret from Dane, it's just something we do when we have conversations between us.

Plus, signing words are so much easier than saying them sometimes.

She bites the corner of her lip, turning her gaze back to Dane.

He wastes no time, shifting his weight, pulling her face to his as he presses their lips together, moaning like he's waited an eternity for it. My cock instantly thickens behind my pants and I can't help but moan myself.

My eyes devour the two of them, taking in the sight of their tongues dancing together, his hips inching forward to hers as they pull themselves flush against each other.

What started as a kiss, inevitably turns into more. Their hands roam each other's bodies like they can't get enough of each other, and I can't keep my eyes off them.

Dane wore these lightweight white cotton joggers. *Yes, fucking white.*

All day I've been able to glance down to see the slight outline of the tip of his cock, but now the full backside of his cock pulls on the center of his pants and there's no hiding anything.

It's fully erect, upright, and hard as fuck behind that thin fabric and I want to reach out and stroke it.

Instead, I cover my hand over my mouth, using my fingertips to rub back and forth over my lips attempting to keep my hands busy.

Dane pushes himself off the bag and holds his body over hers, his movements are sensual, yet frantic, as he reaches down and pulls her skirt up to her waist, dipping his fingers into the front of her lace panties.

He begins to stroke over her clit, eliciting those rare sounds she makes as he curses over her mouth.

"Fuck, I need to taste you." Pulling his hand out, he dips his fingers into his mouth and kneels in between her legs.

I have an unobstructed view of her face with his back and ass directly in front of me.

Fuck.

Fuuuuck.

Her mouth forms a large O and her head falls back as he dives in, devouring her cunt with pleased groans.

"Fuck you taste so good," he says between licking and sucking. "Is your boyfriend touching himself yet?" he asks with a smirk behind his tone. He's not looking back at me, but his head tips to look at her for an answer.

Her eyes shift past his shoulders landing on me and she shakes her head no.

"Shame," he says before diving back in.

Digging my fingernails into my palms I clench my fists.

Because I don't want to touch myself.

I want to touch *him*.

My chest heaves and my breath becomes heavier at the thought, but I push the anxiety filled sensations aside and fall to my knees behind him.

Moving quickly, I reach around him and yank the front of his joggers down, exposing the full length of his cock. He lets out an audible grunt as I wrap my hand around his base and stroke upward.

His body stammers, matching his stilted moaning. When I tug back, sliding my hand down his shaft, I pull his ass into my groin and rock my hips into him.

Another loud moan reverberates from his chest when I roll

my hips, rubbing my own achingly hard cock between the round globes of his cheeks.

"Jesus Christ. Fuck...Please keep doing that," he says in between breaths before diving back in.

Hannah grabs the sides of his head, holding him down as she rolls her hips. She's so close and by the way Dane is rutting into my hand like he did to my leg yesterday, I can tell he is, too.

Leaning over his back, I use my free hand to hold his ass against my crotch as I inch my lips closer to his ear.

I have no idea what's gotten into me, but I want nothing more than to turn him inside out, like he's done with me.

"Does my girlfriend taste good, Dane?" he hums, answering my question with a small nod, it's the only amount he's able to move with Hannah's tight grasp on his hair.

His cock twitches in my grip and I know he's getting close. A rush of excitement runs through me knowing my words and touch are getting him there.

I stop my strokes and grip the base, using my fingertips to massage his balls. "Can you hold out while you make her come?" I knead my fingers deeper as he attempts to nod through another guttural moan. "Good. Because when you're done with her, I need you to fuck my face as hard as I fucked yours through that wall."

"Oh, fuck...fuck." He squeezes his eyes shut as his muffled words drown in Hannah's pussy. My words affect her as much as him and her toes begin to curl, fingers dig into his scalp and her entire body tenses through her orgasm.

I can't help but smirk as he lets out a frustrated groan, attempting to hold back his orgasm.

Hannah comes down off her high as Dane pushes into his palms, bringing his face to hers. He kisses her on the lips and whispers something before he flips over and faces me.

His eyes lock with mine, as he lifts his hips off the floor, pushing his joggers past his ankles. He kicks them off, wrapping his hand around his cock and sucks in a heavy breath.

"I hope you meant what you said because that took everything I had to hold back." He gives himself one long, languid stroke as his eyes flutter and his breath hitches. "Are you going to stay true to your word?" he asks, his body language pleading as much as his words are. He inches closer to me, taunting me with both his question and the thinned skin crown of his cock as he twists his hand over the length and squeezes at the tip.

I don't think. I don't wait. I just act on pure instinct of everything I've wanted from this moment.

Leaning forward, I replace his hand with mine and wrap my lips around the thick crown. He grunts in pleasure as I take him further into my mouth while pushing him back down to the floor. His hand slaps the ground, the other lands square on Hannah's thigh and he grips hard. She intertwines her fingers with his, then shifts her body closer to us. The comfort of her nearness blankets me, giving me the confidence I need to keep going.

I push my face further into him, his cock slides over my tongue and taps the back of my throat. The sweet salty mixture invades my senses and I can't help but groan loving the taste.

I crane my neck further into him, his cock sliding deeper into my throat and the tip of my nose is now flush with his stomach.

I guess I don't have a gag reflex.

"Oh my god, fuck. Fuck." Dane grabs the side of my face, gripping my short hair as he pulls my gaze to his.

I look up at him, a smile must pierce my eyes because he huffs out a smile. "Oh, you smug bastard." I can't help but cough out around his cock as I attempt to smother a laugh.

Keeping the tip lodged in the back of my throat, I bob up and down, massaging it with the soft tissue of my throat as I suck around his shaft.

I'm loving every bit of this. The taste, his tense body, the way he looks down at me, completely powerless.

His mouth drops, brows pinch, and he thrusts deeper. "Oh fuck, I'm sorry," he grits out as the tip of his cock begins to swell. I can feel it start to pulse as he attempts to push me away but I grab his ass pulling him deeper as he comes.

The thick, salty liquid hits the back of my throat and I groan from the unexpected intrusion but continue to suck and swallow, still determined to make him lose all control.

"Oh, Jesus. Goddamn it." He flops back onto the floor, his hands roam over his chest as if checking to see if his body is still here.

I swallow around his cock once more before trailing my lips over his length and pop off the tip, cleaning him as I go.

His entire body shutters and he crunches forward before falling back down again.

"I'm so pathetic. I don't think I've come that fast since I was a fucking teenager," he confesses, a hint of shyness behind his playful, satiated tone.

I can't help but smile as I run the back of my palm over the corner of my mouth and glance over at Hannah. Her gorgeous, normally bright eyes are blown out and her hair is a frazzled mess. Dane's physical state is similar and I can't even imagine what I look like.

I plop down beside Hannah, wrapping my arms around her waist, pulling her into me.

The length of my erect cock presses against the small of her back and she reaches back, but I stop her. "I'm good," I whisper in her ear. Because, I am. "Just let me stay here for a minute."

I don't know if I'm hiding behind her but at least I'm not running. I refuse to feel the same kind of guilt I did last night. Plus, this was a top tier sexual experience and I didn't even come.

She relaxes into me and Dane pops ups onto his elbows as he takes us in.

"I don't know what that was, but I swear I saw the fucking Milky Way." I laugh and I can feel Hannah's body do the same. "That was...wow," Dane adds, giving me a rare timid smile before standing.

Grabbing his joggers, he steps into one leg and freezes as voices carry from the other side of the door.

His eyes widen as he looks at the door, then back at me, and I glance down at Hannah and I. We're both clothed, but her dress is riding well above her waist and the straps of them hang over her shoulders and I have a massive bulge behind the center of my pants that doesn't feel like it's going anywhere, any time soon. All of us look like we've been royally fucked, hair completely unkempt and our skin is flushed.

"Shit," I spit out, pulling Hannah's dress down as she yanks up her straps. She stands, heading straight for her locker, as if she's grabbing something and Dane rushes so fast trying to get his foot into the other leg of his pants he topples over onto the floor with a loud thud.

I screw up my face and involuntarily say *ouch* out loud with a small laugh. He pins me with an overwrought look, as he rolls over and yanks his pants up then reaches under the bed right as the door is opening.

"Found it," Dane yells, as he scooches back toward the bean bag chair and plops on the one opposite of me, smiling, placing a deck of cards on the table between us.

Two people stand in the threshold of the door and fortunately, they don't sense anything as they step through the doorway, with a few more people following behind them.

"Hi guys," a guy with dark skin, long dreads, and a friendly smile says as he shrugs his backpack off his shoulders.

Hannah waves as Dane and I glance over and say, "hey," at the exact same time.

Dane smiles at our synchronized rhythm and I roll my eyes at him.

Of course, Dane being the extrovert he is, stands holding out his hand and introduces himself.

"I'm Dane—solo traveler," he clarifies, and it kind of bugs me. He categorized himself outside of our group and it's the first time he's separated himself from us.

I hate it.

"That is Hannah and Ethan." He points in our direction.

"Hi everyone, I'm Trent," the guy with the dreads replies. He looks at both Hannah and I, then names off all the people in his group, a total of five of them. "We just checked in a day early, luckily they had space! There's another group of eight in the other room."

"Wow, big party," I reply.

"Yeah, this is the first stop for our CGA mission trip," Trent replies, bouncing with an excited smile.

"CGA?" Dane asks, tilting his head with a slight squint in his eye.

"The Celibacy Group of America."

20

DANE

"You should have seen your faces." I laugh, as I take a bite of my jam toast.

Hannah's cheeks flush, yet again, and she throws a raspberry at my face.

"Celibacy Group of America? I mean, come on, that's funny right. Considering what we had just done." Hannah dips her face into her palms and Ethan shifts a bit. I'm still unsure about mentioning our sexual adventures so easily but his reaction is still leaps and bounds better than the first night.

Everything between the three of us has been so natural since the first day, it's only after something happens sexually between Ethan and I that he tends to retract into himself. I've been very mindful of this and tread lightly but after almost getting busted by an entire group of celibate Christians, we all seem to be taking things a little less seriously. It's been light-hearted, fun and absolutely fucking perfect.

Even now, his knee is grazing mine under the table and he's not jerking away. Hannah always seems to be touching me or Ethan and I love that because it's my primary love language.

Hers too, I think.

I haven't figured out his yet.

Either way, I don't want this to end and I hate that after breakfast they're going to go see some sights together and I'm going to hang out with Kobi for a few hours before he flies back to Japan. I mean, I want to hang out with Kobi but I don't want to miss out on time with these two either. Plus, it's the last night and the room is now occupied, so there isn't anything we can do in our room later.

I know I'm living a life of sin according to some and I don't need the Celibacy Group of America reminding me of that. Especially when I want to do all sorts of unspeakable sinful things to my two new friends in the privacy of my own room.

Actually...I could capitalize on this.

"So, hey. Kobi is flying back a day early. He prepaid for the hotel and is offering me the room. He's pretty bougie, so it's probably really nice." I run my hand through my hair nervously—a foreign feeling that I'm not used to. "Do you guys want to stay there..." I swallow thickly, "with me?"

Kobi doesn't have an extra night, but I will damn sure get the best fucking suite in this city if they say yes.

My eyes bounce between the two of them, trying to read their expressions. The silence is excruciating and I find myself trying to think of all the perks to sell them on the idea.

I go to open my mouth but Ethan spits out a quick, "Yes, god yes. I can't wait to have a room with our own bathroom and a tad bit of privacy."

Oh, thank god.

I huff out a sigh of relief that mixed with a chuckle. "Yeah, the last few nights have been rare in a hostel, but a private room all to ourselves—" I wiggle my eyebrows at Hannah because that's far too flirtatious for Ethan, "who knows what kind of trouble we'll get into."

"You've been uncharacteristically quiet about your trip," Kobi says as he steps up a steep ledge. He pulls himself up on a flat rock with ease then turns, holding out his hand and helps me up.

We're both shirtless, a sheen of sweat glistens over our skin as we trek through a dense forest park just outside of Paris.

Traditionally we make this hike whenever we're in Paris together and trek until we reach the edge of the waterfall. It's been over an hour and we're almost there, yet we've only had surface level conversations because I refuse to talk about how invested I am in whatever is happening between Ethan, Hannah and me.

"Just training myself to get ready to teach. I'm trying to be a better listener," I say, telling Kobi a half truth.

"Ha! If I've ever heard of a line of bullshit in my life, it was that line right there. Spill it with the couple you're coiting with," he quips, knowing me too well.

"Coiting? Is that even a word?

"Stop deflecting. You aren't good at it."

I pause, taking in the sights as we peer over the lush trees and listen to the sound of rushing river water. It's the most peaceful place I know, a favorite to visit out of all the places I go, and this time I feel unexplainably different. I feel...happy. And not the fake, goofy happiness that I always show everyone. It's an ease and contentness I haven't felt in a long time. A very long time.

"Do they know how you feel?" Kobi asks without me saying anything further, because he's a fucking know-it-all. We've traveled and spent far too much time together over the years for him not to see a shift.

I chipmunk my cheeks and force out a breath as I place my hands on my hips.

Do they know how I feel?

No, I mean how could they? Why would they? It's been

three fucking days and I'm head over heels for the both of them. I hardly know anything about them.

What I do know is how I feel when I'm with them and that's more than I've felt in a long time.

And for some reason, that's all that matters to me right now.

I shake my head and he hums.

"What do you plan to do about that?"

"I'm going to tell them," I say. "We all go home tomorrow, so I just need to tell them more about myself. I'll tell them I'm headed back to Seattle to teach for a year, then maybe I can spend some time wherever they live and," I shrug, "I don't know, hang out there for a while."

I hate how unsure I sound. Because why would they even go for that or even want to spend time with me after a year. I feel fucking sick and vulnerable and I hate it.

Kobi watches me as I shift back and forth in my stance, knowing I'm completely fucking unhinged by them and losing my mind trying to figure out how to keep whatever it is we have going. I mean, it's possible, right? I can't be the only one feeling this way.

"Hey," he pats me on the shoulder, "I'm sure it's going to work out, just tell them how you feel. Be open. They've been pretty open with you, right?"

Sexually, yeah. But I know nothing about them personally. I don't even know what state they live in.

I nod. Agreeing and answering his question at the same time.

Kobi looks at me with concern and I don't blame him. I'm far out on the line, with my heart on a platter, serving it up to them and I have no desire to pull it back.

"Who's going first?" he asks, glancing down over the side of the waterfall. I peer down and I'm thankful for the change in topic. Jumping off this cliff is easier than expressing my foreign feelings for my hostel mates.

Glancing back up at our surroundings, I don't see anyone around, which is perfect timing on our part.

Every time we're here together, we end our trip by not only making this trek, but jumping into the lake at the bottom. It's a rush of excitement knowing we shouldn't be doing it but the fall itself is at least a couple hundred yards down.

When you finally hit the water after the freefall it's addictingly cleansing.

Even so, taking the leap still makes my heart pound out of my chest and I love the adrenaline.

We both look down over the cliff. "Is my eyesight going bad or does it look further than usual this year?"

My lips form a tight line. "It does, actually. But I think it's less our eyesight and more our old age."

"You first this time?" he asks.

"Ehhhh, maybe you can go first," I squeak out.

As we debate, voices echo between the trees and I can tell there's a large group making their way up. It sounds like a park ranger on a megaphone giving a tour.

Hell, it's probably the fucking CGA group haunting me here too.

"Oh, shit," Kobi says as he looks over his shoulder then back at me.

Time to go.

Both of us jump at the same time, leaping over the edge. A profound sense of freedom rushes through me, replacing the initial fear and it's exhilarating. Falling is the scariest, yet most intoxicating feeling I have ever experienced. The last few days with the two of them have felt exactly the same, except instead of my body, it's my heart. Which is not nearly as strong in handling an impact.

Regardless, I know whatever happens it's going to be worth the fall and I want to share everything I feel with them.

My eyes roam over my gorgeous surroundings and I feel

grateful for another amazing summer, knowing I have one more extraordinary night to experience before heading home.

I expel all the breath from my lungs as I hit the lake and allow the water to wash over me in waves, feeling refreshed physically and emotionally. I'm ready to dive in head first with them, if they'll have me.

21

HANNAH

"Are you ready?"

I ask Ethan for the third time as he looks around the room, which is now a chaotic mess due to the sheer amount of people in it.

I'm so thankful Dane invited us to stay with him, especially after being spoiled for the last few nights with no one else in the room.

We only have one more night in Paris, and as much as I'm not looking forward to the end, I'm still excited for tonight.

Ethan is pacing as he packs his bag, looking in places he's already checked and I can tell he's nervous. I know there aren't any expectations for tonight. But if it's anything that naturally happens between us when we're alone together, things will go farther than ever.

We exit the room with our backpacks snug tight against our backs and close the door behind us. Stopping at the front desk we hand both of our keys over to the same front desk gal that we checked in with and she smiles as she takes them from us.

"Checking out?" she asks me and I nod with a smile.

"You still have one more night paid for, is everything okay?" she inquires softly as she taps on her keyboard.

"Everything was perfect. This is by far our favorite place we've stayed." I peer over at Ethan, surprised by how open he's being, but he's right. Not only was the location amazing, but the company was too.

"It's our policy not to rent out the beds if they were prepaid so we'll leave that bunk open for you in case you need to return for any reason tonight. But, if we don't see you, we do hope you'll come back on your next trip."

"Absolutely," Ethan replies to her as I tap my chin with my palm and push out, thanking her, and we push through the lobby doors onto the sidewalk and walk toward the address that Dane texted me.

It's a perfect summer day in Paris; there's a small breeze and the sun is warm as it hits my skin the moment I step onto the sidewalk.

Ethan cups his arms around my elbow, pulling me into the shade as he zips open the side pocket of his backpack and pulls out a small tube of sunscreen.

"Come here, love." He calls me to him but he makes the step closer to me and squeezes some of the lotion on his fingers. He takes his time rubbing it softly over my scar, massaging it into the skin with care and detail as if it's his most important task in life.

I can't help but smile as his tongue darts at the corner of his mouth, fully concentrating before he snaps the lid closed and says, "there," in the most satisfied tone.

He tilts his head as he peers down at me and the level of love he has for me shines bright, even hidden behind the shades that cover his eyes. I feel it more and more every day and what happened with Dane on this trip brought us a deeper understanding of each other.

Somehow, bringing in another person made me feel more connected to him than ever.

He glances to the left, squinting as if trying to see how far the distance is. I take in his stern demeanor that has softened over the last couple of days, appraising his golden hue that glows from more than just the sun-kissed skin from our back-packing trip. His thick, dark hair has grown out longer than I know he likes and rebel pieces stick out of the sides of his backward baseball cap.

When he returns his gaze to me, I can't help but smile at how unkempt yet happy he is. It's unusual for him to be both at the same time.

"You like him?" I sign.

His brows pinch together as his lips press together. Sucking in a deep breath he nods.

"Me too."

"We're okay right?" he signs.

"Better than okay."

"Good," he says softly with a smile.

"Anything goes for me tonight," I add.

His brows lift and there's a small twitch at the corner of his lip before he looks down the street again.

"It's the last night."

"No inhibitions."

He gives me a soft, grateful smile, the one I see often when he feels supported and loved. Unlike the fake ones he feeds his father when he reprimands him on every decision he's made, and continues to make, in his life.

I hate how discouraging he is, and I wish his father saw him for the amazing man he's become. But I don't want to focus on that now. We have enough to worry about when we get back to the states. For now, I want us to enjoy the last night of our trip before we go home.

Leaning down, he presses his lips against mine and I fall

into him like I always do, loving how protected and loved he makes me feel.

He kisses me with meaning and purpose, and when he pulls away, his lips still hover over mine as he whispers, "No inhibitions."

22

ETHAN

There's a long pause, Dane's eyes peer over the steel blue plastic partition with a hardened look behind his normally bright blue eyes.

"A3." My stern gaze doesn't stray from his.

"You asshole, you sank my battleship," he finally says with both defeat and a playful anger in his tone.

He's more competitive than I expected but something tells me he doesn't mind losing considering what we bet on. Or shall I say, what Hannah made us bet on.

"Whoever loses has to massage my feet."

When she signed it to us and I repeated it out loud for him, we both just peered over at each other with the same thoughtful look. How can I purposely lose at *Battleship*?

Regardless, we're both too competitive to take an "L", but the punishment isn't exactly *punishment*.

Dane closes the cover of the game and stands, rubbing his hands together with a big fat grin on his face. He must have not shaved today because the stubble that decorates his jawline makes him appear slightly older and more mature than his usual youthful demeanor.

I know Hannah appreciates the look because when we got here she immediately stepped into the hotel room and ran her fingertips through it with more appreciation than I expected. It probably should have made me jealous but I couldn't help but smirk instead.

The only thing I'm jealous of is his ability to grow said beard.

"Get your gorgeous feet over here woman," Dane calls out as he plops down on the couch in the middle of the insanely large hotel room that Kobi previously stayed in.

By the look of this hotel room, he must do well as an international translator. Everything is white or cream colored, brand new, and so clean I feel like it's never been stayed in.

I watch Hannah pad over to the couch and gracefully sit down on the opposite end of where Dane is sitting, then places her bare feet up on his lap and she leans back.

Clearly hating her choice of placement, Dane grabs a hold of her hips and pulls her closer to him, then places the entirety of her legs across his lap so he has full access to not only her feet but her shins, knees, and thighs.

She smiles back at him as she sinks into the cushions. Her eyes roll to the back of her head as he kneads his fingers into the meat of her calves. I swear his number one goal in life is to pull those tiny little moans that vibrate from her throat that he claims to love.

I don't blame him. I love them too, but I hate the reminder that I'll never get to hear her voice again. Especially when so much of the reason is my fault.

I didn't cause the accident but I can't help but think about what I could have done differently to prevent it. Things would be so much different right now. Hannah would still be able to speak, I'd still have baseball, and I wouldn't be spending the rest of my life working for my father at a job that I hate.

I shake those thoughts away, trying to stay in the moment

and not trail off into the thoughts that steal so many of my nights.

A few minutes pass by as I watch them communicate the way they've learned how with each other. Somehow Dane just knows how to ask her questions she can easily answer with just her body language. Sometimes I see her sign out of habit but she'll quickly make a facial expression or nod a certain way that Dane just gets.

He gets her.

He gets us.

Suddenly I feel like I'm missing out on whatever is starting to happen between them and I don't want to wait for them to pull me into it and for me to act reluctant even though my body wants nothing more than both of them.

Silently, I stand, reaching into my bag grabbing the necessities I bought at the store earlier, knowing the inevitable when it comes to the three of us.

Kicking off my shoes. I step around the couch, placing myself in front of Dane then slowly kneel directly in front of him. His breath gets caught in his throat as I reach for the middle of his lap. He shifts as his Adam's apple bobs and I can't help my lopsided grin as I take ahold of Hannah's foot and begin to rub into the arches.

"Fucker," Dane whispers, smiling back because he knows I did that on purpose. I guess his sense of humor is rubbing off on me a bit.

We do this for who knows how long. Hannah writhing under both of our hands as they roam from the tips of her toes all the way to the base of her hips while Dane and I look between her and each other.

The sexual tension is high, we both feel it and for the first time since we met, I don't hate it.

It's on the tip of my tongue. The question I've been wanting to ask him since the first night. I glance over at Hannah and her relaxed, hooded eyes sear into me because she knows me well enough to know that I'm holding myself back.

She gives me a soft nod, so small I could have easily missed it, but it's enough to muster the courage to ask what I've been thinking about for the last four days.

"Did you mean what you said...about being a top and a bottom?"

His eyes flicker down to my lips, as if he's trying to read the words because he doesn't believe his ears. The column of his neck bobs as he swallows thickly and nods.

"Yes," his answer comes out husky.

There's a long pause. I didn't plan out what to say after I got an answer, but thankfully, he saves me from my thoughts.

"What do you want?" The question is kind and soft, laced with genuine curiosity.

"I don't know," I reply honestly.

"Okay." His head bobs up and down slowly in understanding. "What do you feel more comfortable with?"

"Doing the fucking, not getting the fucking," I reply quickly, because that's the truth. It's not that I don't want the latter, but I'm definitely more comfortable with the former.

His head bobs slowly again, still rubbing the soles of Hannah's feet.

"That's normal." His voice is light, honest.

He's clearly the more experienced one here, although my personality is a bit more alpha than his, his sexuality screams dominance. Not in a demanding way but with more knowledge and understanding of how I'm feeling in this situation.

The thought that he's had this before with others makes me clench my jaw and I pause caressing Hannah's leg so I can clench my fists.

His eyes scan over my face, down to my hands, then back up to meet my eyes.

"I want you. I want both of you, more than I can express.

This is the most fun I've had in a really long time and I want tonight to end however you'll allow it," Dane admits in a way that surprises me. It's vulnerable and for the first time I see an uncertainty in him that makes me feel even more comfortable.

Because somehow he does that. He makes us both feel so goddamn comfortable and I have no idea how.

No inhibitions.

I let those words repeat in my head as I sit up on my knees and lean into him. His eyes widen as he sits up a little taller and I can't help but smirk at the power exchange. He's always been in control. He's been in control even when I wrapped my hand around his cock from the other side of the barrier that separated us.

Even last night, when he devoured Hannah as he bent over in front of me. He held the power then, taking control of the moment and pulling me into the gravity that he's created since the moment we met.

Tonight I want him to know how much I want it.

Not waiting for any more seconds to pass, I crush my lips to his, kissing him for the first time, feeling the foreign sensation of masculine lips and whiskered hair that scores my skin. Our tongues mash together and it's deeper and more rugged than any kiss I've had before. It feels all wrong compared to what I'm used to, but so perfectly right at the same time and when he moans into my mouth it gives me the confidence I need to keep going.

I let go of Hannah's feet, trailing my hands up his tight chest. I strip off the shirt he's wearing, only breaking our kiss for a brief second before coming back in again and he's frantically reaching for the front of his pants, ripping open the fly as he pushes his hips up slightly so I can tug his pants down.

Hannah sits up, removes her top, and leans toward us. I blindly pass his pants to her as she tosses both articles of clothing over the back of the couch.

Pulling away, I ask, "Do you have any lube?", even though I have some. I'm curious if he bought some for tonight.

He smirks tilting his head. "Don't you know how it goes?"

I squint, confused.

"He who holds the lube, gets to top."

I'm unable to hold back a smile as I reach into my back pocket, pulling out the small bottle of travel sized lube and condoms I shoved in there a few minutes ago.

"Well, shit. Looks like you win." I love the lop sided grin he gives me. It's both sexy and mischievous, and I would bet my life that he has a bottle of lubricant in his bag but is holding back from admitting it for my benefit.

I glance over at Hannah, who's biting her lip watching us like we're aphrodisiacs.

"Get naked and on the bed," I say to her with meaning behind my teasing tone.

She raises her brows before saluting me, then stands seductively as she begins to strip off articles of clothing.

She lifts her arms over her head, taking out the hair tie that holds her messy bun. The silky strands of her dark chocolate brown hair fall over her shoulders as she crosses her arms behind her back, unclasping her bra, it tumbles down the front of her body and onto the floor.

Hooking her thumbs into the waistband of her loose cotton shorts, she pushes them down, they easily fall off her hips and down her long legs, resting at her ankles. One foot steps out then the other as she kicks the fabric to the side, leaving her in nothing but these cheeky little boyshorts. Her plump ass peeking out from the bottom and I swear both Dane and I bite our lips in an exaggerated groan.

She gives us a seductive look over her shoulder before she turns the corner into the room and we both quickly kick ourselves up, him off the couch and me off the floor, racing each other to the room.

23

DANE

Our shoulders collide against each other as we both force ourselves through the doorway into the bedroom, following the most captivatingly gorgeous woman I've ever seen.

There's something about Hannah that just exudes a confidence that I don't see in most women. She's sweet and kind, yet seductive and sexy.

She doesn't need words to express that, it oozes out of her with every step, every smile, and it's addicting. Watching her is all-consuming.

And Ethan. Fuck.

The change in him as each day has passed is truly indescribable. Another addiction I don't think I'll be able to ever get enough of.

It makes me want to experience something new with them everyday.

My impatience shows as I tear off the rest of my clothes, scattering them across the ground as I stride quickly past Ethan, beating him to the bed. I'm already naked by the time my knees graze the end of the bed and I dip into the mattress, hovering my body over Hannah's.

I'm excited and anxious. I've been waiting for this moment all day—hell I've been waiting for it since we first met—now that we're all here and willing, an unfamiliar nervousness passes through me. I want this to be as good for them as it will be for me.

My heart pounds behind my ribcage and I feel just as much adrenaline as I did jumping off that cliff earlier today. The only time I've ever felt this alive in the bedroom is when Celeste and I first started experimenting together.

I press my lips to the center of Hannah's chest, trailing my tongue over her soft skin. Moving from one breast to the other, lapping up the taste of her sweet and salty skin. Hovering my lips over her body, I blow over the areas I've licked and she visibly shivers as goosebumps bloom everywhere.

Sitting back on my heels, I grab the condom that Ethan tossed on the bed and sheath myself with it. The mattress dips beside me as his naked body crawls next to Hannah, his fingers trailing up her leg, hovering at the apex of her thighs that I'm sitting in between.

Fuck, they're a sight.

His scarred hand pushes one thigh further away from the other, spreading her legs wider for me, for him, for both of us.

His finger slides through her slit, arousal glistens around her lips and I can't help the pleased groan that reverberates from my chest.

"Fuck, you're stunning, Hannah." My words make her blush and a tint of pink highlights her cheeks, trailing all the way to the scar that she wears with conviction.

"Yes, our girl is so fucking beautiful," Ethan says as he presses his mouth to hers at the same time his finger circles her clit.

Our girl.

I can't help the stupid ass smile that forms over my face and I'm glad neither one of them can see me right now.

I sit up, giving my hard cock a languid stroke and I scooch in closer to her, spreading her legs even wider, allowing Ethan's fingers easier access to that sensitive bundle of nerves that's making her arch and bite that sexy, plump bottom lip of hers.

I feel like I've waited so long for this moment, and my impatience shows yet again. I lean forward, the latex covered tip glides into her entrance and I grunt as her walls swallow my crown.

Ethan continues to circle her clit as I slowly press into her. Our mouths fall open in unison. She's wet, so fucking wet, but even with her arousal coating the condom I can feel how tight she is. I grind my teeth together, pulling out and press back in and groan at how fucking good this feels.

Ethan cups his hand around her leg, pulling her thigh higher, spreading her wide. I press my thumb into her exposed clit and push in deeper.

"Fuck, yes. Fuck our girl, Dane. Make her feel good,"

Are you fucking kidding me right now? This man has hardly said one single dirty fucking word for the last four days. Yet, the words he just uttered make my spine tingle and my cock throb painfully as I thrust into her.

"Goddamn, you motherfucker." My words are clenched, as I hold back.

"You like that, huh?" He presses into his palm, pushing himself closer to me as I continue to piston into Hannah, her pussy clenching around me as I continue to plunge into her.

His body is flush next to mine, his lips only inches away from my ear as he dips his hand in between my body and hers. He palms her mound as he spreads his fingers around my girth, squeezing them together, I have to work harder to press my cock into her tight hole, going past his fingers into her wet cunt and back out.

I slam my eyelids shut and huff out a deep breath. This feels so fucking good and yet again, the knowing sensation that they bring out so easily begins to build. Starting at the base of my spine, down between my legs, tightening my balls with each thrust.

"Don't come yet," Ethan whispers as he pulls his hand away and the relief is instant. Opening my eyes, I peer over at him, his dark eyes laced with an intensity I've never seen. He pulls his fingers into his mouth, licking them clean, then presses both into my mouth, pushing down on my tongue.

"I want to feel your ass contract around my cock when you come."

"Goddamit," I muffle as I suck off his fingertips and push into Hannah. The base of my cock is flush with her body and I stay there for a moment to catch my breath.

Leaning over, I take her mouth in mine. I need something, anything, to distract me from his fucking words and I think he can sense how easily I'm falling apart.

He takes full advantage of my vulnerable position, shifting as he stands behind me. The snap of the bottle echoes through the room and I lift myself up, hovering my bent body over Hannah's.

She cups her hands around my face as the cool liquid drips down between my cheeks. She clenches around me, I know as an attempt to distract me. It works as he massages the slick fluid over my back hole, but I still flinch when he presses the tip of his finger into it.

One finger, two...I grunt and groan as he slips in the third and fucking hell, it's been so long, but it feels un-fucking-believable.

"Is this okay?" Ethan asks, his words desperate and needy.

My mouth falls open and I nod.

Hannah watches me, bringing her mouth close to mine as she kisses the corner of my lips. She's so worked up just watching him get me ready and I can't wait for her to see her boyfriend fall apart when he finally takes me.

The pleasure outweighs the pain when I see how much these two both love what we're all doing to each other.

It's true, what I said. I've always been a switch, being a top or bottom depending on the person or the mood. But, I know what I want, and I take charge in most cases because I've most often had sex with women who like being more submissive or men who have never been with a man.

Ethan taking charge is foreign to me; I don't hate it—it's just been a long time.

Glancing over my shoulder, Ethan's blown out pupils and feral gaze set me on fire. The way he looks at me with such need and desire. I want him to do everything he wants and not hold back.

Removing his fingers, he lines himself up tapping the tip on the globes of my ass. He quickly grabs a condom, presses it to the tip and pulls it down over his shaft. His eyes roll to the back of his head and I can't help but enjoy the view because this man is just as gone as I am.

"Please tell me you're ready," he asks but doesn't wait for an answer. He's already lining up the crown to my ass, pushing the tip in. "Oh fuuccck," he drawls out and his desperate words feed my need.

He drives in deeper, not all the way, probably half, but fuck it burns. I press my forehead into Hannah's chest and grunt. She runs her fingers through the sides of my hair and I feel everything.

The burn of his cock, the butterflies in my stomach, the shivers in my skull.

He stalls for a moment, keeping a tight grip on my hips.

"It's been a while," I tell him honestly, as I look back again so he knows that I'm serious. I don't do this with everyone and it's been a long time for me.

My confession pleases him with the drop of his jaw and squint in his eyes.

He struggles to hold himself back, but he does for me and that does something inside my chest. Fuck, Kobi's right. These two are taking over my soul and there's nothing I can do to stop it.

"Please, fuck. Can I move?" he asks but remains still as he lets me adjust. Another moment passes, the throbbing of his cock and the agony in his voice provide me with the desire I need to keep going.

I push back into him, and when I do my cock pulls out of Hannah, giving me double the friction and the sensation burns through my veins like a wildfire.

"Fuuucccck," I hiss out a long breath and continue to roll my hips back and forth.

"Jesus Christ, you feel so fucking good." Ethan admits, groaning through each word.

Hannah's back arches off the bed as she grips the side of my head, pulling me deeper into her neckline, making my body arch further, allowing Ethan to go deeper.

I muffle inaudible words into her chest as Ethan mutters profanities between his groaning.

"Oh fuck." Thrust. "So good." Thrust. "So deep." Thrust. "Mmmmmppf. Fuccck, goddamn it." Thrust.

The sounds this man makes will be my fucking undoing.

He pistons into me, his movements getting choppier, needier. It pushes me back and forth into Hannah, her wet cunt swallowing my cock with each pass.

Her walls begin to tighten around me and her whole body tenses. I tip my head up, her bright blue eyes are full of lust and so much of something deeper. A need, a longing. It's everything. Every night I've witnessed her come undone and she gets more and more beautiful each time.

She tosses her head back, squeezing her eyes shut as her pussy flutters around my cock.

"Hannah, Jesus." My chest heaves as I attempt to breathe through the vise grip she has on my cock. Ethan pushes his entire body into mine, the weight of his chest is flush against my back and the angle of his cock is perfect, as the crown pierces my prostate. "Oh, fuck, you're gonna to make me come."

"Fuck yes. Come for us," he says in my ear but with his gaze locked on Hannah. I don't know if he's saying it to her or to me, but both her and I have lost all the willpower to hold back now.

The loudest groan I've heard yet reverberates from Hannah's throat. My eyes widen at the melodic sound of it as an unavoidable whimper floats out of Ethan and my cock throbs as I eat up the symphony of noises. This mixed with the micro-thrusts Ethan is performing on my G-spot and his flawless tempo, I'm over the edge. I swear he's studied exactly what he needs to do to make a man completely fall apart. Because, that's exactly what I do.

"I'm...fuck, I'm coming," I grit out, my entire body tensing as my toes curl and muscles contract.

Hannah reaches past my head, her arms wrapping around all of us, as if trying to get our bodies even closer together. Her right hand pulls Ethan's face flush against my upper back while her left hand digs into the flesh of my shoulder. Her fingernails cut crescent shaped moons into my skin at the same time Ethan groans through his own climax as he bites into the muscle that sits as the base of my nape.

The perfect amount of pain mixed with the high of my orgasm has me begging, screaming, telling them how good it feels. "Never stop, never fucking stop," are the last words I mutter before my weak body falls limp next to Hannah. Ethan follows, his body melting into the mattress behind me.

Hannah's eyes are closed, her body heavy as her chest heaves. I run my finger over her cheek and tuck her hair behind her ear. That grants me a small smile that I mirror and before I can think otherwise I tell them, "I'm changing my flight. I'm going to stay another day or maybe two." I swallow, feeling vulnerable because I've never wanted more time like I do with them. I've never chased it, but this, this is a burning desire I can't resist. I need them to stay with me. I just need a little more time with them. "Can you...can you stay with me?"

She tilts her gaze to me, then it shifts over my shoulder to Ethan. I'm holding my breath because I know it's not just her choice but his too. I have no idea what's going through his mind right now and I refuse to look back. I keep my eyes locked on hers, sending silent prayers into the universe that they say yes.

Her smile grows wider and she nods and I'm obnoxiously grinning now. It's stupid but fuck it. This is everything I've been missing.

We melt further into the mattress and I'm still sandwiched between them, my body high and happy, and for the first time, we all fall asleep together.

24

ETHAN

My eyes peel open and squeeze shut immediately when the bright sunlight hits my irises like a million needle pricks.

I palm my face and rub my eyes before slowly opening them again and as they adjust I take in the plush comforter, king size bed, crown molding that surrounds the base boards of the room, and the clean marble floor.

My body sits up, the comforter pulling down revealing Hannah's naked sleeping body. Her dark hair is a stark contrast to the crisp, white linen sheets. Her lips are slightly parted as her chest rises and falls in the relaxed state she's in, far from the moments we were before we fell asleep last night.

Memories flash behind my eyes. Her face. His face. The metallic taste of his blood when I couldn't control how powerful my orgasm was and literally bit into his flesh, breaking the skin.

I peer over my shoulder behind me and it's empty. Running my hand over the sheets, there's not an ounce of heat and I instantly feel uneasy.

Ripping the comforter back, I step out of the bed and pad

lightly over to the bathroom, peering in and that's empty too. A plush, white velvet robe hangs on the back of the door, with a lack of options, I grab it considering for far too long if I should put it on.

I've never worn a robe in my life. My father has one, it's red satin with a black trim, similar to the one Hugh Hefner wears in all his Playboy mansion pictures. Except, my father is far from that kind of wealth, even though he pretends like he isn't.

I don't want to stride around the room naked so I wrap it around myself, tying the belt at my waist, feeling uncomfortable in my own skin as I make my way to the main room.

Coming here last night was fun, but the morning after feels strange. Surreal. Nothing like the days after in the hostel.

I don't know if it's the discomfort level of my current surroundings or how we gave into each other. It felt natural last night. Easy.

In the light of the day, it all feels so...different.

Searching the hotel room I come up empty. Dane is nowhere to be found and a sense of panic rolls over me. I make my way back to the bedroom and round the opposite side of the bed where Hannah still lays.

I reach to wake her but a notepad on the nightstand snags my attention. Picking it up, it reads:

> *Went to run a quick errand and pick up some breakfast from the best patisserie in Paris. Don't forget to change your flight. I changed mine :) Be back soon. - Big D *wink*

My body relaxes as I take in his words and can't help the small grin that forms when I exhale out a deep breath.

I don't know what I thought when he wasn't here. I guess it

shouldn't matter but I feel relieved regardless and I'm not quite sure how to process it.

Grabbing my phone I look up our flight reservations and login. I run through the options and see there's a flight tomorrow night and the morning after that.

Glancing over at Hannah's sleeping form, she looks so peaceful and so at ease. The way her eyes gleamed with hope when he asked if we could stay longer was more telling than I expected.

Not only has she needed this vacation to get away from the busyness of our life back home but it's the first time she's let loose since the accident. Hell, even my rigid ass isn't constantly looking at the clock or figuring out what's next on our agenda.

I've loved what this trip has brought out in us. What *he* has brought out in us.

I want to choose the latter, giving us two more nights here. Plus the later flight is dramatically cheaper and I've created a habit of saving every penny. I hope that works out for Dane because I really don't want to go back to a hostel after staying in a private room.

Reaching in my bag I dig for my wallet so I can see how much cash I have. I want to make sure I have enough to cover at least one night here.

I remove a few items, continuing to dig but I come up short. Pretty soon my bag is empty and I'm still missing my wallet. I can't change my flight without my credit card and I need my ID for everything. Closing out of the website and leaving our flights as is, I scan through my bag again and still nothing.

"Fuck." I run my hands through my hair, my eyes bouncing back and forth as I recall my steps.

I haven't used it since the hostel. I must have left it in the safe there. "Shit."

Pulling the cloth belt apart, I slip on my boxers, shorts, and a shirt from the pile on the floor. I slip on my sneakers and run to the room, adding to Dane's note.

> *Had to run back to the hostel. Forgot something. Love you. - Ethan*

I hate to leave her to wake up by herself but I need to go back as soon as possible.

Dropping the pen, I press a quick kiss to her temple, grab the spare hotel room key, and jog back to the hostel. It only takes about twenty minutes to get there at my running pace. I pass by the front window and I see the same front desk gal—I think Dane said her name was Sally—pointing to the computer as she talks to another employee behind the desk.

I feel instantly relieved; hopefully she'll remember and let me check the safe. She said she wouldn't rent out the bunks and I really hope it's still there.

Entering through the front door, there's a small narrow way that creates a blindspot for anyone coming in. It seems to be common in some of these old buildings in Paris. I never really noticed it before but as I hear Sally talking I remain frozen behind the wall barrier.

"Dane was here this week?" the lady I don't know asks Sally.

"I swear he should just rent a bed for half the year, he's here that often anyway. I wish when I was younger I lived as freely as he does." There's a brief pause and some tapping.

"Did you enter the total wrong? You only had the three guests for these days but the total revenue shows all the beds were rented...twice," the other lady asks.

"Oh no dear, that's correct. The first night Dane checked in with only two other separate travelers. He came down that first night and rented out every single bed in both rooms until that large group was reserved. He even paid for me to cancel the other reservations and not only refund what they paid but give them a severance for another hostel or hotel room."

"Hmm, interesting. Why would he do that?"

She pauses for a beat. "Dane's requested some strange things in the past so who knows."

Holy shit.

That first night, he came down here to talk to her. He rented out every single bed. He made her cancel the other reservations. So what? So he could be alone with us?

My thoughts run rampant reliving that night. It was after the glory hole. He had showered. He must have known then it was me. He saw my scar and knew right away.

My chest feels heavy as my mind runs through each of those moments, trying to recall the conversations.

Did he trick us? Does he do this often? She said he stays here all the time. Is this his thing?

Fuck!

The door opens and two people with large backpacks attempt to squeeze their way through the door. I immediately step forward, exposing myself to Sally and she immediately recognizes me.

"Hey," I say, awkwardly.

"Hi, welcome back." Her eyes peer to the door and when the other two people that aren't Hannah and Dane come into view, she looks back at me and says, "aren't you missing that beautiful girl of yours?"

I smile, with a half chuckle, mostly from feeling awkward.

"Yeah, but I—I left my wallet in the safe. Can I check it?"

"Of course, run up there and check. We haven't rented out your bed or locker so nothing has been touched," she replies, kindly.

"Thanks," I say as I quickly turn around. My feet shuffle over each other, the rubber soles of my sneakers squeaking on the tile floor. I make my way up the stairs into the room and stride straight for my locker. Entering the code I programmed the first night, it beeps open and there's my wallet.

I breathe a sigh of relief knowing I have it back and shut the door.

I take a step back and pause, glancing around the room. Now it's full of other people's stuff and I realize how stupid I was to think this room would have been empty for days on end. Hostels are never fucking vacant like that.

He tricked us. He knew how long we were staying and renting it out so he could force himself into our world. Taking us to that fucking expensive dinner, showing us all around Paris.

He should just rent a bed for half the year, he's here that often anyway.

I feel like a fucking idiot. This is what he does. Stays in hostels, finding a guy or a girl or a couple that he likes then just goes after them. None of this meant anything for him except for a way to seduce us. He knew I was fucking vulnerable after that first night. He knew everything from the fucking beginning.

Fuck. Fuck!

This is going to kill Hannah.

I make my way down the stairs. I'm grateful Sally is helping the two backpackers at her desk. I hold up my wallet, thanking her with a quick tip of my chin as I beeline for the front door trying to avoid any eye contact.

I'm through the threshold and around the corner, running a faster pace back to the hotel. I never changed our flight earlier and I'm so fucking grateful for that. The sooner we leave, the better.

25

HANNAH

I scrunch up my face and thickly swallow the rest of my tiny espresso, or shall I say *Nespresso*.

I've never had this version of hotel coffee before but it's an extreme contrast from the grainy, yet sour and watered down coffee from the hostels.

This though, this is like getting punched in the face with a coffee bean on steroids.

Placing the cup and saucer down, I pad my way back to the room. My eye catches back onto the note they both wrote to me.

It's silly, I know. But the amount of joy I feel that both of them wrote me a note makes me feel like a giddy teenager.

I'm more in love with Ethan than ever and Dane brings out so much fun in both of us.

Over the last four days I've seen more of the old Ethan—the Ethan before the accident—than ever, and that puts a smile on my face.

All the time I spent in physical therapy he spent berating himself. He was healing too, but mine was so much more severe that it took a lot longer for me to recover. He's gotten better over the years as our life has returned to normal, but since he'll never play baseball and I'll never talk again, there's always something I think he feels is missing in both of our lives.

His childhood love was baseball. It's been a lifelong obsession and he was destined for the MLB. Now, he never even watches it on TV.

I miss it sometimes, hearing the announcers, seeing the players and watching the excitement of the game. I used to love watching him play and fell in love with the game but anytime I put it on now he finds a reason to do something else and ignores the television.

My injuries may have been more life threatening and physically altering, but his injury ruined his future. I'm still on the path I want to be on, now it just has a deeper meaning behind it.

A low buzz steals me from my thoughts and I glance over in the direction of the door. My tight lips attempt to smother a smile. I don't know if it's Dane or Ethan, or maybe the both of them will come through together. That thought makes my smile unavoidable.

But it drops instantly when the heavy door swings open, the back slams hard against the back wall with a loud thud and Ethan comes through it completely frantic and disheveled.

He's heaving, a light sheen of sweat shines over his forehead. This isn't a post run Ethan, this is a panicked Ethan.

"What's going on?" I sign as I walk toward him.

Glancing up, his eyes catch mine, then glance around the room.

"Is he back?"

I shake my head.

"Good. Go pack. We're leaving," he says and I rear my head back in shock at his unusual abrasiveness.

"Why? What happened?" My movements are harsh, demanding.

I don't want to leave.

He peeks his head out the door and down the hallway before closing it, then stalks my way. He reaches out for me and guides me to the room, pulling our backpacks out from the closet.

"I'll explain on the way to the airport. Pack." He tosses the pack on the bed, which is still heavy from most of my belongings in it.

Turning, I cross my hands over my chest and pop my hip out. The death glare I'm giving him is top tier and he knows I'm not fucking moving until he tells me what the hell is going on.

"He used us. He fucking used us." He shoves a shirt into his backpack, followed by a few toiletries.

My brows pinch and my arms fall to the side. My heartbeat speeds up trying to understand why he's saying that and what he means. I shake my head, naturally in disbelief because what he's saying doesn't make any sense.

"He rented out the hostel, paid for all the other people to go away so he could have privacy with us. He probably followed me from the sex club that night. Fuck, I don't know, but he's a fucking stalker and he's manipulated our surroundings to seduce us and get us alone. The lady at the hostel says *that's just what Dane does.* He stays there and just finds people. Fuck, I don't know. We just need to get out of here."

My racing heart pounds harder as it drops to my stomach.

That's what he does?

"Is that what she said?" I step closer to him, signing my question softly.

"She said, he stays there half the year. I overheard her talking to another person that worked there. They knew him, like *knew* him." His face softens as he takes me in.

My eyes drop to the ground and I feel...I feel...heartache. But that's stupid, right. After only a few days. It shouldn't feel this disappointing. I shouldn't have a heaviness in my chest and a sadness lingering in my head.

As I peer back up, Ethan's angry. He's had time to think about all of this on the way back to the hotel and he's processing it with so much anger. I just feel sad and devastated because what we have is *something*. It is. This isn't surface level for Dane. It can't be.

Ethan starts packing the rest of my things and pulls out a pair of leggings and a shirt for me. I'm still frozen, my thoughts are running through my mind like a movie trailer. Flashbacks of all the days we spent hanging out together and the nights we spent exploring each other.

Maybe I'm delusional but it felt so strong. So real. I loved how beautiful he made me feel and how much Ethan shifted into the old yet newer version of himself with him.

"I don't believe this wasn't something more for him. For all of us."

"Baby," he steps into me, placing a hand on my hip and another on my cheek. "This was fun, exactly what we came to do, right?" I nod. "It was never going to be anything more."

He says that but does he really think that this was nothing? I saw how he looked at Dane. I saw how he lost control with him, how we both did. I saw my old, playful Ethan for the first time in a long time and I know he's just as bothered by this as I am.

I take in a deep breath lifting my chin with a fake confidence I don't feel.

I want to fight back. And for the first time, in a long time, I want to scream and yell.

Expression of anger is so different when you don't have words or a voice and I hate how it builds up and internalizes.

I'm not sure if I'm mad at Ethan for forcing us away or for

the thought that this was all a set up for Dane to do 'what he always does.'

I hate this. I knew it would come to an end, but this was not what I expected.

"Come on baby, it's time to go."

26

DANE

"Are you out of your fucking mind?" Kobi's words blare through the speaker as I exit my favorite Parisian café.

"What?" I shrug, peering at him through the screen before looking both ways to cross the street. "It's not like I pulled a Hudson and got drunk married in Vegas to a complete stranger."

Kobi rolls his eyes. "No...that's easily fixable by filing some papers. You permanently tattooed your skin with remnants of them." His eyes are wide, giving me a condescending look.

"I don't know why this surprises you. It's not like it's the most impulsive thing I've ever done. Plus, look at it." I shift the camera over to my shoulder to show him the inked scratch lines and small crescent moons from Hannah's fingernails, then move the phone to the crease in my neck, over my trap muscle. "They're perfect."

"You tattooed his bite mark on your neck, Dane."

"It's not my neck, it's my trapezius, totally different spot."

"You know what I mean," he palms his face, "and yes, you're the most impulsive person I've ever known but it's always been with your life or travel or your random purchases. Never with people or relationships. Tattooing someone else marks on you—"

"It's hot, right? I think they'll like it." I interrupt him because he knows the only other tattoo I've ever put on my body was for Celeste.

I avoid looking into the camera and shuffle quickly over the sidewalk toward the hotel.

Luckily, it's not busy this early in the morning because I really want to get back to them before they wake up.

I snuck out last night, which would have been weird if they caught me leaving at that hour. I did end up falling asleep between them, but I woke up after only an hour of sleep and when I saw the marks they both left I couldn't get the idea of keeping them permanently marked there forever out of my head.

Like my own personal matching scar to theirs.

I texted the tattoo artist I know in Paris and luckily she was still open. I paid her triple her going rate so she could start and finish before the sun came up and I couldn't be happier with how they turned out.

It's official. I'm obsessed. I'm head over heels sinfully consumed by everything about them and I'm ready to tell them after last night.

Let's just fucking lean into this. That's what they say right?

The bolt of excitement that ran through me when they agreed to change their flight, let's just say I'm thoroughly impressed with my self control, considering all of my normal control has been non-existent when it comes to them.

"Are you sure they don't know who you are?" Kobi asks softly.

I get why he's asking. People that know who I am when they meet me want something from me. Most often money or the connections I have.

Getting the payout, and continuous royalties I receive for my code, was by far the most exciting but debilitating thing I've ever done in my life. It's given me the freedom to live how I want, but handcuffed me when it came to my love life. Not that I needed much of one since I haven't had anything serious since Celeste.

Naturally, my 'one-date Dane" nickname sort of became a trend and the media awarded me with the title; the most eligible bachelor most likely to never settle down.

Back then I didn't care much, not when the only person I ever wanted was Celeste. I used my fame and money as a tool and rode the media rage well, telling any girl—or guy—that I wasn't interested in anything more than just having some fun.

All of them always said they understood, but it ended in one extreme or the other. They would only hook up with me because they wanted to put that notch on their belt or it was a feeble attempt to make me fall in love with them, like they thought they would somehow be different.

As active as that lifestyle is, I still feel lonely. And even though my friends thought I was off galavanting around the world, hooking up with someone different every night, that's been far from the truth. Lately, I've been alone more than I'm not. Hiking, or exploring by myself.

Maybe that's what got me to agree to teach in Seattle and stay put for a while. It's something new I've never done but it's also near all of my friends, except Kobi.

There's something brutally ironic about constantly traveling, meeting new people and always being around others, yet feeling utterly alone. Keeping people at such a distance so they don't know who you really are. It's exhausting and I'm ready for a change.

Seattle will be a perfect restart for me.

"They have no clue. We've kept all the personal stuff out of it. They don't know where I live or what I do. They still don't know my last name," I finally reply, relieved I can see the hotel just a few feet in front of me.

"This is sudden. That's all I'm saying." I glance into the screen, Kobi's emerald green eyes pierce through me with concern.

I stop in front of the building, the look reflected in the bottom corner of my thumbnail is vulnerable, honest. "I've missed this. This type of connection. I missed caring about someone so deeply that making them a priority was easy." He smiles back at me at the admission. Even with his pushback on my whirlwind romance I can see the happiness behind his eyes.

He was closest with me and Celeste. After everything happened he sort of took on the big brother role in my life. It was a strange feeling at first, being that I'm an only child, but he's always kept an eye on me and made sure I was okay. Because I think out of all my friends, he always knew deep down, I was never okay.

I don't need his approval on this, but I really want his support.

"Well, tell them then. Make sure they know how you feel and do whatever you need to do to make it work."

I can't stop the shit-eating grin that beams over my face. "I gotta run, I'm heading back into the hotel."

"Have fun brother, call me later."

"Thanks Kob," I say, still smiling as I end the call. Tapping the 'up' button on the elevator, it dings and opens immediately and I step in.

I wonder if they're awake or still sleeping. If I were to guess Hannah is still sleeping but Ethan is probably awake and over-thinking every single moment from last night. Probably pacing the room with his coffee, debating on all the ways he will try and ignore me today. Ignore his feelings.

But I won't let him.

Not anymore.

I'm out of the elevator even before the echo of the ding fades.

My heart beats wildly out of my chest with nerves. I know we have something but thinking them is completely different than admitting the words out loud.

Maybe I'll sign it to them instead, proving to them it's just another way this is meant to be. That we were destined to meet, to explore this.

Scanning my keycard, a low buzz and green light grant me entry and I step through the door cautiously.

The curtain is pulled slightly open allowing a sliver of light through the dark room and a lamp in the corner is lit. One I didn't turn on, so I know someone is or was awake.

It's eerily quiet though. Uncomfortably quiet. There's a stillness in the air that's only present when no one else is.

I get a sinking feeling in my stomach, one that pulls it down with such force it ricochets to my throat.

The low hum of the miniature refrigerator is the only sound in the room and Hannah's clothes that were strewed along the floor are gone.

"No," the words come out breathy. Defeated.

I rush to the bedroom but I already know. I know before opening the door. I know before my eyes take in the bare, unmade bed and I know before I see the empty closet with only my backpack sitting there. I know as I plop down on the edge of the cold mattress and suck in the stale air that they left and they have no plans of coming back.

I know all of this, but my heart feels like it breaks all the same.

27

DANE

One Month Later

I take in a deep breath before I chipmunk my cheeks and exhale. I've been having to do that more often lately as the first day of class gets closer.

It's not that I'm nervous about teaching. I've been contracted by companies in the past that have acquired my code and I often put together presentations for a multitude of different teams within those companies. So that part is nothing new.

Teaching at a University though, that's different. I feel like I have this obligation to not only make it knowledgeable and useful, but fun and passionate as well.

The hard part is, my love for life and that unrelenting passion I've been known to live every day with, is hanging on by a literal thread. I've got a vapor grip on said thread with more fake smiles and forged chuckles than I care to admit.

I need to get my shit together or else this heaviness that sits on my chest like an immovable boulder will make me self-implode.

I've been there once before and I don't want to go back.

Shifting my head from side to side, I roll my shoulders, up and down, then close my eyes. It's gotten better. Not seeing flashbacks of them—but they still come.

I push it away, practicing everything Mimi has been teaching me in her meditative yoga classes. I started taking them when Kobi called Seamus and told him what happened, which just pissed me off even further. I could have just pretended they never existed and none of my friends—that I now see on a daily basis—would have known any different.

Seamus immediately showed up at my door, we got shit faced drunk—which was the highlight of my month, considering that man hardly drinks anything that debilitates him in any way.

It was like old times, at least I felt like my old self, even if it was only temporary.

At some point during our drunken stupor, he talked me into taking Mimi's yoga classes and I've been hooked since the first class.

Mimi is Seamus' wife and an amazing yoga instructor. I met her last year when Seamus bought the house next door to hers —not unintentionally actually.

They met ten years ago at some summer camp, but they lost contact, not knowing where each other went until he saw her at our local lifestyle club, owned by another friend of mine here in Seattle.

Seamus is an ex-Navy SEAL and the most structured guy I've ever known, but after Mimi—the free spirited yoga instructor—came back into his life, well, let's just say I've never seen him so chaotic.

There was this tantric massage class...I chuckle to myself at the memory. Yeah, it's good to be close to friends right now. As much as I hate the whirlwind experience I had and how much my heart hurts, my friends quiet the noise a bit.

I've always been a bit messy and disorganized, but the chaos has never lived in my head like it does right now. My emotions flipflop between lonely and heartbroken or so angry that the fury consumes me. I miss the fun loving guy I used to be. I didn't have a care in the world, and now, now I just want to turn it all off.

I wish I would have never met them.

My body sucks in a deep breath just to push it out harshly, almost subconsciously, like I don't have any real control over it. They awakened feelings I've pushed down for so long and I hate that I'm reliving loss.

Taking one more look at my reflection, my newly cut short hair is still a shock, but I don't hate it. The phantom hair sensation is real though. I still attempt to tuck it behind my ear, and it's barely long enough to do that but it only hangs an inch or so over my ear and my natural waves are more apparent now with the shorter strands.

The phantom touch of her hand on my body and his cock in my mouth is fucking surreal, too. I know for a fact those aren't real, but I still get the overwhelming feeling of loss after the ghost of a moment passes and it takes me back to square one.

Either way, a change was needed and I want to be taken seriously. Especially when I'm standing in front of a group of people who will probably challenge everything I say since I'll only be a few years older than a majority of them, and younger than the rest.

Grabbing my keys, another new sensation occurs since I haven't had to carry keys other than that of a hotel room key card in...well, a really long time.

They feel heavy with both the keys to my newly purchased condo and the 1993 Porsche 911 Carrera convertible that I decided I needed to get myself around. Not that my condo is far from the University, it's within walking distance, but it rains a lot and I've enjoyed having the convenience of it being that I'm on a structured schedule.

Plus, this car is fucking gorgeous. Taking her on drives along the coastline have reeled in my sanity more than I expected.

Starting the car, it roars to life with the rumble of an old but well-loved and well taken care of vehicle. I put the top down, being that there's not a cloud in the sky on this rare Seattle day and exit my garage. The wind feels crisp, refreshing, and in another rare moment, I smile.

Maybe I could start to feel like my old self again.

I continue down the stretch of roadway, allowing the breeze to rip past me, turn my music up a notch too loud and enjoy the drive as I make my way to the restaurant.

It's the first time in well over a year all the guys and I have been in the same place. Kobi is back in Japan and can't be here, but the rest of us are all living here now, so there shouldn't be as many excuses for us not getting together. The last time we were all together was for Jake's *not-so-bachelor* bachelor party and Hudson ended up married.

I smile again at the thought. Yeah, a night out with friends is going to be the perfect distraction.

"Dane! Where's your hair?" Ember stands as I walk up to the table where everyone is already seated. The entire group glances up and jaws drop.

Seriously, you'd think I tattooed my face or something.

"It's just hair, it'll grow back," I say, giving her a side hug and a kiss on the cheek before I take my seat.

Jaws are still on the floor when Cruz finally speaks. "Well, I love it."

There's a whiskey on the table for me so I pick it up and

'cheers' him. "Thank you, Cruz, and sorry I'm late. I'm still getting used to the roads and driving and planning for parking and everything that comes with having a vehicle," I add. It's an adjustment when you're used to backpacking.

"We're just glad you're here," Mimi says. She's sitting next to me and rubs my back in a friendly gesture. We've become close since I've been taking her classes and doing some private one-on-one work with her as well.

I don't miss Seamus' death glare, neither does she. Mimi kicks him under the table and mouths, *relax*, at him.

"So, Mimi, how are you feeling?" Elena asks a very pregnant Mimi.

"Surprisingly, I'm feeling great. I'm just so excited to meet this little one." Mimi looks down at her belly, rubbing big circles over it and Seamus has a look of pride laced behind his usually gruff scowl.

"You still don't know what you're having yet?" Christian inquires. He's the resident CEO billionaire and *'most eligible bachelor'* according to the Seattle Post. That was until he went public with his poly relationship with my buddy Jake from college and his wife, Elena.

"It's going to be a boy," Seamus answers factually as he takes a sip of his water.

Mimi smacks his arm lovingly, "Oh, you stop. If it's a girl—"

"It's definitely going to be a girl," I add.

"She's never leaving the house," Seamus interrupts and the entire group chuckles.

That sounds about right. Mr. Navy SEAL over here will be even more protective of her than he is of Mimi and he's a bit over the top when it comes to her.

"How's the club, Ember?" Seamus asks, diverting the conversation to anywhere else but on him.

"Great, it's so good actually. Memberships are skyrocketing and last month we had to start a waitlist. It's wild. I never expected it would blow up like it did," she replies modestly but with excitement and passion that I love to see in people. It's contagious and I love feeding off that kind of energy.

"I did," Christian quips. Technically, the club was her idea but Christian's company, Ford Enterprises, owns it. "Afterburn is your baby and one of our most profitable sectors. We're opening one in New York and the next one will either be in California or Florida. She's managing all of that from here. It's so impressive," he shares with the group and Ember blushes a bit as she gazes up at Hudson.

Speaking of a whirlwind romance. Ember and Hudson met and got married over the course of a weekend in Vegas and he still looks at her the same way I saw him look at her the first night they met.

My chest tightens and my body does that involuntary breathing thing again.

Seamus shifts his gaze to me, because nothing gets passed him. I ignore his stare and glance around for the waitress. When I catch her attention, I tap on my whiskey neat holding up two fingers for a double.

I don't typically drink bourbon, but lately the burn feels good. Like a tad bit of burn is what my body craves for the torture I feel. Like it's needed to balance out the emotional pain.

"You okay?" Seamus' voice cuts through my thoughts and even though I knew it was coming I wasn't ready for him to ask.

I blink heavy, paste on that signature smile, then turn in his direction.

"Yeah man, I'm all good." I clink my empty whiskey glass with his ice water and take a swig of the contents getting nothing but ice cold cubes.

"You're a really bad liar," he replies.

"Yeah, but I'm good at a lot of other things." I wiggle my eyebrows at him, using my overly flirty personality to avoid anything I don't want to talk about. It usually works, but Seamus is a fucking robot, so he just glares at me.

"You can show me what you're good at," Cruz replies, eaves-dropping on our conversation and when I glance over at him, he's wiggling his eyebrows, mocking me.

It makes both Seamus and I laugh and for a fleeting thought I consider it. We've known each other a long time; it could just be a little friends-with-benefits hookup. Cruz is gay, single, and pretty damn attractive, actually.

He's got this Clark Kent look to him with a little latin twist. His tan skin tone is a little darker now that it's the end of summer and he just came back from a Caribbean vacation.

We've both always been single but he's always been so close to the group, being that he assists Elena or Ember, or maybe everyone at Ford, I'm not exactly sure. But he knows everything about everyone and he seems to be everywhere all the time. Never missing an event, party, or gossip for that matter.

We're similar but vastly different which is why we became fast friends who just flirt whenever we hang out. We both know nothing will ever happen for a multitude of different reasons and our friendship has always been, and will always be, platonic.

I roll my eyes and smile at his comment and I know the entire group is stunned by my witty-less comeback. Typically Cruz and I banter back and forth, flirt then give each other a friendly hug before calling it a night. But I have no energy for it tonight.

The waitress sets down my whiskey, sliding the glass over the wood surface of the table, creating the only noise, making the moment awkward as hell. I quickly take a sip, ignoring the silence and I hate that everyone knows what happened a month ago.

It's been a fucking month. Get over it.

One-date Dane is losing his fucking touch over a four-night

stint with two people I should have never fucking started anything with.

I round my palm over my collarbone, right at the base of my neck and stretch from side to side. The tattoo still feels tight and the sensation is a blinding reminder of the permanent ink I put there from Ethan's mark on me.

He branded me, or I branded him on me, I suppose. It's my own fault. All of it is.

"Are you ready for class, *Professor* Campbell?" Mimi asks and I'm thankful yet again for the question that pulls me out of my thoughts.

"I am, actually. I'm really excited. It's a big change, something totally different. I just hope I don't fuck up these kids for life."

Hudson chuckles and adds, "You're going to be the best thing to ever happen to them. You bring something new and fresh and I'll put money on the fact that these kids look forward to your class. College is boring. Dull professors, redundant lessons. What you'll bring will be an energy they aren't expecting. I can't wait to see how your semester turns out."

"Thanks Hud." I clink my glass against his.

And I hope he's right, because I need something to look forward to, and something to take my mind off everything else.

28

DANE

"Professor Dane Campbell here to see the Dean," I say to the distinguished lady at the front desk. She peers up at me, removing her bifocals and she stands with a smile.

"Professor Campbell, I'm so pleased to meet you. I'm Miranda, the Dean's personal assistant. He mentioned you were coming and to bring you back the moment you arrived. Follow me," she says as she waves her hand toward the hallway.

The University is as I expected it to be, a modern campus, part of it newly constructed and the older buildings completely remodeled. The Dean's office was part of the historic building that was built on campus so it remained intact with just a few upgrades. Dark Oak lines the floors and walls with glass panels and prestigious awards displayed throughout.

Polytech University isn't known for its sports teams or athletics, but has a plethora of academic awards including all the most modern awards for any school of innovation with a strong focus on robotics and engineering.

Hence, why I'm here.

My code was the first AI code to ever integrate into standard systems, creating a brand new way for computers to think and act. Add in my ridiculously high IQ and extroverted personality, I'm a bit of a unicorn in the engineering world.

It's also why the Dean is paying me triple the salary of most of his teachers. He felt like my name alone would bring in students to apply for the MBA course.

And he was right.

They had a record number of applicants and have a waitlist for next semester. I just never promised him more than a year because I'm not sure I could stay still that long.

"Here we are," She gestures through the doorway as she holds it open and I smile thanking her as I walk through it.

"Please let me know if there is anything you need, Professor Campbell. We'd like you to consider more than just one year here at our University and want you to feel at home."

"Of course, thank you Miranda." I nod and continue walking into the Dean's office.

"Ah, there he is!"

"Dean Reynolds," I reply, holding out my hand as I take a step toward him.

"Oh, enough with that. You've always called me Tom." He reaches for my hand, gripping it firmly, pulling me in for a small hug.

I've known Tom from before he was the Dean of Polytech, when he ran CodeCanvas, one of the companies that purchased my program. We worked together to integrate it into their systems and got along well. I wouldn't say we're friends, per se, but we definitely go way back and I trust working for him.

After he took over as Dean he mentioned in mixed conversation how exciting it would be if I came to teach. How the students would flock to the school for someone like me. It was just a quick mention in passing over drinks with mixed company, but everyone agreed with him that it would bring in more interest from the students.

I still don't understand my fame. I never have. I guess I've never cared much. People seem to love the idea of meeting me, maybe because I was so young when I created the code that 'changed the world' or how much money I got for it. I'm not sure, but even with my extroverted personality I've hated that kind of attention. Mix that with the shame of what it's grown into, some days I have more regret than pride.

"Tom." I dip my chin, keeping myself polished so I appear confident and not disorganized like I usually am. "I'm happy to be here. I hope my plan for the curriculum will suit the schools needs, and the students as well."

"I told you before, we're looking for something fresh and new and I want you to challenge them in whatever way you feel is necessary. I'm throwing the standard curriculum out the window and giving you the freedom to inspire these students. I want you to do what you will with it."

"You got it." My shoulders are feeling tense; I'm being far more professional than usual. I think he knows that but I don't want my flighty personality to come off disrespectful.

"I only have one request." My eyebrows raise inquisitively. "Don't date a student. They might be of age, and it's not necessarily against the law, but the last thing I need is some scandal at my school about a teacher and a student when it's totally unnecessary and completely avoidable."

I wonder if he gives this speech to all the new teachers or if it's just me because of my reputation.

"That won't be an issue," I reply simply, because it's true. I have zero desire to date anyone right now.

One-date Dane has morphed into No-date Dane and frankly, I'm currently pleased with this title. I have no plans to give away my already shattered heart.

"Good to hear. I'll walk you to your classroom." He holds out his arm and I take the lead walking back through the threshold of the doorway and into the hall. We exit the historic administration building and cross the quad into the newly constructed technology center in the middle of campus.

We make small talk, striding in pace, as we make our way through the building. He stands tall and proud as he tells me about the University and how this specific building was constructed. He doesn't have to say it, but I know he reserved the largest classroom in the most pristine building on campus, just for me.

"I know you have a busy schedule, I appreciate you dedicating time to teach here this year." Luckily his back is turned to me as my brows raise in response to his statement. *Yeah, busy backpacking the world with zero responsibilities and even less obligation.* But people will conjure up their own idea of what my life is like now, and I'll just let them continue to think I'm noble and busy and doing something worthwhile with my time. I've enjoyed every aspect of my life until recently, when I started questioning how much of it I've been wasting.

He stops in front of a frosted glass entry that looks more like an entrance into a modern cathedral than a class room. "I hope you'll consider making this a permanent thing because we'd love to have you longer than just the year." He pats my shoulder then grabs the shiny metal handle, pulling the door open. "Welcome to your classroom, Professor Campbell."

29

ETHAN

I glance around the room taking in all the modern decor; it's by far the nicest classroom I've ever been in.

It's already full with students, only a few empty seats remain. Stadium style seating that ascends up toward the back of the room and overlooks the center. Everyone is whispering amongst themselves in their groups because apparently our teacher is some hotshot billionaire with a genius IQ who created some AI code that revolutionized computer technology as we know it.

At least, that was the explanation I overheard someone saying on the way to class.

I don't really care who it is. I'm not exactly here by choice. If I can't have the career I always wanted, I might as well do whatever is financially more stable, regardless of how miserable I am doing it. Even though I'm already working for my father, he demands the MBA title on my business card because, 'it looks better to clients' if I have it.

Reaching in my bag, I pull out a notebook and a pen. I highly doubt we'll have much of anything except intros and orientation but at least I can doodle a bit before it starts.

Glancing down at the pen, inscribed on the side is *Bonjour House*.

The words seep into my vision and the memories of walking in and out of the hostel are so vivid I can smell the lavender scent that lingered in the lobby. The way Hannah smiled the moment we saw it because it was the coziest hostel we checked into. The naked man dressed in nothing but a towel, humming to himself like he didn't have a care in the world.

I can still see the reflection of light off the droplets of water that cascaded down his back. The way his muscles flexed when he moved. I close my eyes and can still see his face staring up at me when he took my hard cock to the back of his throat.

A chair screeches next to me, ripping my thoughts back to the stale room. I have so many regrets about how we left, but I revert back to what I heard at the hostel and begin to feel so much rage for what he did.

I just hate more than anything that I can't stop thinking about him.

Hannah and I haven't even talked about it, it's like we pretend it never happened because whatever did happen was deeper than we ever expected. I know it was for her, even though she probably doesn't want to admit it to me. I think she's afraid of hurting me or that I would be jealous of her feelings for him.

Some days I want to tell her I don't have an ounce of jealousy. In fact, there was something about watching him with her, not just sexually but when they would interact, flirt, and talk to each other. There was something that we all brought that just made it feel...right.

I shake my head because it doesn't matter. It'll never be anything more for us. Nothing about having some side piece in our relationship makes any sense. Plus, if my dad found out... that would be bad. Really bad.

So, it's a good thing it ended the way it did.

I just need to find a way to erase the flood of flashbacks. They're a special kind of torture I wouldn't wish on my worst enemy. I hate how he drew out all my fantasies, everything I've been suppressing for so long, so easily. It's like he knew everything I wanted and pulled it from me effortlessly.

The glass door to the classroom opens and my breath gets trapped in my throat in the form of an animalistic choking sound. Immediately I shrink down into my seat as the man I've thought about every day for the last month strides across the room.

Am I fucking hallucinating?

The classroom goes quiet, a few shushes and whispers echo through the room as he makes his way further into the class.

His hair is shorter, clean cut. He's dressed in navy slacks and a white button down shirt with the sleeves rolled up his forearms. Nothing like the outfits he wore in Paris; in fact, I wouldn't recognize him if not for that goddamn signature smile and those bright blue eyes like beacons.

He doesn't climb up the stairs and pick a seat. No, he fucking strides to the center of the classroom, stopping behind the teachers desk, placing his leather bag on top of it, like he's done this a million times before.

I slide further down my seat as he peers up, his eyes skimming the entire room before he grants everyone that stupid smile and announces, "Good Morning class, I'm Dane Campbell, your Professor of Business Development and Analytics this semester."

30

DANE

"I would introduce myself further, but by the silence in the room I have a feeling most of you already know more about me than I would share with you here anyway." A few collective, awkward laughs spread throughout the room.

It doesn't take much to pinpoint the few women in the front that are desperately trying to get my attention; by the landscape of cleavage paired with the short dresses and high heels they are wearing, I would bet my entire fortune they aren't here to learn about business analytics at all.

"With that being said, I'll call out a few of your names. If I do, please stand up and tell me what your major is and where your favorite place to travel is." That gets a few more awkward laughs, because it's a random question, but I find that makes it easier to open up conversation if you know something simple about someone.

Glancing down at my class list, I run my finger over the column of names. "Jodi Adamos," I call out.

My luck, one of the girls in the front row stands up. She makes a feeble attempt to pull her dress down, covering a little more of her legs, but exposing more cleavage. The dress is skin tight, leaving nothing to the imagination. She turns like she pulled a neck muscle with the restriction of her outfit and waves to the class.

"Hi, I'm Jodi." She smiles at me biting her lip. "My major is PR Management and Marketing and my favorite place to travel is anywhere I can wear a bikini." A few guys in the class hoot as she giggles, and you can practically hear the eye roll from some of the other girls in the class.

Scanning the student list again, my eyes catch on the name Ethan. The name comes out as a whisper before I clear my throat and announce, "Ethan Russo."

I shift a few things on my desk then peer up to see the students looking around but no one stands.

Grabbing the corner of the paper, I lift to review the second page to see the total number of students before grabbing my pen to make a note. Chair legs squeal against the tiled floor, the sound traveling through the room before a deep voice says only one word. "Here."

I don't need more than that to recognize the tenor of that voice. I heard so many variations of it in words, moans, and whimpers. It plays on repeat in my head.

My gaze lifts to see *him*. He's standing there, chin high, stoic, un-fucking-readable.

I feel the need to reach out and touch him. Instead, I pinch the top of my hand, digging my fingernails into the skin and yup, felt that.

You've got to be fucking kidding me.

I glance down at my desk then back up, placing my hands on my hips feigning indifference.

"This is an MBA college course Mr. Russo, it's not high school roll call. Name, Major, and your favorite place to travel," I reply with a glacial tone. His jaw visibly clenches along with his fists but I don't care.

I need to discard his presence as easily as he discarded mine.

Even from a distance I can see the column of his throat bob as he swallows thickly. The recollection of that same movement when he took my cock down his throat for the first time hits me.

"Ethan Russo, Accounting major with a minor in Communications." A long pause before he says, "Paris," then slowly takes a seat back down.

Paris?

Did he just fucking say Paris? By the look on his face he shocked even himself.

Paris used to be my favorite city in the world. Now, I completely hate the idea of going there again. I don't say that but I want to.

Instead I ask, "Why Paris, Mr. Russo?" with my most inquisitive curious voice, my eyes never leaving his.

Yes, please tell me why Paris is your favorite place to travel.

Movement at the front door catches in my periphery and I turn to see the side view of a curtain of dark chocolate hair, a button nose peeking from the side, and radiant blue eyes that I don't need to see straight on to recognize.

She enters the room without looking in this direction and plops down in the seat directly next to Ethan, sliding a folder on his desk with a smile before it fades as she tilts her head to inspect his impassive, unamused expression.

Her head turns, following his line of sight and our gazes collide in a tsunami of emotions. She glances around, taking in our surroundings, back to Ethan then me.

Hannah sits up straighter, pressing her lips tightly together as she reaches out and grabs Ethan's hand as if they need each other to be in the same room with me.

The fury radiating from both of them shocks me to my core. *They* left *me*. Alone in my Paris hotel with nothing but silence, regretful memories, and the itch of their marks freshly tattooed on my skin.

I peer down at my student list, goddamn there are so many names. Glancing back up, it hits me how many people are seeing this exchange. For a moment it felt like no one else was in the room and now I'm suffering from claustrophobia.

I skim the rows of names. "Hannah Parker?" I say aloud. When I glance back she nods once. "If you expect full credit for my class, don't be late again." Her brows pinch and a pained look crosses her face that hits me square in the chest.

I hate treating her like that but, fuck, I'm so goddamn pissed off right now.

Moving past this, I call out a few more names just to get some more conversations going and break the ice.

Then I take some time to talk about the standard curriculum created for the students, in which I show them the workbook that I was given. I read a few boring lines from one of the lessons, then open the window and toss it out.

I mean, Dean Reynolds did say I could throw it out the window. Sometimes I can be very literal.

"This course won't be your typical college class. I will challenge you personally and professionally. Universities all over the world will be issuing degrees with the same cookie cutter ideals. I want you to find the passion to do something different. Offer the world something they've never seen before and be crazy enough to go for it."

As I glance around the room, some students are smiling and excited, others jaws are slack, probably questioning my tactics.

My eyes can't help but shift in their direction. They've been attempting to have a private conversation, signing to each other, except for the fact that I've been reading everything they're saying.

They both had no idea who I was until now, which is a relief even though it doesn't fucking matter anymore. Neither one of them knew I was going to be here and this is all just as shocking to them as it was to me.

Making my way back to the front of the class, I ask, "Questions?"

Hands shoot up all over the room, excitedly. I huff out a chuckle because I know it has nothing to do with business analytics.

"Alright, I'll give you guys a few minutes to ask me some personal questions. Then after today, we'll be focusing on the actual subject of the class. Go ahead." I point at a young kid in the middle of the room as I take a seat on the tall stool next to my desk.

"Is it true you created Nova in your college dorm?" he asks.

"Yes, I was addicted to perfecting it so I spent more time in my dorm than not," I reply, leaving out the reasons why.

I avoided the world, people...everything. Code was easy. Emotionless.

In my periphery Hannah signs to Ethan. It's distracting but I can't not look and eavesdrop.

"Ethan, he's a genius. How did we not know?"

I smirk, pointing at another student. "You?"

"Is it true your IQ is higher than Albert Einstein?"

The things people write in papers these days.

"He tricked us. He lied to us."

I squint, taken aback by Ethan's statement. What the hell does that mean?

"I don't think his IQ was ever officially recorded but I love the comparison. Yes." I tip my chin at the girl practically bouncing out of her chair in the front row.

"We should stay and talk to him after class."

"No, we're not."

"I hear your nickname is one-date Dane. So, does that mean you are single?" She giggles.

I school an annoyed expression, as the inside of my eyeballs do an internal roll at her question. Still, I can't help but shift my gaze over to the two people I can't seem to stop focusing on.

Even now, I'm drawn to them and I hate how easily my stomach flips when our eyes meet.

His dark orbs are burning with the same fury I saw when he would try to hold himself back from how much he wanted me and it feeds my desire to want to push him even more. Her gorgeous ocean blue eyes publicize every single one of her emotions and I see them flash by in an instant. Confusion, adoration, need.

I quickly turn away, my gaze back on the girl desperately waiting for an answer and as I skim the room I can see a few others are just as curious. I don't want my relationship status to distract everyone and hell, maybe if I lie it'll get a few of the non-serious ones to drop.

"I'm...taken." I fake a kind smile to the room, regretting it immediately.

Ethan flinches.

"*What?*" Hannah mouths as she signs to no one specifically, looking very perplexed.

"Oh," Tight Dress Girl says with disappointment, sitting back down.

I'm taken?

Who even says that?

Although, it's not a complete lie. I am emotionally predisposed by two people who ran away from me after finally giving into everything we ever wanted in a hot hotel room in Paris.

Soo, yeah. I suppose I am taken.

I can practically feel the rage radiating from the left corner of the room where Ethan is sitting without even looking that way. I muster the courage to glance that direction anyway and, if looks could kill, I would most definitely be dead.

Pointing to another girl in the opposite corner of the room, far away from death eyes, I say, "Yes?"

"Is it true, you're a millionaire?" she asks with the same curiosity as the girl in the front row.

"Millionaire?" Hannah signs.

Ethan shakes his head, tossing his hands up in a defeated, annoyed motion.

Billionaire sweetheart.

I say to myself but provide a PC answer instead, "Don't believe everything you read in the paper." Perusing the room again, I announce, "Yes, last one," then point at a young guy dressed in a pink polo and beige shorts.

He stands and waves to the class, his hand trembling with nerves.

"Hi everyone, I'm Spencer. I just wanted to ask Professor Campbell. Um…" He pauses, rubbing the back of his neck. "Do you really know Christian Ford as well as the tabloids say you do?"

Ah…yes. I was waiting for this. Ever since Christian announced the opening of his lifestyle club there's been a lot more in the paper about him and his relationship with Jake and Elena.

However, before my Paris trip, I was spotted at the club, arriving only with Christian after an unexpectedly long day of competitive golfing—with my fellow billionaire—and the paparazzi had a field day with that one.

"Christian is a great friend of mine. He's in a committed relationship and very public about it."

"You mean, the threeway he's in with that married couple?" Someone, I can't tell who, says with disgust laced in his tone, loud enough for the class to hear.

Without turning my head, I shift my eyes in Hannah's direction. She's looking away as if she feels guilty and Ethan shifts uncomfortably in his chair.

And now I'm pissed. I hate when anyone speaks negatively about other people's choices or sexuality. Especially people I know and love.

I still don't know who said that, but I reply anyway, addressing the entire class.

"It's called a polyamorous relationship and it's completely normal and acceptable. I suggest you do your own research before you make assumptions or judgments on what it looks like." I walk around my desk, exposing myself to the class.

My sexuality has been blasted in different newspapers and articles, some of what is said a complete fabrication, some of it true. But confirming it face-to-face with people whose respect you're trying to gain is always difficult, regardless of how comfortable you are with it.

"To answer your roundabout question. I'm a proud bisexual man. I believe love is love and it doesn't matter if it's a man or a woman that sets your soul on fire, you shouldn't restrict your-self from loving that person the way you want just because of their sex. Everyone is entitled to their opinion, and their choice. All I ask is that you respect each other and each other's opin-ions in my classroom."

That quiets down the room, except for the hand signaling between Hannah and Ethan that I try to ignore but they blare louder than any words could.

"This is bullshit," Ethan signs.

"It's going to be okay."

"I can't listen to him for an entire semester. He's a liar and a cheat."

What the fuck?

I'm a lot of things, but a liar and a cheat is not one of them.

"I need this class."

"We're dropping this class."

"No."

"Yes."

"Stop!" I slam the side of my palm into my open one and yell the word at the same time.

Hannah's eyes blow wide and Ethan cranes back in his chair.

"I've had enough of your side conversation. If you have something to say, say it to the class." I speak the words as I walk toward the two of them, also signing each and every word clearly.

My heart is pounding hard behind my ribcage and I don't know if it's the fact that I'm yelling in the middle of my class or if it's because I'm so close to both of them I can hardly think straight.

Hannah stands with her chin held high, jaw tight and eyes hard. The confidence she's grown to show in moments of confrontation radiating from every cell in her body.

"Can you read this?"

Her hand movements are soft and skeptical, like she doesn't really want the answer.

I shut my eyes, knowing my answer is going to throw me straight into the category of a liar, just like they said.

Maybe I am one and the realization hits me hard. Reopening my eyes, she's scowling now because she knows the answer but needs me to admit it.

"Answer me."

Lifting my chin, I clench my palm in front of me, nodding with both my head and closed palm, signing, *"Yes."*

It's as if her entire body loses its foundation. Her shoulders sag and her chin drops as her eyes bounce from side-to-side recalling all their nonverbal conversations.

She shares a look with Ethan before looking back at me, fury burning in her eyes, but her expression is pained.

"The whole time? The whole time!"

Ethan stands but I point at him not taking my eyes of Hannah. "Sit. Both of you."

His fists clench as he side-eyes Hannah. I know he wants to say something but I don't give him the chance before turning around, glancing at my watch and excusing the class.

It's almost an hour early but I don't give a shit.

"Class is dismissed, I'll upload your assignments in the portal and see you next week." A few of the students hoot and holler with the early dismal, a couple others look between me and Hannah before standing and making their way out.

The shuffling of papers and bags blend with the squeaking of rubber soles on the tile floor as the students rush out, almost as if they need to exit before I change my mind.

There are still a few students lined up to exit but the room is pretty much vacant now.

Hannah begins to pack her things as Ethan stands again. It's funny that they think they're leaving.

"You two. My office."

They share another glance, their expressions angry and I don't blame them but I'm not letting them walk out of here like this.

The even funnier thing about my demand is I don't even know where my fucking office is. The Dean offered for me to come get acquainted with the campus and decorate my space early, but I've never proactively done anything earlier than I needed to. I figured I would just do it after I started teaching and now I regret my procrastination because I feel all out of sorts with these two here.

I peek behind me, seeing two doors and walk confidently over to the first one, opening the door to a fucking closet with cleaning supplies.

Closing it quickly, I grip the door handle of the other, walking through it with purpose, hoping they didn't see that. I leave my office door ajar as I round my desk and place my hands on my hips, which feels weird. So, I lean forward palming the hard wood of my foreign desk slightly hovering over it and my dick twitches.

Nope. Nope. That's not going to work either.

Fuck, I'm a goddamn mess.

Hannah walks through the door first; Ethan trails right behind her and now that it's just the three of us again, my heart does that weird thing it did in Paris. Beating uncontrollably and wild as my stomach turns into a butterfly graveyard.

"Nice closet, *one-date Dane*," Ethan says sarcastically, calling out my nickname simultaneously with the fact that I know nothing about my classroom or surroundings. "I thought maybe you were bringing us in here to introduce us to your girlfriend...or boyfriend," Ethan adds with a hint of jealousy behind his tone.

"Who?" My brows furrow, confused.

"You said you were taken."

"Oh." I attempt to pull back my non-existent hair into a manbun, then stop midway when I remember I don't have that much hair. "I'm not taken. I just said that so my single status wouldn't be a distraction in the classroom."

"Sure," Ethan says incredulously.

What the fuck is his problem?

Steeling my spine, I cross my arms over my chest, reigning myself in.

I have no idea why they left so suddenly but the shift in his demeanor is screaming that I did something wrong. Knowing there's nothing I'm going to say in our current state to talk him down, my gaze shifts to Hannah.

She's just as breathtaking as the first time I saw her. She's wearing a dress similar to the one she wore on our dinner date at the Eiffel Tower. The memory of her smiling, eating each dish like she savored every moment, and the flashback of that confident wink to the women at the table next to us before she even more confidently leaned in and kissed me in front of them and Ethan. *Fuck.*

I can physically feel my body sag with the memory of melting into her and my eyes soften. I fist my palm to ask her why they left but Ethan interrupts me before I can sign.

"Don't look at her like that," Ethan manages to grit a threat through his clenched teeth.

I'm angry that he's saying that to me. I'm angry that he's standing in front of me, acting like he didn't beg for me. I'm angry that my cock is so easily ready for them yet again and I'm fucking angry that I can see the dark pools of his irises and labored breath—not from need— but for how much he's hates me right now.

My body is unyielding as I round my desk with urgency, standing toe-to-toe with him.

Ethan is taller by an inch or so, but my presence is commanding and dominating. It feels as if I engulf him, but he's easily breaking my barrier with the scent of his smoky, woodsy cologne that wafts around me.

There has always been a tense energy between us, a push and pull we somehow mastered in Paris but now, it feels dangerous, explosive. Especially when I can see the bulge behind his zipper, because just like my traitorous body, he can't help it either.

"Look at her like what?" I tilt my head, challenging him, stepping into his space. "Like I don't know the way her eyes squint and that dimple appears on her chin when she's turned on?" My feet push forward, forcing him to step back as I lower my voice. "Like I don't know what she tastes like on my tongue?" Another step. "Like I haven't heard a groan fall from her throat when she comes?" I inch closer. "Don't look at her like I don't know what her pussy feels like when she clenches around my cock."

Ethan's flush against the wall now, trapped between my

towering form and the immovable structure. His eyes saucer in surprise and he's momentarily paralyzed.

Pressing my palms into the wall, I cage him in. "I guess I shouldn't look at you like I don't know what your cock feels like pulsing in my ass, either." My lips graze his ear as I press my body flush against him. "I should forget those sexy, thunderous sounds you make when you lose that control you try so hard to maintain." My hard cock finds his, and it's just as erect and needy as mine. I roll my hips into him and he huffs out a choppy breath as his jaw slacks.

Ethan's eyes flutter, shutting for only a moment as if he's relishing in my touch. Shaking his head with a growl, he steps forward, reaching his hand up to the base of my throat. He grips hard, then flips me around, slamming me against the wall.

31

HANNAH

He's an imposter. That was my first thought when I saw him standing in front of the class as my *professor*.

This man, the one wearing a button down shirt, neatly tucked into his fitted navy slacks, adorned with a belt and matching leather shoes, wearing a wrist watch. Yeah...a watch. A watch that keeps actual time. Dane knew nothing of time in Paris. He didn't care about it.

So yeah, I'm fully sold on the fact that *this man* is the evil twin of *my* Dane. The difference with this twin is his sleek, clean haircut, which looks just as good as the shoulder length shaggy mess he pulled off before. This style still shapes his shark-fin jawline with utter perfection providing him with an even more tailored, sophisticated look.

Evil Twin Dane's hands fist Ethan's shirt as Ethan pushes forward, grabbing his neck and flips him around, pinning him against the wall. They're both expelling an anger from deep in their bones and the tension between them sets me on edge.

Dane lets out a strangled grunt as Ethan slams him again, back into the same spot he was just in, then wraps his hand tighter around his throat, pushing hard into the soft flesh of his neck. "Don't. Don't fucking do that." Ethan's pained voice matches the pain behind Dane's eyes and I can see how much they are both struggling.

"You lied to us. You tricked us," Ethan whisper-snarls.

Dane raises his arms; at first I thought he was going to push him away, but his hands freeze at the side in surrender.

"I never lied." His response is labored and raspy from the tight hold but his words are clear.

"No?" Ethan tilts his head, his gaze menacing. "You didn't buy out the hostel to trap us there with you, to seduce us just to throw us away whenever you were done with us." Dane's face falls. His eyes bounce between Ethan's eyes then to mine and they're laced with guilt.

"That's what I thought," Ethan says, tightening his grip.

The deep pink flush you only get when you're struggling for air paints Dane's face. His expression is both stunned and sad, like he's giving up and letting Ethan take what he needs.

"*STOP!*" I repeat slamming my open hand on the other. "*STOP!*"

Ethan can't see me so I rush forward pulling him off Dane. I cup his face to turn his gaze to mine and the anger pooling in his eyes fades the moment he focuses on me.

He relents, stepping back, leaving me in between the two of them.

Turning my attention back on Dane, he's leaning over, his hands pressed into his knees for support, slouching forward in defeat as he tries to catch his breath.

He finally stands to his full height, his chest still heavy as he runs his hands over the sides of his head, pushing back the short strands of his hair.

I need this class. I need this credit to finish my MBA and I can't have anything get in the way of it. I'm so close and I've worked too hard.

Ethan needs it too, he just doesn't care about it as much as I do. His father is forcing him to do this, while I've dreamed about it for years.

My eyes plead with Dane as I walk toward him. Looking up, our eyes connect and I can see *my* Dane again. He appraises me with admiration and a softness I felt in Paris and it makes my heart flutter.

"I need this class," I sign, feeling vulnerable. He hurt me. He hurt us. But I can't have anything get in the way of this. Taking a deep inhale, I squeeze my eyes shut before opening them with even more desperation.

"We won't bother you or say anything during your lectures. Just let us stay in this class and get our credits. Please. Let's just forget what happened. Forget Paris."

"It's impossible to forget," Dane huffs the words out in a whisper so low, it's like a confession to himself. He stands to his full height, teetering his head from side-to-side as his palm roams over the column of his neck, massaging the marks Ethan left from his tight grip.

"Forget Paris?" he asks, looking at us, like the thought is unfathomable. I see the sadness, the Dane I knew. The one with the messy manbun and free spirit. The one that felt like he was all in with me, with us.

"Forget everything," Ethan bites back as he reaches for my hand, slipping his fingers in between mine then leads us toward the door. "Hannah needs this credit. Stay out of our way and we'll stay out of yours."

32

ETHAN

I meant what I said when I told him to stay out of our way. But, I hate that he's actually fucking listening to me.

In Paris, it was like he didn't have ears. He constantly pushed my buttons, threw me out of my comfort zone—like he's never heard of what a boundary line is—and challenged me every moment he could.

But here, he's done exactly what I told him to.

Stay out of our way and we'll stay out of yours.

It's been five weeks since the discovery that Paris Dane is *the* Dane Campbell. The Dane Campbell that invented Nova, the first ever and superior code that allowed for the first introduction of AI into our world.

Any companies that utilize it to build on their own AI coding have to pay him royalties. So, yeah, he's a fucking billionaire.

Dissecting all that information after our first class—when I nearly choked him to death, had me running through a roller coaster of emotions.

I have no idea why someone with his kind of wealth would

stay in a hostel other than to do exactly what he did. Seduce us, trick us, take advantage of us.

But, did he?

As much as I hate admitting it, and would never admit to him, I know I wanted it. I wanted him. It was the best part of our entire trip and I hate that Dane Campbell and everything we did still lives rent free in my head.

I glance up at Hannah who's completely consumed in her study book, then look around the café on campus. It has a large open area with tons of different types of seating options for the students who like to hang out between classes and study or do homework. It even has a few private spaces for groups that are working on projects.

It's comfortable and we've found ourselves migrating here after most of our classes.

After we both graduated, Hannah was top of her class, obviously. We opted—well she opted—to apply for her MBA because not only does it look better on a resume, it was something she's always wanted to do. Especially after the accident.

It's probably the only area in our life where we're exactly opposite.

Where she found her passion, I lost mine.

As bitter as I am, I'm happy it wasn't the other way around. And I'm even happier that she's still here with me. Because, we almost lost her. After we both healed and started learning sign language it was sort of a solidifier for us. Nothing would tear us apart, emotionally or physically.

So, we always knew that we would stay together, wherever we went. School, work, it didn't matter, we would find a way to move and live together. Neither one of us wanted to do the long distance thing. So, when baseball was no longer an option, it made the decision to stay in Seattle easy. She can finish her degree and I work for my dad.

He hated my love for baseball and wanted me to stop playing from the minute I joined Little League.

He never went to any of my games, nor did he support my desire to go pro.

After the accident I had no other option. I never had anything to fall back on and because Hannah needed so many surgeries, the medical bills just kept compounding.

My dad knew I couldn't take care of them so he offered to take care of them, only if I paid them back, with interest, and worked for his company so he could have the father son team he's always dreamed of.

Not that he cares much about me or a father and son working together. He just likes the image it portrays.

Somehow he thinks that makes us look more approachable, likable. But there's nothing likable about Edward Russo. He does things that benefit him only and the first opportunity he has to hold something over your head, he will.

Back then, I didn't care. I just wanted Hannah to get what she needed. I don't regret it, but the debt he holds over me, reminding me almost on a daily basis, is excruciating.

Regardless, I'm stuck, paying him back for the rest of my life, currently taking an MBA course because he thinks the title will look good on a business card, all while working in a field that makes me sick to my stomach.

I'm living my life with no choices of my own, just doing what he says because I have to.

His firm, Russo & Company, is one of the largest accounting firms in the United States and they represent some of the biggest companies worldwide.

The people that work there are nice enough, other than my father of course, but there's no joy in it. Not for me at least. However, if it supports Hannah and provides stability for our future, that's exactly what I'll do. If I can't be happy in my career, I might as well do whatever I need to do for her to be happy in hers.

I mean, I'd rather be crushing fastballs and reviewing baseball statistics but I can hardly stomach watching a game, even though I can't help but follow all the highlights and players.

So, the fact that I have to meet my father at Ford Field ballpark to watch the Seattle Smashers in their first playoff game in less than an hour is only a slight slap in the face.

Is this a father son relationship building outing? No. He has a potential client he's meeting so he has to appear like a standup, present father. He only brings me along for the image, to tell them how proud he is in front of their faces, just to turn around and remind me how much I disappoint him in private.

"Are you feeling okay?"

"Don't really want to go."

"I know."

Hannah grants me one of her soft, pity smiles that only appear when we're talking about my father.

"I have lots of studying. I'll be here for a while then head back to the apartment and I'll be home when you get back."

"Okay, baby. I love you." I kiss her on her forehead and head out of the coffee shop.

Skimming the campus, it's always bustling with students moving back and forth between buildings. I find that a lot of them spend most of their time here, studying, or working on big projects, so more often than not, it's busy.

My eyes catch those familiar dark blonde locks exiting the main building. He pauses at the top of the steps as he slides his hand into the pocket of his slacks and pulls out his phone.

Tapping on the screen he lifts it to his ear, that trademark smile unveils itself, as his lips move in conversation with whoever is on the other line.

I turn away, hating to see how happy he is talking to

whoever the fuck is calling but I can't help myself, so I look back again.

This time he's pulling the phone away from his ear, his gaze is trained on me, and I bask in the attention. He's avoided my gaze in class, not looking at either one of us during lectures, taking the *stay out of our way* comment literally to heart.

So, snagging his attention now makes my stomach flip, even though I don't want it to. I turn away and increase my stride, finding my way into the parking lot and around the barrier away from his dangerous gaze.

Over the past few weeks there seem to be a lot of rumors flying around about Dane. Some about his past and previous relationships, others about what he does with his money and how he goes off the grid.

I hate not knowing the truth and I want more than anything to ask him what's real.

If the three of us were real.

33

DANE

I cross the campus, heading in the opposite direction Ethan was going. Naturally I keep stealing glances back over my shoulder to see if he's still within view.

Of course he's not because the moment he saw me looking at him, he sped up like an escaped convict needing to flee the country.

I've done everything he asked. Okay, he asked one thing. But still, it's one of the hardest things I've ever had to do in my entire life.

Restraint that I've had to endure these last few weeks, watching him and Hannah come in and out of my classroom. Handing me assignments with nothing but statistical numbers and meaningless words, as I pray for some sort of olive branch hidden on the paper.

A penciled heart, a 'we miss you', or maybe a *"I'm sorry we left you alone in Paris after the best night of our lives"* note. Perhaps their fucking phone number.

That would be nice.

But, nothing.

Nine more months.

I only teach for nine more months. If a woman can literally grow an entire human from a tiny little nucleus into a ten-pound baby with a functioning brain and beating heart, I can certainly reset mine within that time, right?

Yes. Yes, you can Dane Campbell. You've been through worse.

Wrapping my hand around the cool, metal door handle, I pull it open and hold it for a couple of students walking out with coffee cups in their hands.

"Thank you, Professor Campbell," they say in unison.

I nod and smile, then step in through the doorway; my eyes instantly lock on those familiar ocean blues surrounded by chocolate brown waves.

Jesus Christ, I can't catch a break. Both of them are fucking everywhere.

Campus. Coffee shop. My fucking dreams.

She immediately dips her chin back into her text book and I swallow thickly as I continue to the counter. There's a line so I'm stuck standing in it, directly in front of her table, as I stay completely quiet.

Her face is buried in her book that she hasn't turned the page on since I walked in so I know she's just staring at it, taking nothing in, and I want nothing more than to talk to her.

"Next," I get called up to the counter.

I request my usual as I hand them a ten dollar bill, "Cappuccino, please."

Stepping aside, the pick up counter is even closer to her table. Now I'm standing so close I can smell that signature citrus scent she carries around with her.

I suck in a deep breath as if trying to imbed it in my nasal cavity when I hear someone call out, "Excuse me?"

I turn around and there's a man leaning around Hannah. "Is this chair taken?"

I don't think he wants to sit, I think he wants to take it for another table, but I'm not taking the risk either way.

I can't help myself as I round the corner of the square table, hitting my leg on the pointed edge, before flopping down on the seat like it was musical fucking chairs.

"It's taken." I smile up at the guy, praying he doesn't recognize me, before looking back at Hannah who's wide eyed and shocked.

"Hey." I face her direction, turning my back to Mr. Seat Stealing Guy.

"*Hi.*"

"How are you?" I ask, my voice raspy like I haven't talked in a while but it's just nerves.

She stares at me for a beat, her eyes working through different emotions. I can tell by the way her brow furrows, then relaxes before her lips press into a tight line.

If she wanted to, she could just push me off the table, especially after what she's heard about me over the last few weeks. I'm not stupid. I hear what the students say about my past dating history. My *one-date Dane* reputation now seems to be a running challenge for some of them.

Her now knowing all of that along with the fact that I paid to have the hostel at no vacancy so I could be alone with them for days, just adds another reason why they shouldn't trust me.

"*I miss you guys,*" I sign, telling her the words that have wanted to spill out for weeks.

Squinting her eyes as if in pain, she tilts her head then looks away.

My hand immediately shoots forward. My fingers pinch the corner of her chin to turn her face back to look at me. I don't want her to avoid my words or my gaze because I've never felt so strongly about a statement before.

A glass shatters in the background and I yank my hand away, realizing I'm in a very public place with a fucking student.

I palm my face in frustration and lean my elbows on the table.

"I'm enjoying your class," she signs and I swear to god a euphoric explosion ignites in my chest.

Small talk is fine. Any talk is fine.

An unnaturally huge smile beams out of me.

"Yeah?"

She nods, short and quick, and I can see a smidge of a smile.

Her hand covers the column of her neck, lightly roaming over the scarred area of her skin and I can tell she's just as nervous as I am. Fuck, she's stunning in all her ways. I love that she's confident but timid at the same time. I love how loud she speaks without saying anything.

"Hannah—" The words get caught in my throat and I pause. "Can we—"

"Professor Campbell, your cappuccino is ready!"

I whip an unavoidable glare at the barista before turning back to Hannah, then glance down at my watch. Shit. I have to go.

Rubbing the nape of my neck, I lean closer to her. "I have to go, I'm meeting a friend and I'm late."

The column of her throat rolls as she swallows and I don't miss the annoyed look in her eyes before turning away from me.

"It's a guy friend," I spit out immediately, as if to tell her it's not another woman but she side-eyes me and I realize she knows it doesn't matter if it's a guy or girl. "A platonic guy friend." Jesus, I sound like an idiot.

"It doesn't matter."

But her body language says otherwise, and as much as I hate that she's feeling bothered, I really fucking like it.

"You're jealous?" I sign with a smirk.

"No."

"You are. Admit it." I press my shoulder into hers.

"Stop it." She palms my shoulder back playfully, finally smiling at me.

"Oh, you like me." Her fun loving look instantly fades with my statement.

"That was never the problem."

Annnd she pours ice over my playful banter in a reminder that, although I didn't really lie to them, I didn't really tell them the truth either.

I nod once with a tight-lipped smile before standing and grabbing my cup at the pick-up counter.

Turning back, I stop at her table. I want to sit back down but I won't. This might have not been the exact way I wanted this to turn out but the fact that we're talking at all, well, it's a start and I'll take what I can get right now.

Even though she's still mad, this little conversation gave me more hope than I've felt in the last two months.

"See you tomorrow, Poe." I wink as I turn toward the exit; I don't miss the blush that appears on her cheeks at the sound of her nickname.

I've been focused solely on ignoring them, trying to forget everything that happened and getting over the fact that I fell so hard for them so fast.

But now, I feel revitalized. Thinking of all the ways to prove to them that I'm not the person they think I am.

34

ETHAN

There's something about a baseball field that provides an endorphin release like nothing else. The earthy smell of the dirt, the sound of the cleats digging into the grass and the feeling of overall satisfaction when the crowd starts filling the stands, happy and cheering.

Every memory I ever had came flooding back the moment I stepped into the stadium, except it wasn't the same happiness I've always felt. Dread, laced with an overwhelming feeling of sadness knowing I was so close to walking into a stadium just like this one, but as a player, not a spectator.

I glance over the field from the biggest suite in Ford Field where the Seattle Smashers are warming up, holding a beer in my scarred hand instead of a baseball. Dressed in a suit, instead of a uniform. And I hate every fucking minute of it.

I don't belong here. I don't know where I belong to be honest.

But I know it's not in the top-tier suite, listening to my father spew used car salesman pitches to whomever is on his roster to impress.

"Ethan!" My father calls me and I internally cringe at the abrasiveness in his tone.

Steeling my spine, I walk over, my eyes oscillate between the two men he's speaking with and I hold out my hand as I approach.

"Ethan Russo, nice to meet you," I introduce myself, shaking the hands of two men as my father provides me with their titles first—because that's far more important to him than their name apparently.

"Ethan, this is the CFO of Ford Enterprises, Quincy Morris, and the CCO, David Ferguson." They are dressed in Smashers jerseys of what I assume is their favorite player on the team instead of the suits you would be expecting. It makes me feel even more out of place because my father said nothing less than a three piece suit would be acceptable for this *meeting*.

Of course, I opted out of wearing a tie because that's excessive. I didn't hear the end of it until everyone showed up and he finally had to stop berating me about it.

He even griped about the choice of color. I chose navy over charcoal and that's apparently disrespectful because, oh who the hell knows. If I chose the charcoal one he would have complained that it wasn't black.

I'm feeling more and more claustrophobic and this crisp, white, overly-starched button down might as well be a straight jacket. I unbutton the top buttons and turn my neck side-to-side, blowing out a stalled breath as I attempt to reset knowing I still have a few hours of this before I can leave.

"So, Ethan, do you follow baseball?" Quincy asks with a respectful, easy going tone.

Only with my entire soul.

I may not put on the games anymore but I still secretly look up all the highlights and details, following all the teams, players, and stats. I know more about the MLB than I should, I just don't get the chance to talk about it anymore.

Fortunately my father sees someone he *must* say hi to and excuses himself.

"I do. I have my whole life," I respond directly to Quincy with a modest tone because I don't want to seem overly excited about this conversation.

"Me too, me too," Quincy quips, excitedly, like we just became best buds. "What do you think of Hudson Byrnes?" He hikes his thumbs over his shoulder as he turns his back to me, his jersey sporting the name BYRNES.

"Oh man, his minor league stats were unmatched. Coming back from an injury like that and maintaining the numbers he did..." I shake my head, "Unbelievable. I think I did a secret happy dance in my bathroom when the Smashers picked him up last year."

I continue spouting off facts and details of all the players. Both Quincy and I rally back and forth about historic plays and our favorite games. I don't know how long it's been, but the team is finally warming up on the field and the suite is getting a little more crowded.

Slipping off my jacket, I drape it over the chair in front of me, getting more comfortable as I roll my sleeves up over my forearms.

"Ethan!" my father yells yet again, but this time it's not as curt, there's an eagerness to it that tells me he's with someone super important and I need to be on my best behavior.

I turn my body in his direction, preparing myself for anything. Except I was wholly unprepared for the sight of *him*.

Dane hasn't noticed me yet. He's looking over at *the* Christian Ford, CEO of Ford Enterprises and leaseholder of this baseball field. My gorgeous professor is chuckling and patting Christian's arm like he just told him something funny.

I look to my left and right for an escape but I can't get away and when I look back at my father the threat behind his gaze is serious.

Fuck.

"Excuse me," I say to Quincy and take a step toward their huddle. It's my father, Christian Ford, and Dane *fucking* Campbell.

I step into the empty space completing the circle. Dane's eyes flicker my way, back to Christian, then his head snaps back in a double take, his smile fading.

"This is my son, Ethan Russo. Ethan, this is the CEO of Ford Enterprises, Christian Ford." Giving my father a wiseass glance for the unnecessary introduction, I miraculously hide an eyeroll as I shake his hand with a smile. "And, obviously, you know Dane Campbell," he says, turning as he snaps his fingers at one of the banquet servers.

"Do I?" I say sarcastically, with only enough volume to be heard between the two of us.

Seeing him here now, dressed casually in a baseball jersey, beer in hand, is similar to how I remember him in Paris. His shorter hair is a reminder that it's not the *same* guy, this version is currently my professor. But it's not styled like it is during class, it's messier and stupidly sexy. He looks a bit more carefree and his shoulders are at ease. His whole demeanor is a stark contrast from the tense Dane that I've grown to know over the last few weeks as my professor.

Still, I hold my hand out trying to remain as professional as possible in front of my father, clearing my throat and speaking louder. "Of course. Good to see you, Professor."

A smirk crosses his face and I have no idea how to read it.

"His accolades, awards, and contribution to our world is truly extraordinary. I hope you know how lucky you are to have him as a teacher," my father adds.

Dane's smirk grows, then he winks using the eye hidden from the view of Christian and my dad and I can't help but clench my jaw at his cockiness. There was a part of me that loved seeing it in Paris. Now, I want to punch that confident look straight off his stupid, kissable face.

My father turns his body toward the waitress and starts spouting off drink orders.

Dane leans in and says, "I see you have to be on your best behavior. This is gonna be so much fun."

35

DANE

"Stop fucking around," Ethan threatens me while his father isn't paying attention. "This is serious."

"Not for me. For you though," I glance over at his father then back at him, sucking air through my teeth, "holds the leash tight doesn't he?"

"Dane. Stop."

I push further because I'm getting under his skin and I've missed this banter we had in Paris. "He's been begging me to manage my portfolio for a really long time. I wonder what he would say if he knew—"

"Just...don't..." He sighs deeply, anxiety dripping from every nerve in his body. "Don't...say anything...please." His eyes plead with me as easily as his words and it immediately puts me on edge about Edward Russo.

Ethan is a grown adult, yet he cowers to his father like he's a teenager with no decision making skills of his own. It's a side of him I haven't seen and I instantly feel very protective.

"So, Dane, how's my son performing in your class?" Edward asks as he waves off the waitress like he's annoyed by her presence.

My eyes bounce between the two of them and when I glance over at Christian, he squints at me and I can tell he suspects a shift in my demeanor.

Clearing my throat I respond, "he's super attentive, a perfectionist at everything, always aims to please." When I glance back over to Ethan there's a distinct flush in his cheeks because he knows I'm not talking about his mediocre classwork and half-ass tests he barely tries to pass.

Hannah is truly the top student in the class and academically exceeds in everything we've worked on so far. Ethan? He just seems to be there.

"Great to hear, keep it up Ethan. You'll be working your way up my firm in no time." He pats him on the shoulder in a gesture that's for a stranger.

"Actually, before I forget, can we exchange numbers and keep in touch after the game?" Edward asks and this is a great opportunity to snag Ethan's number.

"Absolutely." I tap into the contacts of my phone and hold it out to Ethan first. He rolls his eyes, grabs it, and adds his number before passing it back to me. I quickly shoot him a text to make sure it goes through then Edward reads me off his number, looking over my shoulder the entire time to make sure I don't mistype anything.

Quincy calls Ethan over and he gives me another pleading look as if he's silently begging me to be on my best behavior before he graciously excuses himself.

Edward continues to talk about nothing I care about. Christian being the businessman he is, listens intently but I can tell he's also completely unamused.

The rest of the afternoon goes along this way. Christian and I try to skate away from Edward to find peace without the constant solicitation of our portfolios and watch the game, well sort of. I find myself just watching Ethan as often as I can get away with it.

He hasn't been networking like the sleazeball his dad is. He's been engaged in the game, talking mostly with Quincy and David, his eyes catching every move, every play.

He talks about the game like he knows more about the MLB than the MLB does. I can hear him spouting out player stats, facts, historic events, game plays.

He knows every-fucking-thing.

The only time I've ever seen him this lively, this enthusiastic, is when he converses with Hannah or talks about her.

I can't help but grin as I side-eye him. He's smiling wide and laughing and fuck, my heart stutters in my chest at the sight.

The crowd cheers as Hudson Byrnes, one of my best friends and catcher for the Smashers, steps up to the plate. It's the bottom of the seventh, we're down by one with two outs, and he's got Ramos on second. The first pitch flies toward him at ninety-nine miles an hour and, *crack*, he slams it into the outfield. The entire suite stands yelling, arms outstretched in the air, watching as it floats over the field and out of the ballpark.

"Fuck yeah!" Christian and I high five. I look over at Ethan, he's hollering with a smile a mile wide.

Hudson is rounding the bases, the crowd is going wild, but my eyes are glued to Ethan as he animatedly comments on the play. I can't hear him, or read his lips, but it's clear in his body language how excited he is. How passionate his words are. His arms are floating up as if imitating the way the ball flew out of the stadium. The way his fingers are pointing to each other as if he's naming off stats and all this makes me so much more curious about him.

His father steps up to his side, he was probably the only one in this entire suite that didn't have any reaction to Hudson's home run and it just goes to show he cares nothing about the game, building relationships, or having a good time, he only cares about getting the client.

Ethan visibly stiffens and his smile fades. Edward has a pierced look in his eyes while he says something to Ethan, his jaw clenching as he avoids his fathers gaze.

After a solid minute of getting reprimanded his father finally steps away and Ethan looks down huffing out a long breath, then peers over at me seeing that I saw the entire exchange.

He looks embarrassed and storms off, heading straight down the hallway in the suite where the bathrooms are. Of course, I'm following right behind him.

He disappears inside the men's bathroom but right before the door closes all the way, I sneak my hand through the opening and follow him in, allowing the door to shut behind me.

Turning around, I lock the deadbolt. It clicks into place and Ethan spins around and I can tell how pissed he is. Not just at me for being in here but for that entire conversation I just witnessed.

"What the fuck are you doing?" he screams. "Get out!"

"No."

I step into his space as his feet fumble back until he's against the wall.

I don't waste any time because I know we don't have any.

"What's going on with you and your dad? And what's with this whole other side of you? You knew more facts and looked more alive than I've ever seen you while you watched the game." I'm towering myself against him, making it known that I'm not leaving until I get the answers I want.

He stays silent but his blown out irises tell me so much. Sure he's mad, but he likes this dominating side of me, even if he'll never admit it.

I gently place my hand on his chest, pushing him flush against the wall, then creep my hand up at the base of his collarbone, pushing a little harder.

"Answer me," I say with a little more grit because I want him to know how serious I feel about this entire situation.

"If I do will you leave me the fuck alone?"

"Probably not."

He sinks against the wall in defeat with an annoyed eye roll.

"My dad wants me to get my masters. For the title. So that's what I'm doing."

"But why do you care? You clearly don't want to work for him."

His eyebrows furrow. "How do you know?"

"It's fucking obvious. You have more passion about this bathroom sink than you do about investment portfolios. And how the hell do you know so much about baseball?" His eyes saucer wide. "Why aren't you out there playing?"

He pauses again as if the words are on the verge of flying free but he's still holding everything back.

"Why, Ethan?" I push into him with both my body and my words.

"Because of this!" he screams, holding up his scarred hand. "I was supposed to be the number one draft right out of high school. I was lined up for everything I ever wanted. Until prom night, when that fucking accident ruined both our lives and..." He pauses, a look I can't read flashes over his face and I can tell he's shutting down.

"And?" I push more.

He sucks in a stuttering breath. "Now, I can hardly grip a pen, much less a baseball, and she lost the ability to speak for the rest of her life. I owe it to her to do a job that allows me to take care of her, even if I fucking hate it."

If I know anything about Hannah, it's that she loves wide open and wants nothing more but for Ethan to be happy. Not once has she ever indicated that she holds a grudge or feels bitter about her circumstances and I highly doubt she cares about a posh lifestyle of designer clothes and expensive cars.

"Does Hannah feel that way?" I ask him. "Does she want you to work for your father?"

"It doesn't matter. It's the only option that makes any sense for me." He presses his palms into my chest with a weak attempt at trying to push me away.

Smacking his hands away, I lean into him. My lips hover over his jawline between his ear and mouth. I can't decide if I want to talk the sense into him or kiss it out of him.

This is a dead end conversation. He's already sold himself on the idea that this is what is best for him and Hannah, even if it makes him miserable his entire life.

"Go to dinner with me after this," I state more as a fact than a question. My lips brush his ear as I push my hips into him and he visibly shivers at the contact.

He might hate me, but his body loves me.

"No," he breathes out.

I smirk. I knew that would be his answer.

"Fine." I straighten myself up and step back, creating a cold distance between us.

"Fine?" His eyes take me in questioningly.

He tilts his head, waiting for a punchline.

"Yeah. Fine," I repeat as I wave my arms, gesturing toward the door.

"Okay, fine." he repeats again slowly, still questioningly, as he stands up straight, brushing his hands down his button up and walks toward the exit.

He looks back over his shoulder and I know he's curious that I'm just giving up on pushing him right now. I get why. I push on everything, but I know he'll never agree to going out with me.

I know someone who will though.

Unlocking it, he grabs the door handle, swinging it open and his entire body stalls before a whispered, "Oh, fuck," falls from his lips.

36

ETHAN

I pull the door wider, unsure of how to respond as Christian Ford leans against the wall as if he were waiting for his turn in the bathroom.

Dane cranes his neck in my direction to see who's on the other side and says, "oh hey," like it's not a big deal that Christian Ford is watching us walk out of a locked solo bathroom. We both peek out, look down the hall and see Christian's bodyguard standing at the entrance, not allowing anyone through.

In synchronized motion we turn our gaze back to Christian as we step out of the doorway. His eyes bounce between us and I can't read him. This guy is tall and intimidating and I have no idea what to say as I stand here suspiciously. Dane on the other hand has his signature smile without a care in the world.

"You're welcome," Christian says with a smirk, then slips between us passing through to the bathroom and shutting the door behind him.

Okkkaaay. So, they're cool like that.

Then I remember Christian is in that poly relationship with the other couple and it makes me wonder if Dane—No, I'm not going there. I don't want to consider that at all.

Dane doesn't wait for me as he walks down the hallway and passes the bodyguard the size of Egypt, then makes his way to the bar where my father is standing.

He's being weird and I have no idea how to read him. He gave up way too fast after he asked me to dinner. It's so unlike him.

I glance at the scoreboard; it's the last inning and we're still up by one after Hudson Byrnes' two-run homer. I continue my way over to where Dane is standing because he beelined straight for my dad and that's strange considering he vehemently avoided him the entire game until now.

Not that I was paying attention to him.

As I step up, Dane rolls back onto his heels and rubs circles over his stomach. "All this excitement has me famished. I'm *starving*," he says that bit with way too much exaggeration and I peer over at my father who I swear has fucking dollar signs flying out of his eyeballs.

"Let's go to that new restaurant around the corner, I've been dying to try it out," my father replies in a surprisingly calm tone, considering I know how badly he wants to get Dane alone.

"Only if Ethan comes, too," Dane says as he turns his gaze to me with a full blown smile.

This motherfucker.

My father grits his teeth as he lasers into me. "Good idea. It'll be a great real life learning experience for him."

"I—I'm not really hungry. You guys should go." I smile back at Dane because him being stuck at dinner with my father genuinely puts one on my face.

"Nonsense. You're coming," dear old Dad replies, not giving me a choice. "I'll call ahead and get us a reservation." He steps away as he places his cell phone to his ear, not taking any chances with this opportunity.

"What are you doing?" I pin him with an—I don't even

know what kind of look. I'm fucking pissed that I'm stuck spending more time with my dad and now we have to discuss all the money Dane has and properties he owns. *Great.*

"Anything I want," he replies with a confidence I'm jealous of and it's just so him.

The crowd cheers loudly and the scoreboard lights up. The Smashers brought home another win and the entire stadium is going crazy.

My father comes back telling us they have a table waiting for us and holds his arm out to the exit. Dane says goodbye to Christian and we head out, using a back entrance that isn't as crowded. I take a minute to text Hannah to let her know what's going on with an angry face emoji and she just responds with a laughing and face palm emoji.

Great. She's enjoying this, too.

I guess she knows if anyone can make this dinner with my father more entertaining, it's Dane.

Right when we walk in, the hostess greets us and immediately takes us to a corner table in the restaurant. My father must have name dropped Dane Campbell because the restaurant is packed and I guarantee you this wasn't easily available.

The table is square with two chairs on each side. I step to the opposite side of it, placing myself closest to the corner where I'd prefer to remain in solitary so I can just get through the evening. Instead of Dane sitting across the table like I expect, he slides into the seat directly next to me with yet another fat grin on his face. My father sits directly across from Dane, pleased with the full frontal attention.

We go through the pleasantries with the waiter and order food and wine. We finish the first bottle before the appetizers arrive and Dane orders yet another bottle of wine, topping me off again.

"Stop trying to get me drunk," I reply under my breath.

"Why? You're so much more fun when you're drunk." His

hand discreetly covers the top of my thigh and my knee jerks up, banging the bottom of the table.

My dad glares in my direction even though he has no idea if that was actually me, but my dad blames me for everything.

"Ope, sorry about that. Big legs," Dane replies like he was the one that hit the table and then expertly steers the conversation in another direction. "So, Edward, tell me more about your company."

Edward Russo rubs his hands together like a mad scientist and spews out his elevator pitch like he's practiced it a million times. Except, it's not really an elevator pitch because those are supposed to be summarized quickly. He just keeps talking and talking. I find myself taking more sips of wine as I watch both of them.

God, I hate this. Wining and dining clients. Kissing ass for a living. The managing money part isn't horrible but how am I going to build relationships with clients when I don't want to build relationships with anyone.

I only ever like talking to Hannah. And more recently Dane.

I curse myself at the thought.

Dane is engaged with my dad, more engaged than I've seen him today and I wonder if he's actually considering working with his company. It would be a huge account for my father.

I flinch again at the heat of Dane's hand as it crawls up my thigh. It was more gentle this time so I didn't kick my leg up but it feels too soft and intimate. He's still looking at my father with a completely composed expression, you'd have no idea he's groping me under the table.

I place my hand over his, gripping tightly as I attempt to push his hand off my leg but he holds strong, dipping into my inner thigh and cupping between my legs.

"Umpf," I grunt out and then cough a couple of times grabbing my water. "Sorry...swallowed my own spit," I reply with the first thing that comes to mind. My father is clearly not pleased.

"No problem," Dane replies, "you were saying?" He turns back to my father, expertly hiding the fact that he's palming my cock.

Dane continues a rhythmic pace as my dad names off stats and numbers and other facts that I can't pay attention to because I can only feel his hand on me. You would think the fabric of these expensive trousers would be enough armor to protect me from such a simple act, but they're far from dense. In fact, I swear they're made out of fucking tissue paper with the way I can feel all the ridges of his fingers dip underneath and around my now hard cock.

My eyelids flutter as he wraps his skillful hand around my length and tugs, the fabric providing an unexpected pleasurable friction.

"Oh, fuck," falls from my lips as a groan rumbles in my chest.

My dad ignores me, and thankfully I can't hear anything he's saying because the pleasure builds in my groin as Dane continues at a slow, but punishing pace. He stops and I huff out a heavy breath as if I finally come back to earth.

"You okay?" Dane asks, sans any clue he's stroking me off right now.

"I'm good," I reply, my voice husky and thick.

"Food is coming, don't forget your napkin." Using his other hand, he tosses a napkin at my lap and I pat it down under the tablecloth, trying to act normal when nothing is fucking normal right now. The hand hidden underneath the table begins unbuttoning my pants and releases my zipper.

I give him a pleading look, which he ignores, as a rush of cool air hits my cock before he wraps his entire hand around it, stroking it from base to tip.

Smothering another groan, I jerk forward, pretending to adjust my seat as I pat the napkin.

My dad is still talking, how I don't even know but I don't care because if I don't come I think I might die.

I shift my gaze to take in Dane's profile. His eyes are still bright with a pleased expression but his pupils, they're a shade darker than usual. His sharp jawline is clenched like he's enjoying every minute of this but hates holding himself back.

He side-eyes me as his lips tip up in a smirk, then he rubs his palm over my tip coating himself with my pre-cum then jerks down the length of me. I grunt again and my father pauses, looks at me, then continues talking.

Dane knows how loud I am in bed. I'm not good at being quiet.

Fuck.

Grabbing the drink menu, I place it in front of me as I lean my elbows on the table and palm my forehead, looking down pretending to read.

I steady my breathing as Dane picks up his tempo, twisting his hand over the tip then back down the shaft. My cock thickens and Dane hums, acting as if he's agreeing with something my dad said, but I know that hum. He's turned on, too.

I want to grab his cock under the table, give him the same treatment he's giving me, but it's too late. The knowing sensation builds at the base of my spine and I try to hold back but my cock jerks as my hips thrust up and I spurt cum into the napkin covering my lap. I hum out a long moan and exhausted breath, still pretending to study the menu. Another pulse of cum, then another as I hiss and groan between my teeth.

"What's gotten into you?" my father asks, annoyed at my disruption over him.

"Nothing, this menu is great," I reply as I close it and place it across the table from me.

Just then the waiter stops by with our meals, placing our dishes down in front of us.

"Bon Appétit!" he says as he turns on his heel and walks away.

Dane and I share a look, recalling our dinner in Paris that had just as much sexual tension swimming at the table and he chuckles. I can't help but do the same in my post-orgasmic state, even though I'm still put-off by the fact that he jerked me off across the table from my dad.

"This meal looks fantastic," my father says as he dives in, not waiting for anyone else at the table.

Dane finally removes his hand from my lap. He doesn't grab his napkin. No, that would be a far too normal thing for him to do.

Instead he looks down at his plate, swipes his cum-coated finger over the mashed potatoes and sauce, then locks eyes with me as he presses it into his mouth. He sucks his finger clean with a slurp and a pop, humming his approval.

"You're right, Ethan. This is delicious."

37

HANNAH

Ethan: Be home in ten.

He's mad.

Ethan is very expressive in his texts because it's a big part of our communication but this text is nothing of the sort.

I know he was stuck going to dinner with his father and Dane and I can't even begin to imagine the thoughts that flooded his mind as they made their way over to the restaurant.

Dane reminded me at the coffee shop exactly why I liked him so much. I got a dose of his easy going and fun personality mixed with that carefree spirit I loved so much. I missed him and felt terrible that we left him like we did but I know it was for the best and it was what Ethan needed.

Plus he did lie to us, or at least, refrained from telling us who he was. I can understand that now knowing who he is and how much money he has. I can see why he would seek out anonymity.

That part doesn't bother me as much as buying out the

hostel. We still don't know what his true reasons were, but if I were to guess he didn't have ill intentions like Ethan thinks. It was an impulsive act driven by desire, just like everything Dane does in life.

Plus, leaving Paris and our actions behind was always what we planned to do at the end of the trip. There were never any expectations but as much as we tell ourselves that, I know Ethan feels the same as I do.

If the circumstances were different, it could have changed things. And now that we're all back in the same place, at the same time for an extended time period, the only thing holding us back is the fact that he's our professor—a taboo little detail —and the little fact that Ethan refuses to address his sexual desires and feelings toward Dane.

I've had all night to ponder these thoughts and after carefully considering all the details, I know I want us to try and pursue something with Dane, even if it's just something casual between the three of us. No one else needs to know.

I just want what we had in Paris. We're all adults, I know we can figure this out and if my encounter with Dane at the coffee shop today tells me anything, it's that he would be fully onboard with this plan.

I don't want to risk getting caught or getting in trouble. I can't afford to not graduate but I also don't want to give up on the idea of what this could be. It's crazy, I know, but something feels right when we're all together.

I love Ethan, but I also miss the person he became when Dane was with us.

I *crave* both versions of Ethan and, admittedly, Dane too.

The front door opens and shuts abruptly. He didn't slam it but he didn't really care to stop it from closing harshly, either.

I walk into the living room where he's kicking off his shoes and tossing his keys on the sofa table. He looks rightfully disheveled. His hair is a hot mess like he's been running his hands through it a bit too much and his dress shirt is untucked, hanging haphazardly over his pants.

"Hey."

"He fucking jerked me off. At the dinner table. In front of my dad!" My face blanches and my jaw drops. "I mean, like under the table. He just started stroking me and I couldn't do anything. I just had to sit there like nothing was happening as my dad talked about numbers and bank accounts and interest rates. It was infuriating. God, he pisses me off." He places his hands on his hips, expelling a massive breath as he cranes his neck up to the ceiling.

I can't help it. I attempt to cover my face but my shoulders jerk as a fit of laughter overtakes me. That is such a Dane thing to do and I can only imagine how furious but needy Ethan was and, god, I wish I could have seen it.

This must go on for a minute before I see his face soften as he attempts to smother a smile.

"Oh, you think that's funny." Ethan peers down at me, taking a slow step in my direction. His voice is less angry now and a little playful.

I squeeze my lips in a tight line and nod.

"You brat." He lunges for me, using his fingers to tickle the sides of my body because he knows it's like pure torture for me. I shake my head, laughing as I duck away and shuffle my feet into the bedroom. I throw myself on the bed, attempting to hide behind the blankets.

"Stop," I sign as I peek over the top, still laughing.

"No way, baby. You're in for it now," he says, stripping off his shirt. As the buttons splay open, there's a distinct stain on the front of his pants, presumably where he came on himself and I hold my stomach and roll over, laughing even harder.

He shakes his head with that beautiful smile of his and I can't help but thank Dane for bringing this playful side out in him again tonight.

I toss away the blankets and take my sweater off, leaving me in just a bra and panties. Spreading my legs, I bite my lip and crook my finger inviting him in.

He prowls toward me, his chest and ab muscles flexing as he moves. His usually put-together hair flops over his forehead and I love how chaotic he looks.

Pulling my underwear off, he tosses them to the side and trails kisses up my thigh.

I crook my finger under his chin so he can look at me.

"Did you like him touching you?"

There's nothing but lust dripping from his eyes and even though I already know the answer, I want him to say it.

Closing his eyes, his chest rises with a heavy breath and he nods.

"Show me."

I circle my legs around his body, pulling him into me. The underside of his hard length rubs against my center and I can't help but roll my hips into him further.

He continues rubbing against me, his cock glistens with my arousal as he tells me what Dane did and how good it felt. There's a bit of shame in his voice but it's full of lust and need and burning desire.

He finally enters me, the full length of his shaft gliding in as he thrusts his hips and moans deeply.

God, I love his sounds. I can only imagine how quiet he had to remain at the table and I bet Dane got such a kick out of it.

I cup his face and bring his lips to mine, our eyes connecting as he fucks me slowly with so much meaning.

"You want him again, don't you?" His voice is breathy, like he didn't want to ask but can't help himself.

I nod as my walls begin to contract around him and I can feel my orgasm building.

"Me too, baby. Me too," he admits and I feel like it's a confession that's been waiting a lifetime to arrive. Like he's finally allowing himself to be okay with how he feels about his sexuality, about Dane.

I come hard thinking of all the things we did and the potential of what this could mean for us. He grunts into my neck, his moans echoing through the room like a promise to whatever it is we just talked about and for the first time since we left Paris I feel hopeful.

He flops over to my side and I wrap my leg over the top of his.

I don't know what got into him after tonight, but it's a shift that I couldn't be happier about.

"I have an idea on how I want to get him back for what he did tonight." He turns to me with a smile. "Trust me?"

38

DANE

The wait for Tuesday morning to arrive was excruciating.

I deserve an Olympic gold medal for the restraint I showed not using his number that's burning a hole in my phone. Seriously, going the entire weekend without texting him with a snarky remark is next level maturity that even I'm shocked by.

Not to say I didn't attempt to, more times than I'd like to admit.

The text messages went something like:

> Me: Can I get a side of semen with my mashed potatoes please?

Delete

> Me: Is that a pepper grinder or are you just happy to see me?

Delete

> Me: Mmmm. Sweet and salty.

Delete

> Me: You kinda left me hanging….

Delete

> Me: Can I take you out properly? Both of you. I swear I'll behave.

Delete

My desperation over the course of the weekend shifted from wanting to continue to push his buttons to just wanting to hear from him. I half expected to get a call or message from Hannah because she's always been that middle ground for us, but it's been crickets.

"Hey, Professor Campbell," Jodi calls out from behind me. Her heels clack against the tiled flooring in a rush to catch up. "How was your weekend?"

"It was good. How about yours?" I reply with a monotone expression. I've learned to minimize my excitement and refrain from engaging too much with the students, especially ones like Jodi who are clearly interested.

"Kind of boring. Maybe you could take me out, show me a good time?" She looks up with an innocent expression I know all too well.

"I'm sure you have plenty of friends that can do that." I pick up my pace to my classroom door.

I wrap my hand around the cool brass handle and hold my arm open to allow her to pass through. "Ladies first." She wears her pout as thick as she wears her makeup but manages a fake smile as she passes by.

I follow her through the doorway and my eyes quickly scan the room. There are only a few students—the punctual ones—already here.

I peek over to where Ethan and Hannah usually sit and I'm shocked to find their chairs empty. It's uncommon for the students to sit somewhere else but it's always a possibility. I glance around the room and still nothing.

They are always early. Hannah is the best student in the class and there hasn't been a day where she's been late, other than that first day when she had to go to the office before class.

The same unsettling feeling of being left alone in that hotel room wafts over me and I hate the deja vu it brings.

He wouldn't have dropped the class, right? Even if he did there's no way he would have convinced Hannah to drop.

I second guess my thoughts. Disappointment blankets me as the students begin to pile in and I glance at the clock.

So, it's official. They're absent.

Pulling out my phone, the screen is blank and empty and I hate the silence. Maybe I pushed him too far this time.

I palm my face and suck in a deep breath.

"Good Morning," I announce.

A few grumbled *mornings*, followed by a few *heys*, is the standard good morning melody of college students after a long weekend.

I ask the students about their weekend and a few rave about the Smashers back-to-back wins. Others have their heads tucked into their arms as they lean on their desk, with zero motivation to be here.

I feel you.

I start the lecture, using my dinner with Edward Russo—leaving out any names, of course—as a topic of conversation. Edward was driven, a true salesman in his determination to get my business. But, when is it too much? We chat about strategies on selling yourself, your brand, your idea, and the students liven up a bit.

I assign them in groups and ask them to come up with a joint pitch. I want them to work as a team and find a way to convince me. Convince me to need what they have. I want to feel that passion.

This isn't necessarily a sales class per se, but in life we need to learn to sell ourselves, our brand, and they need to know how to build relationships and talk to people, so I came up with this as a way to push them out of their comfort zone. Most of these students are only comfortable behind a computer; it's time to get them out in front of it.

As the students converse amongst themselves, my cell phone lights up with a text from Ethan. My heart beats heavily behind my breastbone before it jumps to my throat. A mix of excitement and worry battle each other and I find myself urgently reaching for my phone.

I click open the message; there's no text, only a video. I squint then glance around the room, everyone is consumed in what they are doing so I click the volume button down then tap *play*.

The video is aimed at the floor then pans up as I see a very familiar dark wood desk come into view. *My desk.*

I glance over my shoulder at my office door. It's shut and I'm trying to recall if I locked it when I left last week.

Turning back, the video pans to my *quote-a-day* flip desk calendar showing today's date—*I sure as hell didn't change that*—and a quote; "One day your life will flash before your eyes. Make sure it's worth watching." - Gerard Way, then the clock showing the time. I glance at the clock on the wall of the class-room. *Ten minutes ago.*

What the hell?

I snap my gaze back at the video and Hannah appears on

the screen. She's sprawled out over my desk, her pink dress is bunched around her waist, legs spread open touching herself.

I smother my feral expression as I clench my phone, my cock thickening instantly behind my pants.

Goddamn it. I turn around to look at the door as if I have X-ray vision and could see through it. Is she still there? It has to be Ethan recording, right?

Just as I internally ask myself the question, the camera flips around and Ethan's face comes into view, smirk on full display.

"Enjoy your class," he says, as he records himself diving into Hannah, his tongue flattens as he presses his face in between her legs and the video ends.

Fuck.

If that wasn't the best fucking invitation of my life, I don't know what is.

Looking back at the clock, there's still thirty minutes left of class.

Fuck it.

"Class dismissed!" I close my laptop and place it in my bag. They all look up stunned and some go back to talking like they plan to stay in my goddamn classroom. "Class dismissed," I repeat. "Work with your groups and prepare for a practice speech on Thursday. This project will be part of your final so take it seriously." Finally they stand and start to exit and I'm practically bouncing on my toes as I walk the last student out and lock the door behind them.

I'm at a roadrunner pace as I walk through the classroom. Reaching the office door, I grab the handle and use my body's momentum to walk through it, but it doesn't fucking open. Instead I crash into it, my shoulder zinging with the pain of the impact.

"Ow!" I groan as I grab my keys out, flipping through them frantically.

"You stop, you stop right now!" I call out from behind the door as I fit the key into the hole and turn the handle.

39

ETHAN

Dane comes barreling through his office door and even though I was expecting it, it's still quite a shock to see how worked up he is.

"Stop." My tone comes out surprisingly calm and even. It halts Dane dead in his tracks and he looks stunned by my demand. His chest rises and falls with labored breath as we share a look before he glances at Hannah then back to me.

Hannah's dress is hiked up to her waist, her beautiful bare ass sits on Dane's desk and I love that I'm on the other side of it. It feels powerful and all-consuming.

I wrap my hands around the front of Hannah, slowly unbuttoning the top of her dress as she lays out in front of him. The soft fabric flops to the side the lower I get and by the time I unclasp the last one, the dress falls off her shoulder exposing her breast. She's braless and so fucking beautiful but I keep my eyes trained on Dane. His tongue darts out over his bottom lip as he attempts to take another step forward.

"No." His eyes snap up to mine and I can't help my lopsided grin seeing how much he's holding himself back. I peer over at the clock then back to him. "You ended your class early today, Professor." I tsk, shaking my head as I walk closer to him.

"I had to. I couldn't—"

"Sit," I interrupt, tipping my chin at the chair in front of his desk.

He obeys and takes a seat, remaining quiet and compliant.

Reaching behind my neck, I grab the back of my shirt and pull it over my head. I know Dane is equally attracted to me as he is to Hannah so when his hips lift in his chair as if he's dying for some friction, I can't help but smile.

"Like what you see?"

"Always." His reply is breathy and full of need.

I step closer and lean over him as I place his arms parallel with the armrest.

"Keep your hands here and sit still until the clock hits the top of the hour. If I make her come before that, we'll leave and go about our day. If not," I shrug, "maybe you can help me."

"That's twenty minutes!"

"Our dinner was two hours," I quip back.

He lifts his chin, trying to smother his smirk. "Oh, payback I see. Fine. Bring it on." I raise my eyebrows at him, loving the challenge.

I step around the backside of his desk and reach around Hannah. She lifts her hips as I remove her panties, trailing them down her long legs before tossing them in Dane's lap. The bulge behind his zipper is obvious and I can't help but lick my lips at the thought of it aching and weeping underneath.

I trail my tongue over Hannah's exposed shoulder as my fingers pinch her nipples, her head dips back and a light moan falls from her throat.

"Oh fuck. I love that," Dane confesses, sounding tortured. "Let me help."

My lips inch lower as I wrap them around her taut nipple, but raise my eyes toward him as I lick and suck over the peak.

They both buck, almost simultaneously, as I hover my fingers over her entrance and push in.

Dane's fingers grip the arms of the chair and my body gets a sick joy at how tormented he looks.

"Did you enjoy yourself at dinner?" I ask, my fingers moving in and out of Hannah at a slow, agonizing pace for all of us.

"Yes," he admits.

"Did you make yourself come after?" He swallows thickly as his eyes meet mine. "Answer me."

"No."

"Why not?"

"I wanted both of you, not my hand."

I hum, hiding how much knowing he didn't get himself off turns me on.

"You must be aching." I pull my fingers out of Hannah and step toward him, wiping them over his lips as I dip them into his mouth. I hiss as he sucks around my fingers while he moans and the mix sends bolts of lightning through my body.

Pulling my fingers back, I unzip his pants and pull everything down to his knees. His erect cock bounces out, the thinned, pink crown achingly hard and my mind flashes with so many dirty things I want to do to him.

When I glance up at Hannah I know she's just as high as I am at all of this and it feels just like it did in Paris when we were all so comfortable and everything was easy and fun.

It's the first time I don't feel anger at what happened or question his reputation. His eyes tell me how badly he wants us and I can't help but want to dive head first into whatever it is that's happening between all of us. Fuck my father, fuck the standard, fuck it all.

"Don't touch yourself," I remind Dane, then turn back to Hannah.

Dropping to my knees, my face lines up at a perfect angle with her gorgeous cunt and I dive in, pressing two fingers back in. Her walls clench around me and I know between everything we did before Dane got in the room to now, she's close.

Her hips roll harder into me and she grips the side of my head. Her body writhes underneath me with the sounds of tiny whimpers that mix with Dane's labored breath.

"Ethan. *Fuck*. Please, let me in," Dane begs. "Don't come, Hannah."

His words send her over the top and her orgasm crests as she comes on my tongue, her arousal dripping over my fingers.

"Fuck, fuck, fuck." Dane's tortured voice says so much of how badly he wants us and I fucking love the sensation of being needed so desperately by him.

Hannah's body melts into his desk with a satiated smile. I press into my feet, hovering over her, kissing her exposed skin until I get to her lips. "Ready?" I whisper so only she can hear, and she nods, still donning that gorgeous smile of hers.

Holding my hands out, I help her to her feet and Dane's eyes bounce between us, worry laced behind them with a sense of something else. It's the first time I've seen him so vulnerable, as if our decision to stay or go is life or death.

40

DANE

I f they walk out of here, I swear it will break my fucking heart.

And probably my dick.

I'm trying my hardest to school my expression, like it doesn't matter either way. He has a right to be pissed at what I did. I acted on my needs and desires and didn't care if we got caught by his father or anyone at the restaurant.

Hell, the paparazzi could have been outside the window. It was impulsive and fucking careless but I needed him. I needed to touch him. Have him at my mercy again.

As much as I feel their playful energy, I'm still terrified they'll walk out and we'll go back to square one or, even worse, everything will end.

"You're never going to do that again." Ethan leans into me, his face mere inches from mine.

I shake my head and agree.

My brain isn't registering what I'm actually agreeing to, but it doesn't matter because I'll do anything to get him to stay this close to me.

There's a long pause between us. Our lips are so close I can feel his breath on mine. Hannah is standing behind him and it's the first time I feel like I can't read her expression.

His hooded eyes flicker down to my mouth then back up to my eyes and I want to slam my lips against his, but I won't and it's taking everything in me to sit still.

I can't take over. *I can't push him.*

The words lap around in my head over and over. I close my eyes and suck in a deep breath as if my body needs to suck in the tension lingering between us.

I can only imagine what I look like sitting in this chair. He yanked my pants down earlier, which are still around my ankles and my cock still erect between us. My hair is a mess and the only thing still protecting me from full exposure to them is my now wrinkled button down shirt.

As if he reads my thoughts, his fingers trail over my chest reaching for the buttons. I flinch, not only at the discovery that he's undressing me but also knowing once this shirt comes off, they will see them. My tattoos.

The new permanent additions of their marks on my body.

I don't know if I'm ready for that confession yet.

But it's too late. He's already finished unclasping all the buttons as Hannah walks around behind my chair, reaching over my chest pulling the shirt down my shoulders.

My heart pounds behind my ribcage from the knowledge they are staying here with me and not walking out but also because they are going to figure out how far gone I've been for them and I'm going to have to lay everything out, right here, right now.

Hannah's hands freeze just as my shirt reaches my elbows and there's a small gasp that both Ethan and I hear. Ethan glances up at her, then follows her line of sight at my shoulder, as she traces her fingers over her tattooed marks.

He squints, tilts his head then walks around to inspect the bite mark on the other side, resting just above my dandelion.

I lift my chin to meet his gaze and there's so much behind his eyes. Confusion, need, sorrow. I can't tell and it's making me overthink everything.

Hannah steps in front me and I turn to look at her. She's fucking beautiful. Her hair is knotted and messy, her dress is half hanging off her body, and I've dreamt of seeing her like this again.

"Are those ours?"

As unsure as I feel, I sit up proud and nod. "Yes," I say, but as confident as I am, my voice still comes out raspy.

She shares a look with Ethan before her mouth turns into a tight line then a smile appears. I physically feel the relief as she sits on my lap. Her wet center glides against the back side of my cock and she rolls her hips, pressing her lips against mine.

I wrap my arms around her, pulling her close, moaning into her mouth like I need it to breathe.

"Fuck, I've missed this. I've missed you." I can't help the words that fall out of my mouth as our tongues dance together in the same rhythm our hips are moving.

Ethan grips the back of my head, pulling me back. His gaze is something more certain now.

Need. Unrelenting, feral need.

I don't know if it was him witnessing me and Hannah like that or the fact that he really likes his bite mark permanently inked on me, but I love that fucking look in his eye.

"When?"

Hannah is kissing down my chest, kneeling in front me of, as he interrogates me and it's fucking distracting.

"When?" He pulls harder at the base of my skull.

"The last night in Paris before I came back to the hotel and you guys were gone."

He huffs out an annoyed breath, like he already knew that answer but didn't want to hear it.

Hannah wraps her lips around my cock, licking the tip like

a lollipop before taking me all the way to the back of her throat. I squeeze my eyes shut as my jaw drops but I blink, yanking them back open to keep my eyes on him.

He's struggling or maybe he's mad; I have no fucking clue but the way Hannah is devouring me, I swear I won't have a chance to figure it out before I'm coming down his girlfriends throat.

Before I can even realize, he pulls my head further back and slams his lips against mine. His tongue darts out into my mouth and it's stronger and needier than the one Hannah just gave me.

"Oh, fuck," my muffled words come out garbled and desperate.

He only kissed me once, that last night in Paris. It was on the couch after we played *Battleship* and I remember it distinctly because it felt like such a breakthrough. This feels the same but with more surety than before. More desire and meaning.

"Do you want us?" he asks, hovering over my mouth. "All of us?"

I don't know if he means physically or emotionally but it doesn't matter to me.

"I want everything." It's the easiest question I've ever had to answer.

Ethan grants me with a rare smile and it makes my stomach flutter to my chest. Slowly, he kneels down, keeping his eyes locked on mine as he lines himself up next to Hannah.

Oh shit.

She pops off my cock and he takes it in his mouth, using that magical no-gag reflex to his advantage and I can't help but groan as my knuckles blanch white, gripping the wood on the armrest of my chair.

They both start licking and sucking, the sight un-fucking-believable as they take turns on each side of my cock. His hand reaches down between his legs as he unzips his pants and begins stroking himself.

His arm moves back and forth as he jerks himself and I've never been so jealous of a hand before.

"Let me," I manage to say, my voice husky and on the edge.

He ignores me while he continues exploring the tight skin of my cock with his tongue. Both him and Hannah take turns like a planned expert game of ping pong.

Keeping my focus on his hand, I study the way he strokes himself using his fingers to massage the underside of his tip. I need him as close to the edge as I am.

"Please." His eyes peer up to mine and I'm pleading with him. "Please, let me touch you." At this point with anything.

He shakes his head, denying me, and his silent words slash through me.

"Stand up," he demands, as he stands up himself.

I obey, pressing into my heels and Hannah's body follows mine as she comes to her feet, bent over, her mouth still taking all of me. My legs feel weak with the fire that licks through my veins but I manage to get fully upright as Ethan steps behind Hannah.

He pulls her hips back to meet his. Her body makes a perfect ninety degree angle as he lines his up against her entrance.

Well, I never have to go back to Paris again because *this* Eiffel Tower just became my favorite.

Ethan pushes into her, his body pistons back and forth and I have a mind-blowing view of his cock shining with her arousal, and the desire on his wanton face, as he moves in and out of her soaked pussy.

"That's it, baby, suck his cock," Ethan says as I run my hand through her hair. She glances up at me, her ocean eyes dark and wide as she licks and sucks with expert precision. My eyes trail down her back, up Ethan's tight abs and appraise his thick chest, sprinkled with the perfect amount of hair down the middle column.

Then my jaw slacks open as Hannah twists her tongue around my tip and I hunch forward. Ethan grabs the back of my neck, pulling me closer, pressing our foreheads together causing both of us to rut into Hannah even deeper.

My cock pierces the back of her throat. She gags around me but keeps it lodged tight in her mouth.

"Oh fuck, I'm close," I groan out.

Ethan's eyes sear into mine, our gazes locked in a silent understanding of what this is. A start of something. Trust, need, desire. Everything. All of it.

Those goddamn sounds he always makes bellow out of him. They fall from his lips in waves as he moans, curses, groans, and grunts, pounding into Hannah with a force like he's finally giving in to everything he needs.

It's all-consuming and powerful. Her. Him. The three of us. All mixed together just like it was that night in Paris and I fucking explode. Ethan follows right behind me, grunting as he squeezes Hannah's hip with one hand and the back of my neck with the other, the pain-pleasure combo is fucking addicting.

A sense of satisfaction mixed with indescribable relief blankets me as I fall back in my chair and take in the two of them that are just as satiated as I am.

The last couple months have been so different for me. I've gotten used to the day-to-day routine, and while I don't hate it, I haven't quite fallen in love with it either.

I'm happy that I get to spend more time with my friends but the part of me that was looking for stability and change still feels lonely.

Honestly, I've felt a void since the moment I realized they left that hotel room and it's only partially been filled since I saw them again in my classroom.

"Did you mean what you said?"

Hannah is hardly finished signing the words when I spit out an urgent, "Yes." Hoping she's referring to me wanting everything. "I've never wanted anything more," I say, honestly.

The look they pass to each other is palpable. The concern behind her bright blue eyes and the fear behind his dark ones say everything I don't want to hear.

I stand, pulling my pants back on and begin to button my shirt. They haven't said anything about what they want, but they made a decision to be here and I don't think it was just for payback.

I wasn't expecting to have this conversation but I've never gotten the chance to and I'm tired of waiting.

"I know this is risky...for all of us. I'm committed to the University to teach for the rest of the year." I don't mention how tarnished my reputation would be if I was caught dating, not just one student, but two. Not that I really give a shit, but that won't help sell them on this idea.

"Hannah, I know how important it is that you finish this course and get your MBA." I give her an honest look then turn to Ethan and say it like it is. "I know you're not ready. I was once where you are, but I had someone who helped me, accepted me, and I wish you'd let me, us," I gesture between Hannah and me, "be those people for you." He avoids my eye contact and looks at the wall next to us. That's fine—I expected that, but I'm not going to let him berate himself for something that he shouldn't and pushing me away is just going to make things worse for all of us.

"It's more complicated than that," he says gruffly, still avoiding any direct eye contact.

"We don't have to say anything to anyone. We can keep hanging out and having fun with no pressure. At the end of the school year, we decide if we want it to be something more." I don't say 'or not', because frankly that's not an option for me.

"Sure. Like you won't see anyone else," Ethan states, with a snarky judgment in his tone and I'm offended. How can he not feel how much I want him, want both of them? I clench my jaw and step toward him. I've let him take charge, take control, and he almost choked me out in my own damn office, but I'm not going to let him think that this is some stupid fling for me.

I cup my hand around his collarbone, pushing him back against the same wall he pushed me against reliving a sense of deja vu.

"I chased after you, running to the airport, not even knowing where you were going, in hopes I could find you. I gave myself to you in Paris, *in every fucking way*, then tattooed your marks on my skin, and you think I'm interested in seeing someone else? I've only ever wanted you and her since the moment we met in Paris. I have no idea what else you need me to do to prove it to you."

I press my arm into him, pushing myself off and stepping back. I shake my head and turn around.

I should tell them to get out but I need some air, so I walk through my door without turning back around.

I hate that they don't trust me. I hate the situation we're stuck in and I hate that my reputation is weighing on their decision when the only reason why I haven't been serious with anyone is because no one could measure up to how Celeste made me feel. No one has ever ignited me like she did, not until them.

41

HANNAH

The week went by painfully slow. It was like time knew it needed to torture Ethan and I for opening up our old Paris wounds.

Our intention was to be playful and fun, to bring the three of us together again like we were in Paris and perhaps get a little payback on Dane for what he did to Ethan at the restaurant.

In the heat of the moment, it all sounded fun, but we never thought far enough ahead of what could come out of it. So instead, we just fed an addiction that Ethan and I both wanted and hurt Dane in the meantime.

As much as I want something to come out of this, I know it can't.

I would have no idea how to navigate a relationship with two men. Even though everything between us has come so naturally, so easy, and it's clear they want each other just as much as they want me, but he's our professor. I've worked way too hard to get where I am and I can't risk losing everything if we get caught.

Crouching down, I roll out my yoga mat and kneel down on

top of it. I used to take yoga all the time, but after the accident I had to focus more on physical therapy to help my healing so I stopped going all together. Ethan was going to come with me today but he opted to stay home and work on the project that Dane assigned to the class since he has no clue what he's doing for it. But I know he just wants to relax and watch the commentators talk about game seven of the World Series tonight.

The Smashers are defending their title and ever since he went to the first game he's been openly watching it again. Like that small taste brought back all the love he had for it and now he can't get enough. I can only hope it's exactly what he needs to bring that passion back into his life.

Placing my water bottle on the floor, I kneel down and take a moment to glance around the room. It's been so long since I've come to a class that the studio is now owned by someone else and it looks completely different.

The mirrors that line the walls are all the same but the once sage green and grey undertones have been replaced with pinks and yellows. It's bright and airy and I love the energy it brings to the room.

I crisscross my legs and focus on straightening my spine as I roll my shoulders and circle my neck. Other mats spread out against the wood floor as they're rolled out and whispered voices carry throughout the room.

One familiar voice carries louder than others and I can't help but side-eye in that direction as a gorgeous woman with luscious, dark hair, glowing olive skin, and a perfectly round pregnant belly strides into the room arm-in-arm with *Dane*.

Shit.

I tuck my legs behind me as I bend forward, putting myself in Child's Pose to hide my face.

Is he here with her? Are they together? The rampant thoughts reeling through my mind should be illegal on a yoga mat.

I peek through the strands of my hair that cover my face just as he guides her to the front of the class, kisses her cheek then glances around the room. He swings his mat from one shoulder to the other, looks toward me, freezes, then starts walking to the back of the room, in my direction.

Shit. Shit. Shit.

I press the bottom of my forearms harder into the mat, as if it could make me smaller and swallow me whole. My back arches slightly with the pressure on my arms, pushing my ass back further and I hate that I chose my shortest spandex shorts today.

His bare feet pass by the side of my mat and just when I think I'm safe, his mat slaps the hardwood then rolls out, right next to mine.

Matching my pose, he sucks in a long breath then blows it out loudly.

"I'd recognize that gorgeous ass anywhere, Poe."

Errrg, I internally groan to myself, pushing myself up as I sign.

"What are you doing here?"

"What am I doing here? I've been coming here for months and I've never seen you. What are you doing here?" His whispered tone is as accusatory as my body language.

I don't even have it in me to answer his question because I'm too curious about the instructor.

"Who is she?"

Just then, she glances our direction, her brows pull together then turns away as she plugs her phone into the stereo that sits at the front of the room.

A satisfied grin covers his face and I want to smack it.

"You're jealous," he signs, which pisses me off even more.

I roll my eyes and shake my head.

Because, yeah, I'm jealous, but I'm also confused.

I raise my eyebrows, demanding an answer.

His face is still smug, like he's debating about answering my question but highly considering making me suffer.

"Her name is Mimi. She's the owner of the studio, the best yoga instructor in town, and my best friend's wife." He leans in whispering the last part with a smile and my body physically relaxes. I'm only slightly embarrassed how much I overreacted but I've been confused about my feelings—our feelings—for him and what 'us' could potentially look like.

He means more to me than I'd like to admit and because he's involved with both me and Ethan I feel protective and territorial.

"Oh."

"You're really cute when you're jealous." He winks at me then turns to face the front of the classroom as Mimi begins to instruct us through a warm up.

An hour later and one thing is certain. Dane was right. Mimi is absolutely amazing. She guided us through every pose, the flow felt natural, and my body loved every minute of it.

Dane and I had a few moments where we glanced at each other—him trying to mask his smile while I attempted to hide mine—we failed each time though.

Now, as I lay in savasana listening to Mimi's comforting voice guide me through my inhales and exhales, I can physically feel my shoulders melting into the mat. My eyes feel heavy but my body feels light.

We're still on our mats but Dane's hand somehow made its way closer to mine and the soft touch of his pinky caresses my own. There's an overwhelming amount of comfort in the gesture.

How can we make this work? How can we see each other without risking everything? Is it just not our time? There are so many questions I've asked myself and so many of them revolve around the what if's and what could happen after I finally get my MBA.

Ideally we would stay in Seattle since Ethan intends to continue to work for his dad. Even though I know he hates it. I wish he would just do what he wanted instead of what his father wants him to do.

He might not ever play baseball again but I know he can find something that would make him happier than working for his dad. I get he just wants stability for our future but I'd rather have his happiness. As many times as I've told him that, he's set on getting his MBA—even though he hates school—because his dad insists on the title.

I just hope it's something he can come to find joy in.

Me on the other hand, I feel like the more titles and degrees I have the more desirable I will be. Considering I won't be able to speak or lead teams in the way I want. As much as there's a no discrimination policy when hiring, I clearly have a disability when it comes to working in the corporate world.

But if I can fine tune the code and build out the platform I've been working on, it could change the way ASL is utilized in the digital world and that in itself will be invaluable.

My presentation revolves around what I've built so far but it's a long way from being ready. In fact, I'm embarrassed to bring it up. I feel like I might just get laughed out of the classroom but I'm hoping that maybe sharing it will push me over the hump I'm stuck on.

Just as I realize I'm not pushing my thoughts away and clearing my mind, Mimi's angelic voice softly vibrates through the room. "When you're ready, gently roll to your side and press into your mat, bringing yourself to a seated position." Bodies move throughout the room and I'm now sitting with my hands in a prayer position in front of my chest. "I'd like to thank all of you for coming today, being present and moving your bodies with me. The light in me, honors the light in you. Namaste."

The class repeats the mantra back to her and everyone starts to clean up and exit.

Dane turns to me, signing, "*So, how's Ethan?*"

I knew Dane couldn't wait to ask. I feel like he's always checking on him and his wellbeing. Normally, that would be the case, but I think both Ethan and I have been more concerned with how Dane is feeling after what happened this week.

"*He's good. We were worried about you actually. How are you?*"

There's a small pinch in his brow but he covers it up quickly. It's the same vulnerable Dane I remember from the first night in the hostel when Ethan ran out on us. When he told me about Celeste. It's also the same Dane I recall covering up his emotions with that gorgeous smile of his, attempting to push aside any hurt he might feel.

"*After that class, I feel amazing.*"

"*You were right. She's so good,*" I sign excitedly.

"Mimi," Dane calls out, waving her over. I glance up at him wide eyed as Mimi steps toward us. I have no idea what I will look like when I'm pregnant but I can only hope it's half as good as she looks.

"Mimi, this is Hannah, the girl I was telling you about. Hannah, this is Mimi. She's the owner of the studio and married to my friend Seamus." Dane introduces us like he has every intention of us being friends.

"I've heard so much about you." She smiles as she raises her arm and pulls me in for a hug. "Sorry, I don't do that handshake thing."

I can't help but smile back at her. She's got such amazing energy and I can see why she would get along so well with Dane.

"Dane hasn't stopped talking about you and Ethan since Paris," Mimi adds.

I suppose it shouldn't surprise me how open Dane is but I'm still surprised she's sharing that with me. I can't help but blush and share a shy smile while Dane's expression owns every word like he's proud of that fact.

Tapping on my throat I pick up my phone and type out, **Your class was amazing.**

I turn the phone screen toward her and she smiles wide. "Thank you. I'm so glad you came. Will you be able to come regularly?"

I nod, because I actually bought a class pack and had every intention of making this a regular thing even before I found out how great Mimi is.

"Great!" she says excitedly. "Oh, here." She grabs my phone and types in her name and number. "Text me sometime and we can hang out."

Smiling wider, I nod again. I don't have many girlfriends. Frankly speaking, I don't have many friends at all. I don't get to have normal conversations and because I can't speak, people can't get to know me. It's easier to walk away and not work on a friendship with someone unless they also speak ASL.

"Actually, you should come by the stadium today and hang out with all of us."

My eyebrows raise and I look over at Dane. "Yeah, you and Ethan both. You guys are more than welcome." His words are reserved as if he knows that we would automatically say no. And in most cases that would be my normal response. But after how I've felt this week about how things ended in his office and how hurt Dane was by Ethan's sharp accusation, I'm tired of feeling guilty and holding back.

I think we all are and if I need to push Ethan over the ledge with me, I will.

Plus, game seven of the World Series at the stadium? Ethan will secretly love every single minute of that.

"If you're sure. We'd love to come."

His eyes widen with a smile as he mouths, *yeah?*

"Yay! I'm so excited," Mimi celebrates. "I'll text you all the details."

"Sounds good," I sign and glance at Dane to gesture to him to tell her as I step backward, waving.

Exiting the studio, I get in my car and before I even put it in *Drive* Mimi has added me into a group text with Dane providing me all the details for the game, what time to be there, and shared a screenshot of the location pinpointed on a map.

I don't know if it was meeting Mimi, the class, or seeing Dane but my mood is lifted and I can't help but smile as I walk through the door of our apartment.

It's a small one-bedroom but in a nice area and close to campus. There are a lot of college students that live here purely for the convenience and location.

Closing the door, I kick off my shoes and make my way to the living room. There's a kitchen island that separates the living space from the kitchen and I tend to always make my way there first.

Ethan pads barefoot and shirtless in the kitchen, his joggers sit low on his waist showing off the V-line at his hips and the view is absolutely mouthwatering.

"Hey baby, how was class?" he asks.

"Good. You'll never guess who I saw."

"Ooh, let me guess." He rounds the island, grabbing my waist as he lifts me on top of it. He fits perfectly between my legs as he leans in kissing my neck. "Big-boobed Jodi from class came to yoga class in a mini skirt and heels," he says because she dresses inappropriately for every place we've ever seen her.

I toss my head back and smile, shaking my head.

"Dane."

The playful look on his face falls away instantly and he steps back, running his hands through his hair.

"At yoga huh?" he replies, rounding the island as he pours

himself a cup of coffee. "How is one-date Dane?" His question is snarky and I narrow my eyes at him.

His eyes look up at me and I know even he's ashamed of the way he's talking. I swear to god these two men and their overly complicated feelings for each other will be the death of me.

"You know just as well as I do that he is not what his reputation says."

He remains silent as he sips his coffee.

I know he's felt bad about what happened. What was supposed to be a playful revenge joke turned into something that brought out the real emotions we've all been suppressing. This week has weighed on him just as much as it weighed on me, but when you look at the bones of it, Dane's right. The most complicated factor is that we're his students. But that's not a permanent situation.

"We need to talk about this." I push my hands into the marble island and shimmy my butt over to the other side to meet him.

"Will you just admit you like him?"

He doesn't say anything, just takes another sip of his coffee.

"Okay fine. You don't have to admit it because I know you do. And I know you're just as curious about what a relationship with him could look like. He's been clear about what he wants and if we just lay low through the school year and see where things go, I think that's a fair thing to try...for all of us."

"There are so many factors that don't make sense, Hannah," he replies, using my name as a note of seriousness.

"That's just what you're telling yourself because you don't know how to handle your feelings. And you're worried about what your dad and other people will think."

"Geez, don't sugarcoat anything for me," he says sarcastically.

"But, I'm right." I lift my chin, because I know I am.

"Yeah, yeah. You just like the attention of two really hot

dudes who are totally fucking desperate for you." He pulls me flush with his body.

I shrug with a smile. *"Glad you're finally admitting he's hot."*

"Oh, you shut it, woman." He kisses me again and I know he's feeling calmer now than he was before.

"Let's see where this can go? Tell him how we feel?"

He glances down at his bare feet then looks back up at me and nods, slowly.

"Good. Because we're meeting him at Ford Field for the game in an hour so we should probably get dressed."

42

ETHAN

The mix of emotions that have been flooding through me since Hannah got home is overwhelming. The entire week I've had to stop myself from calling him, texting him, and stopping him on campus to apologize.

But my pride wouldn't let me.

I'm worried about the fact that he's our professor but Hannah's right, that's only temporary. I just don't understand how any of this can work. It doesn't make any sense. It's always just been me and Hannah and I have no idea what mixing Dane into this means for us. What kind of future is that for him, for us?

Does he want kids? We do, eventually. What will people say? I don't even know how I would handle the three-way relationship, much less people being curious about my sexuality.

I've never had to question myself before or address it. So, I have no idea what the hell I would say.

Surprisingly, when Christian saw me and Dane coming out of the bathroom at the ballpark that day, I wasn't embarrassed or ashamed. I was...proud. Dane wanted me, so much that he had to lock me in the bathroom to get my attention.

I've always had the same feeling with Hannah. Proud that she chose me, to be the man on her arm and, for some unknown reason, I felt the same when Dane was quite literally claiming me in front of his friends.

So, I suppose my sexuality doesn't bother me as much as wondering how my dad would take everything. But my dad is such a dick I don't even know why I care.

Actually, I know why. Because since I was a kid he's embedded in me that a man takes care of his wife. The man is the head of the household and financial backer for his family.

The underlying gay jokes subliminally laid the groundwork in my head that a relationship with someone of the same sex was wrong.

Hannah has a bright future with whatever field she chooses. She's brilliant and driven. I know she'll be the top at whatever company she decides to work for, while still managing to be the best wife and mother, all at the same time.

Me? I'm not going to be able to provide her anything if I don't get serious about what I'm doing at my dad's company. The hundreds of thousands I owe him will take years—many years—to work off.

If I don't get a few big clients I'll be working for him until I die. I also won't be able to take care of her and support her like I want and I just can't have that. As much as I know that times are different this day in age, I still want to do all those things and make sure she has nothing to worry about.

I just always thought that it was going to be baseball that allowed me to do that.

"Stop overthinking."

Hannah places her hand on my thigh, pulling me out of my thoughts.

I glance over to her then out the window and have to crane my neck to look to the top of the stadium. It's newly constructed and massive.

Stepping out of the rideshare Hannah looks around in awe as she takes everything in.

There's a DJ outside, vendors, and random pop-ups. People are dressed in either some baseball related costume or their Smashers jerseys, dancing and drinking. There must be thousands of people lined up outside the entrances that are more than likely just hanging out here without tickets, but just want to be present for the win.

Last year the Smashers won their first World Series in twenty-two years, needless to say the crowd was similar and I don't think the streets were cleared for a week.

I place my hand on Hannah's back and lead her to the same back entrance I went to before. Hannah pulls out her phone to present the tickets to the doorman and he lets us through into an elevator and up to the suite.

I'm not going to lie, I feel nervous. The way Dane walked out of his office after we completely defiled it, left me in a massive state of confusion.

Hannah is smiling and I love seeing her excitement when we try new things and even though I was here last week, it still feels surreal.

The elevator doors slide open and we're greeted to the chatter of excited voices overlapping each other. The space is filled with twice as many people as it was last time and everyone is dressed a lot more casual.

It's immediately more welcoming than the first time when my father was here with all the sharks in suits surrounding Christian and his team.

A woman with long, dark black hair and a pregnant round belly calls Hannah's name. I squint in her direction because I don't recognize her or the massive man dressed in almost all black standing next to her. He's about a foot taller than her, with stiff broad shoulders and an even more rigid face. I can't tell if he's her personal security guard or the suites.

Hannah grabs my hand, waves back at her, and we head in their direction.

The mystery girl pulls Hannah in for a hug and tells her how happy she is that she's here. Then side steps leaning into me with her arm open pulling me into the same friendly hug.

"You must be Ethan. It's so great to meet you!"

I awkwardly pat her back as platonically as possible, as I stare up at the shadow behind her glaring down in my direction. I'm a little over six feet, he's not much taller than I am but he feels like a goddamn goliath.

"I'm Naomi, but everyone calls me Mimi, and this is my husband Seamus." She pulls him forward and he reaches his hand out.

"Hey man, good to meet you," he says as I clasp his monster grip and say the same. He's nice enough, but his facial expression doesn't change much. Not until Mimi wraps her arms around his waist and snuggles into him.

"I'm so glad you guys decided to come. Dane will be back any second, he went down to wish Hudson luck."

"Hudson Byrnes?" I ask, a glint of excitement behind my voice.

She glances up at Seamus then back over to me, smiling. "Yeah, they went to college together, well Dane did. Seamus and Hudson were best friends and neighbors from Kindergarten until Seamus went to boot camp. And they're all still attached at the hip. Well...sort of. *He's* currently attached to mine because he won't let me do anything solo now." She rolls her eyes but by the looks of the beaming smile on her face as she rubs her belly, she doesn't mind it so much.

"That's amazing. Did you play baseball, too? I heard he started playing T-ball pretty much after he started walking," I ask.

Seamus doesn't smile but he replies and I can tell by the look in his eye he's proud of his friend.

"I think when I met him he had a baseball in his hand. It's been his dream since I can remember and he's so goddamn good, it blows my mind that he continues to just get better and better."

I shift excitedly in my stance as I go into the stats from his college years, the short stint he had in the majors before his injury, and even some of his minor league stats as well.

I realize I've been talking for minutes on end and when I look down at Hannah she's gleaming up at me. The same proud look that Seamus had in his, she has in hers.

"You sure know a lot about him," Seamus adds questioningly.

He knows EVERYTHING about *baseball*. Hannah types out on her phone and flashes it toward Seamus.

"Is that right?" Seamus' face lights up and there's an instant kindred moment that silently passes between us. "I'm a fan of whatever team Hudson is on but I'll always check in on the Dallas Dust Devils because they were my team growing up. Hudson loved the Houston Mavericks so that led to some heated fights between us."

"Oh man, I bet that broke the friendship a time or two." I chuckle, imagining these two massive guys going at it over rival teams.

We easily dive into conversations about the season and Seamus shares a couple of stories about Hudson when he was a kid.

I peek over at Hannah and Mimi watching them as they converse together. Mimi's patience with Hannah as she types out her answers is endearing.

Seamus and I continue to chat as the stadium fills and time passes quickly. The National Anthem begins to play and we all remove our caps and stand a little straighter as the lyrics filter through everyone in the stadium.

I see the lineup of players on both sides and try to imagine the flood of emotions they must be feeling. To get to this point in their career, standing on a field at game seven of the World Series. It's the moment every team dreams of and in a short while one of them will be celebrating the biggest professional accomplishment of their lifetime, while the other will drown in all the 'what if' thoughts and devastation after a loss.

Baseball isn't in the cards for me anymore. I know it never will be. But I'm starting to see that removing it all together isn't an option either.

"I only ever want your happiness."

Hannah slides her fingers in between mine and squeezes as if she knows exactly what I'm thinking and how I'm feeling.

Maybe there's something different out there for me. Something that doesn't involve me standing in the shadows of my father. Just maybe.

43

DANE

I linger in the corner of this expansive suite for far too long watching Ethan and Hannah talk to my friends like they've known them their whole lives.

Mimi and Hannah I wasn't concerned about at all.

Seamus and Ethan...I thought they'd be standing there looking at the field like two awkward sloths next to each other. But no, they're talking animatedly, smiling, and laughing while a bromance blooms in the air.

Ethan continues to talk, laying out a silly facial expression while he tells a story and Seamus watches him in anticipation as he comes to the punchline. Seamus chuckles then places his hand over Ethan's shoulder to balance himself as he leans forward laughing.

I repeat. Seamus is fucking laughing.

I don't even get him to laugh like that. *What the hell?*

This annoys me even further about these two because it just goes to show how perfect they are. For me and for how easily they slip into my friend group so quickly.

Also, the fact that I've got Hudson as my best friend, I will certainly whip out that card with Ethan, using all my resources to get them to fall in love with me.

It's not beneath me.

Hannah looks unbelievable in her Smashers jersey. Her dark wavy hair flows half way down her back and covers all of the lettering but the number displayed is Hudson's. It's the same jersey that Ethan is wearing, except he topped his off with a backward cap and I could fall over and die from how hot he looks.

I make my way toward the bar and ask for three espresso martinis, smiling at the memory from when we had way too many of these at the club in Paris. The flashbacks of the moments after at the forefront of my mind.

"Are you sitting anywhere, sir?" I point over to where Seamus and Ethan are standing, behind a small row of seats that Mimi and Hannah are sitting in. The game is just starting and I swear everyone is already on pins and needles. "Great, I'll bring them over to you," she adds with a smile.

I suck in a deep breath, centering myself before I make my way over there. I haven't had a ton of time to dive into the feelings I've had about them breaking into my office. Frankly speaking, I fucking loved that part.

It's the moments after that kill me. The judgment on Ethan's face when he thought I couldn't be faithful to just them. It mirrored that of my PR manager whenever she would have to put out tabloid fires that came out as rumors, or questionable rumors.

Again, my past behavior might not be the cleanest, but the fact that no one really knows the entire truth is something I've always had going for me.

I just hate it now that I'm trying to be serious with someone, or someones in my case.

Fortunately, I haven't needed my PR manager much but if anything gets out about me and my fellow students at Polytech, well that's going to be a logistical nightmare for her. I know I shouldn't pursue anything, but I've never been able to stop myself when there's something I want.

It's embedded in my DNA. I want it. I do it. Act now, questions later.

Some people say it's my worst quality. I sort of think it's my best.

I shrug to myself as I push my body off the barstool and walk toward them.

Stepping in between them, I plaster a smile on my face as I wrap one arm around each of them and peer over their shoulders at the field.

"Did we win?" I ask, even though the first pitch hasn't even been thrown yet.

Ethan looks over his shoulder at me, the lopsided grin tells me he's happy I'm here. "Do you even know anything about baseball?" he asks, giving me shit.

"I prefer extreme sports but baseball is okay."

"Ah yes. The Dane Campbell motto of life. The more risk, the more reward," Seamus replies in his best Mr. Miyagi interpretation, not looking at either one of us.

"Wait. Did you just say a joke? I mean it wasn't like a full joke, like half a joke, maybe. But it was still snarky as hell even though it's 100 percent accurate," I reply, still surprised and slightly jealous of the way Ethan has brought out a bit of fun in Seamus.

I pat Seamus on the shoulder as he glares at me, then move around on the other side of Ethan, so now he's standing between us.

"You like taking risks," Ethan states, factually, not questioningly.

"They're usually worth it."

His neck swivels over to me, as if he needs to see my face to determine his response.

"What if it fails?"

"You keep trying."

"What if someone gets hurt?" he asks.

I'm a smart guy and I most often have a witty comeback resting on my tongue. But right now, as we're talking metaphors of the relationship that's blooming between me, him, and Hannah, I want nothing more than to prove how great this could be for all of us.

"I met my best friend in Kindergarten. She was this awkward little thing with the brightest blonde hair I'd ever seen. She brought me a dandelion and told me to make a wish."

"A dandelion?" Ethan asks, his attention fully on me but his eyes flicker to where my tattoo sits on my back.

I can't seem to answer with words so I just give him a tight-lipped smile and nod. His facial expression shifts into something deeper when the realization hits him that I've only ever tattooed myself with things that mean something to me. Things that mean a great deal to me.

"Yeah, my wish was her. I was immediately obsessed and went out of my way everyday to get her attention in any way I could. She was the coolest five year old on the block and I wanted nothing more than to be her friend. We became best friends and spent every single day together. I was in love with her all through elementary school. And I know what you're thinking. We were kids. But I knew she was the one, even way back then, I just knew. In seventh grade, after years of hiding how I felt, I finally told her—risking everything—and she kissed me. It was the most rewarding moment of my life but I regret not saying something sooner," I peer over at him, "If I would have told her sooner I would have had more time, more kisses, more touches before the cancer took her from me."

I can tell by the look in his eye that Hannah didn't tell him about Celeste. I love that about her, knowing she would never tell someone else's story. I suppose she of all people knew I would tell him eventually.

"How long were you together?" he asks.

"All through middle and high school until our freshman year in college." I muster a close-lipped smile at him, trying to provide comfort to him, myself too, as I look down sliding my hands in my pockets. "Even through all of it, still my only regret is not telling her sooner so I could have more memories of what we had."

"Sir." The waiter steps up next to me with a tray of three espresso martinis.

Ethan's eyebrows raise and I don't miss that little smirk that ticks up at the corner of his lip.

"Speaking of memories," I add with my typical goofy undertone, happy for the change of topic, and he chuckles, taking one glass in each hand.

I grab the last one and nod a thank you to the waiter.

"What was her name?" he asks.

"Celeste."

He holds up his glass. "To Celeste. And...taking risks." We tap the rims of our glasses together and just as they connect the crack of the bat sends a ball into the outfield and over the fence.

Hudson Byrnes hits a three-run homerun bringing the score to 3-0 in the first inning.

The entire stadium erupts and Ethan and I cheer along with them. His arm wraps around me as we chant along with the crowd. As excited as I am for Hudson and the Smashers lead, I'm happier with the moment we just had because it felt like leaps and bounds of progress in such a short amount of time, and for the first time I feel a comfort in where this could go.

Hannah comes running, jumping into both of our arms. Ethan and I think the same thing and peck a kiss on her cheek.

Her cheeks flush in heat as we share a look with each other and there are so many unsaid words that float in between.

Seamus is now standing next to Mimi as she glances over at me with a wide, giddy smile and I know I look just as silly as she does but I don't care.

This is the most hopeful I've been since reuniting with them, and even if we have to hide what's happening between us for now, it'll be worth it in the end.

44

ETHAN

There are a few things in someone's life that I hear you get the honor of experiencing.

Marrying the love of your life.

Witnessing the birth of your child.

Watching your favorite MLB team win game seven of the World Series in extra innings with a walk-off home run, live in person.

And this is the most alive I've felt in years. I must have talked to every single person in that suite. I couldn't stop myself, it was like my baseball brain took over and every time one of the Smashers did something I had a back up stat for it.

I spent a lot of time with Seamus and Christian, and surprisingly Christian knew a lot more about the sport in general than I expected. I figured as the sponsor of the field, he would know a little bit about the team specifically, but I couldn't hold in my excitement when he started spouting off unusual facts about baseball's history. I was on literal cloud nine.

"The probability of a pitch hitting a bird is microscopic. My father and I were in the stands and it was the craziest moment in baseball history," Christian says with a smile that only a memory like that could bring out.

That's what I love about this sport. Even if you aren't a baseball fan, there's something about going to a game, sitting anywhere in the stands, and talking with friends as you watch America's favorite pastime.

"I'm so jealous you were at that game. I bet it was crazy to watch replays of that moment." I take a sip of my beer, one that I've been enjoying a little too long that it's a tad warm for my liking, but the conversations have been so good I haven't had time to finish it.

"I think you know more about baseball than anyone I've ever met. Do you play?" Christian asks, just as Dane steps up next to us.

I confessed to Dane the last time we were here that I used to play but that was only because he forced me into it. This is the first time I feel like I just want to talk about it. My past and how much I loved it.

"I used to and you know, I wasn't half bad," I admit modestly as I hold up my hand, "but an injury prevented me from getting drafted."

His lips pull back with a hiss as he looks at the scar on my hand. "Oh man, I'm sorry to hear that."

"Yeah, it wasn't meant to be," I say the words I begrudgingly tell myself, but this is the first time I actually feel okay with it. Maybe because I've had a taste of watching it again. Or maybe it's the game seven World Series high I'm still riding.

I glance around and see Dane walking up to us. My eyes bounce around the room looking for Hannah but I don't see her.

"Hey, where's Hannah?" I turn, asking Dane because she was sitting on his lap for the last few innings.

"She went to the bathroom. Thank goodness because my leg was falling asleep and I would have never asked her to move. I'd rather amputate my leg than do that." We both laugh because that's probably a statistical fact.

Dane and I share a look and smile as Christian taps on the keyboard of his phone then glances up. "Alright, we're all set to head over to Afterburn."

"Well, Christian, it was great to chat with you." I hold out my hand for a shake because that's my queue, but he glances down at it before meeting my eyes.

"You're coming too, right?" he asks, genuinely confused.

"He is. He just doesn't know it yet," Dane replies.

"Oh, Hannah and I should—"

"Great," Christian interrupts me trying to excuse myself from this, patting me on the shoulder. "Hudson will meet us there but our limo is downstairs. Grab Hannah and meet us at the back entrance." He steps away toward the direction of his significant others, Jake and Elena, and I wish I had the guts to ask him about his situation. About how it works.

My gaze shifts to Dane who's standing there still rubbing the surface of his quad. "Hudson will be there?" I ask.

He laughs. "Yes, come on." He pulls me with him as Hannah comes into view and we all head down to the limo together.

"Dane," I call out, getting his attention before stepping into the vehicle. "Um, Afterburn, I've...We've—" I gesture to Hannah.

"It's not open to the public, we're just going there for drinks and to hang out." My body visibly relaxes.

"Oh." I feel relieved. I think.

"Christian closed it tonight so the staff could attend the game but don't worry," he winks, "I'll take you and Hannah another time."

I hate that he reads my thoughts quicker than I can figure them out but as he turns and ducks into the limo, I can't help but smile.

That is until a text message from my father pops up on my phone.

> Edward: I have it on good authority you were at the game again tonight with Christian Ford and Dane Campbell. Why you decided to go with my future clients without informing me makes me think you've forgotten your obligations to me and my company.

> Edward: It would be easy for me to divert everything owed back on her so she can be the one paying for your careless mistake.

45

HANNAH

"These are the private rooms." Dane points down a long hallway with multiple doors before opening the first one on the left.

Stepping in, my eyes bounce around the dimly lit room and I'm immediately overwhelmed. There is a massive, maybe bigger than king size, bed in the middle of the room. The dark wood bed posts have multiple rings attached to them as they trail up toward the ceiling.

A wall display takes up half the area behind it showcasing different types of toys, ropes, and floggers. There's a Saint Andrew's cross on the opposite side of the bed and a cage on the other.

I've never seen anything like this in my entire life. Not that I've spent much time in lifestyle clubs, but I just had no idea this would be what it looked like.

I'm surprised at how clean and classy everything is. The front entrance had a waterfall and peaceful ambiance that let you into a large open bar area with plenty of high tables and seating. Mind you, the club is closed so no one occupied the space when we walked into it but it was pristine and elegant.

As we walked past the bar, there was an area called the Chat Room that donned the old AOL symbol and even had the welcome note and door shut sound as you went in and out of it. Dane said it was a safe meeting room for people who utilize the App that led to the creation of this club.

We passed by a stage area that I didn't ask about because I blushed just looking at it, then passed by the voyeur rooms—expansive rooms similar to this one but with floor-to-ceiling glass windows for spectators—and now we're here in the private rooms.

Now that we're in the room, behind closed doors, the sexual tension is high—as it usually is when the three of us are together, and if I wasn't already blushing at the furnishings that make up this room, I'm flushed by the two men inside of it.

There's no denying the chemistry between us and as much as we all have our moments of hesitation, there's also nothing that feels more natural than when we're spending time together.

I can feel their eyes on me as I make my way over to the bed, sitting down at the end of it. The energy in the room is electric and it sets my skin on fire or perhaps it's just the searing gaze they both have on me.

Sitting on Dane's lap during the game was the most excruciating foreplay I've ever experienced. His fingertips grazed over every inch of my body, alternating under and over articles of clothing. Sneaking under the waistband of my leggings, teasing me endlessly. I squirmed at his touch as I watched Ethan sneaking glances at us, smiling and laughing while talking about baseball for the first time in years. The mixture brought out a happiness I didn't know I could feel.

So now, as they prowl around me, I'm fully intoxicated by the look of desire behind their eyes.

They mirror each other as they step toward me and my pulse kicks up more than a few notches. I graze my teeth over my bottom lip, sucking it in, and I can't hide my smile or the way my body shifts underneath me as they get closer.

Ethan steps to my left and leans forward, placing soft kisses along my shoulder as Dane shimmies to my right, cupping his hand over my face before running his hand through my hair. He leans down caressing his lips against my jawline just as Ethan does the same on the other.

Their tongues brush over my skin, making their way toward my mouth and I can't help but moan as goosebumps bloom over my skin.

My noise elicits a groan from Dane. "God, I fucking love that," he confesses before swiping his tongue over the seam of my lips just as Ethan does the same, all our tongues merging together all at once.

Their hands roam over my body as we kiss, sharing moments between each other. It feels like it did that last night in Paris, when they both finally gave in and the craving we all have for each other outweighed everything else.

"*I want both of you.*"

"How do you want us, baby?" Ethan asks, still kissing my jaw.

"*I want you both in me at the same time.*"

They share a look with each other. Ethan's eyes are wide and skeptical, while Dane has that mischievous look behind his.

"Are you sure, Poe?"

I nod, biting my lip.

"*I've wanted this for a long time.*"

Dane smiles as he stands, walking over to a dresser next to the bed. He opens one of the drawers pulling out an unopened bottle of lube and two condoms.

"Figures you know your way around here," Ethan whispers under his breath, but I can tell in his body language he instantly regrets his words.

Dane freezes, shifting just his eyes to look at him.

"I have a history. A past. I can tell you all the good shit and I can tell you the really horrible, bad shit. But I'm here now with you guys and I don't want to be anywhere else. I haven't wanted to be anywhere else since we met."

Ethan nods, rubbing the nape of his neck.

"I'm sorry. I'm protecting Hannah," he pauses, before confessing the biggest part of all, "protecting myself."

"You don't have to."

There's a brief silence and I take advantage of shifting the conversation. I hope I'm right in my assumption about Dane, because his answer could change Ethan's mind about where this is going.

"I don't want those." I point at the condoms.

Dane's brows raise as he looks at Ethan.

"Hannah—"

"I want to feel you both and I want you both to feel each other. If we're doing this, I want to do this."

Ethan sighs. "Are you clean?"

"I provided a clean test to *Avec Plaisir* the night we met," he pauses, but confidently holds his chin high as he says, "and I haven't been with anyone else since."

I knew it.

I can't help the small grin that passes over my face as I glance up at Ethan.

I've known this beautiful man almost my entire life. We started dating in high school and he's always looked at me with admiration, love, and desire. I can see a shift in him as he absorbs the words that Dane just told him and I love that he's finally starting to trust him.

"I have to tell you though...I haven't ever had sex without one so I make no promises on the length of my performance," Dane adds, as he tosses the condoms back in the drawer, then turns back to me. "Where do you want me, Poe?"

46

DANE

So tonight is the best night ever.

Not only did the Smashers win—not that I care about baseball, more about Hudson—but I spent the majority of my time with Hannah talking and laughing while Ethan seemed to have found his spark again.

I've never seen him so alive and I would give up everything to see him like that everyday.

It's been perfect and the fact that we're all here now, let's just say the night couldn't have ended any better.

Hannah told me to lay down on the bed. So, I happily obliged as she stripped me naked. Then both Ethan and I watched as she removed her leggings and jersey, leaving her in just lace panties and a bra.

God, she's a sight.

Her skin is a notch paler than it was during the summer time, missing that sun-kissed glow from backpacking, but it's flushed with need.

She's always held the control, she always will, but this is the first time she's taken the reins and made it clear about what she wants.

Glancing over her shoulder, Ethan stands behind her and I tip my chin at him as my eyes flicker toward his chest. He's the only one still fully dressed and we just can't have that.

Unbuttoning his pants, he steps out of them then takes off his shirt and tosses it to the floor.

Hannah kneels into the bed beside me, taking the bottle of lube out of my hands. She snaps open the lid, pours some into her hand then closes the lid and tosses it over to Ethan.

I watch him as he drizzles the liquid over his cock and strokes it thoroughly around every inch of the tight skin.

"Umpf, fuck," I hiss as Hannah's cool, wet hand wraps around my length, coating it as she massages it.

Giving my cock this little bit of attention is all I need to be completely on edge. Ethan's dark pupils sear through me the entire time and I can't help but pump my hips to meet her strokes.

She swings one leg over my stomach, straddling me, and I wrap my hands around her hips, rolling her into me.

"Fuck, yes," I breathe out as she rocks her hips like a professional equestrian, the wetness of her arousal mixes with my coated cock and the friction is fucking glorious.

"You're so beautiful." I gaze up at her inspecting every inch of her gorgeous face. My eyes trail down to the scar she wears with confidence. The scar that defines what she's been through and the exceptional gratitude she has for life.

She leans into me, pressing her lips to mine. At the same time her hips lift up and her hand reaches for my erect cock. Rubbing my crown over her wet center, she runs the tip through her arousal then breaches the entrance and my jaw falls open.

It's wet and hot and nothing like I've ever felt before. It's already so sensitive and I can't help but let out a groan as her hips settle down on mine engulfing me completely.

"Jesus Christ," I spit out, throwing my head back against the mattress. "Fuck, that's good."

Rolling her hips into mine, the sensation is unreal. It's tight and wet and I can feel every ridge, every inch of her walls that clench and pulse as my cock pistons in and out.

"Oh, goddamn it, it's so…" I groan, huffing out a long breath, unable to finish with words.

Celeste couldn't take birth control and we always used condoms. I've never had anything serious after so not using condoms was never an option.

This is unlike anything I've ever experienced and I love that I'm having it with them.

Just then, I feel the mattress dip between my legs. Ethan places his hand on Hannah's back and presses her gently forward. Her breasts press into my chest and she uses her tongue to lick around my jawline.

The sensation of them on top of me as Ethan leans further forward is like a weighted blanket I never want to be rid of. My eyes connect with his and there's a fire ignited behind them. The same overwhelming desire fills my bones like it did the first time and I want nothing more than this as a staple in my life.

My eyes don't leave his as if he can read what I'm thinking through my dark, needy pupils.

Trust me. I want this more than you'll ever know.

Hannah sucks in a harsh breath, her eyes squint as her walls grip my cock.

"Relax for me, baby," Ethan hisses out, his thick crown rubbing against the base of my cock as he tries to stretch her wider to accommodate us both.

Shifting my gaze, I cup her face and pull her lips to mine. Her eyes squeeze shut and I swallow her throaty groan that makes my cock twitch, just as Ethan's breaches through and slides over the backside of mine.

"Oh, fuck. Oh, fuuuuucck," I grit out. Her wet heat engulfs us both. Everything is so tight, so wet, and so fucking unbelievable. Ethan's jaw drops, his forehead dips down between Hannah's shoulder blades and we all still, feeling nothing but our throbbing cocks against the tight wet walls of her stretched cunt.

"Goddamn it," Ethan breathes out, pulling his hips back and pressing in slowly, softly with an ease that's both powerful and gentle.

I. Feel. Everything.

The heaviness of them on my body. The lightness in my head. The beat of my pulse rushing through my ears. The ridges of his cock caressing mine as he pulls out and back in. The way her pussy swallows us both as he thrusts in and clenches as he retreats.

My hips find a mind of their own, matching his as they piston a little faster and his moans, the ones I love so fucking much, ascend as his cock grows harder.

My eyes bounce between Hannah and Ethan as I revel in this moment and I can't help myself. I can't help the words bubbling from my chest and there's no stopping them as they leave my mouth.

"Tell me I'm yours. Tell me you want this as much as I do."

Ethan's eyes blow wide as they flicker down to Hannah, but she doesn't look back at him. She grips my chin, pulling her lips to mine, answering my question the only way she can.

The mattress dips next to my head and when I open my eyes, Ethan's leaning down even closer to us. The angle of his cock changes, pulling a small moan from Hannah, her pussy clenches as her walls throb around us, her orgasm slamming into her. Her fingers dig into my flesh, the same area as before where her permanent marks are inked.

I'm already so close and the way that Ethan's eyes are devouring me I swear I'm hanging on by a thread.

"You're ours," Ethan confesses, his voice husky and needy and his words drip with intention.

My cock grows harder, the rough ridges and soft skin of Ethan's cock mixed with the excessive arousal from Hannah's orgasm is destroying every ounce of my restraint.

"Fuck, I'm coming," Ethan blurts out loud and a long moan follows, as if his confession was his own undoing. I know it was mine. The sensation is fucking unreal as my raw cock pulses against his, our cum coating Hannah, and each other.

Their bodies fall to each side of me as our labored breath remains to be the only sound left in the room.

A few minutes go by in comfortable silence and my mind is quiet even though all my nerve endings are still on fire.

This is what ecstasy feels like.

Floating.

Knock. Knock.

"Come on lovebirds. Hudson's here!" Mimi's voice is low and muffled but her words are clear and I've never seen Ethan sit up so fast. Hannah and I share a look and smother our smiles as Ethan's giddiness shows.

"*I've never seen him dress so fast,*" Hannah signs.

"*Me either,*" I sign back.

"Oh shut up," he says, tossing our clothes at us. "We gotta get out there," he adds, rolling onto his heels, unable to hide his excitement.

"*I'm kind of jealous,*" I sign, as I dress slowly.

"*Me too,*" Hannah agrees.

"Oh my god, you guys suck." He throws his head back then looks at the door like he's worried we don't have time.

We have plenty of time. I've already told Hudson everything about these two, but I've shared a lot about Ethan and what I know of his baseball history.

Hudson is just as excited to meet him and I know the two will be practically inseparable once they do.

"Fine, fine." I slip on my pants and jersey quickly as Hannah does the same. I flip the light on the wall to the blinking red option, signaling it needs cleaning, then we walk back out to the bar area with Hannah between us, both of us holding one hand connecting the three of us and I've never felt so complete.

47

ETHAN

My heart is going, quite literally, a million miles an hour. Not only am I still on a high from the most mind-blowing orgasm I've ever had, but Hudson Byrnes is here.

He's hugging and smiling at everyone that's circled around him. His 6 '4 height towers over almost all of them and ironically he's the only one not in a Smashers Jersey but in a World Series Championship shirt with the Smasher logo across the front of it.

A small wave of jealousy hits me but I can't help but smile at the happiness that surrounds everyone.

"Hud!" Dane calls out, practically jump-scaring me, making my heart pump even harder.

"DC!" Dane steps forward breaking the circle and gives Hudson one of those bro hugs that only two guys do when they're close and care about each other in a platonic way.

"You fucking did it, back-to-back champ!" Dane says excitedly.

"It's the team, man. Everyone's at their peak," Hudson says, running his hand through his dark brown hair which is still damp from the shower he probably had to take after getting drenched in Champagne.

"Hey, is he here?" Hudson asks Dane.

Dane nods with a smile and points to me.

I swear to god my eyes saucer out of my head as I look at Hannah then back at Hudson as he makes his way in our direction.

"Ethan," Hudson holds his hand out, "I'm Hudson. I've heard so much about you, it's good to meet you." I shake his hand, still in shock so the only words that leave my mouth are a rusty sounding, "You too."

"Hannah?" He looks at my gorgeous girl, still flushed from the earlier events of the night and she smiles, nodding, not nearly as starstruck as I am. "It's great to meet you." He leans in and gives her a gentle hug.

Turning back to me, he places his hands on his hips. "So, in Game five you think I could have gotten that last out in the ninth inning if I were a tad faster when Silva stole second base?"

My jaw drops as I glare at Dane. "You told him that?"

Hudson laughs and pats me on the shoulder and we fall into some easy conversation that brings back memories of talking to all my baseball mates from high school.

An hour goes by, maybe two—I've completely lost track—we've made our way to the bar while Dane and Hannah talk with others in the group and I swear neither one of us has shut up about the series. We've been reminiscing on different plays that made the difference, making their win possible and the conversation is like a happiness drug I want to overdose on.

Looking over my shoulder, I steal a glance at Hannah as she yawns, dipping her head into Dane's nook. I know it's been a long day and it's time to head out, even though I could talk ball all night with Hudson. He's so down to earth and easy going. I knew that about him, but in person it's like he's one of the guys and doesn't even know how famous he is.

"So, I hate cutting this night short," I look at my watch and it's well after midnight, "Er, I mean cut this night off at all, but I should get her home."

Hudson glances over at Dane and Hannah both on the verge of passing out.

"He's invested, you know?" He turns back to me. "In both of you."

I chipmunk my cheeks as I run my hand through my hair. "It's complicated." I pause for a minute before adding, "My father—"

At the same time Hudson says, "Professor or not—" our words overlap each other and we both stop talking, his brows pinch together questioning why I would say my father versus the huge glaring fact that he *is* technically my professor.

"I mean...yeah, that's a huge problem. I think we need to lay low and just decide where to take things after the semester." I take in the two of them as I've done throughout the day today and I *know* Dane is invested. I've always known, I just haven't been willing to admit it or accept my feelings for him. "We are too. We want to figure this out. I'm just not sure how yet."

Hudson smiles and it's a genuinely happy one. Like he was worried my response would hurt his friend and I immediately mirror his grin because it feels good to say that out loud.

"Just keep him in the loop about how you feel. He'll stand by your side the whole way, he just needs to know."

I nod as he pats my shoulder. "I know it's a bit premature but Afterburn is having a New Year's masquerade party, are you and Hannah going to come with Dane?"

It's still early November and we haven't even gotten through the holidays but bringing in the New Year with the two of them, starting our year off together as the clock strikes midnight, I don't think I've looked forward to anything more.

"Yeah, yeah I think we are."

48

HANNAH

I know they say as you get older time seems to move by so much faster, but the past two months have quite literally flown by. I thought because we had some time off for Thanksgiving I would feel like we would have some down time but not once have any of us had a day to ourselves.

I've jammed in more credits and added an online course to help finish the coding for my program as best as I can. It's ready for the final presentation that Dane has assigned to us and to say I'm nervous is a blatant understatement.

Most of the students are presenting a fake idea or proposing a product that doesn't really exist. Others have taken someone else's product and plan to pitch to sell it to Dane and his selected group of colleagues to judge these presentations, grading them on knowledge, likability, creativeness, and overall marketing of said product.

The project wasn't to create something to sell, the assignment was built so that we can find our voice and sell our brand. But this program is everything to me. It *is* me. It speaks *for* me. Quite literally.

Ethan knows I've been working on this for quite some time. I haven't shared anything with Dane on it.

I didn't want any guidance, or favoritism or anything that could be viewed as unfair, especially with how serious things have gotten between the three of us over the last six weeks.

We're still not public, that's not possible for us, but we're committed. Dane is never seen without a smile on his face and Ethan, well he's an entirely different person. He's my old Ethan again, the one before the accident, the one that doesn't carry the guilt of the crash and the weight of the world on his shoulders.

He still hates working for his father, and that's seemingly gotten worse. His father keeps putting more and more on him at the office, and still pushing him to get his MBA. Ethan is working longer and longer hours, barely passing the classes that he doesn't want to take, all to appease his father that will actually never be pleased.

I hate this situation he's in, but he insists it's for the best.

At least lately, when he comes home to the two of us, I shower him with love and Dane somehow makes him laugh so the frustration of his day job and dealing with his father seems to fade quickly.

Usually we stay at Danes because he has a condo with a doorman and security, whereas our apartment is typically swarming with other college students and the one time Dane came over he got caught leaving our building the next morning.

Luckily no one saw the apartment he left from but there were rumors that he was seen leaving the building so that no longer happens.

I take a deep breath as I watch my reflection in the mirror. My presentation is so deeply personal, it exposes me more than my scar does. This program means everything to me, to the world of ASL speakers and people like me that feel trapped and silent. It'll help ASL speakers grow into the corporate world more naturally, without feeling set back and left behind.

When Dane informed the class that everyone would have presentation time, there was a brief glance in my direction and it was the first time I've ever seen pity when he looked at me.

Because, of course, how am I going to sell myself to someone.

I knew instantly I had to keep perfecting my program and now it's finally ready. Sure, it still needs work but it's not like I'm selling the actual program. I'm making a statement.

I might be silent but I have a lot to say.

The class presentations are long, not because you get so much time to present, but because they have to cycle through so many students.

At the beginning of class Dane informed everyone they had two minutes to find a way to convince the panel to invest in them.

The assignment was not a real pitch, so the shock factor that Dane sits at the front of the class with Christian Ford of Ford Enterprises and Baker VanBuren of VB Technologies we were wholly unprepared for.

I've met Christian before so he's not as intimidating in this setting as he should be. But Baker VanBuren is the CEO of VB Technologies that specialize in utilizing technology for advancement in major medical breakthroughs. I've read about him and his company in multiple different magazine articles and his company is nothing short of amazing.

They were introduced as great friends and colleagues of Professor Campbell's and part of the grading panel.

So, if someone wasn't nervous before, they sure are now.

A majority of the class has already gone, Ethan just finished and he presented an idea he had for a mobile application that mocked the fantasy football league, but for baseball. Ethan isn't the most dynamic personality because he's reserved, but when he talks about baseball he shines. So, although his product was far-fetched and a bit silly, the panel liked him.

Which is the whole point.

I look friendly because I wear a smile but when I can't speak most people don't give me a chance.

"Hannah Parker," Dane calls out my name, as he appraises me with concern. The order of presentations were random, ironically I was last, which is usually the worst because most people are 'over it' by this time.

My eyes shift nervously over to Ethan before I stand and straighten out my dress. I grab my laptop that's already set up and ready to go.

"Do you need the white board or projector?" he asks as I walk up to the front.

I point at the projector and set my laptop down plugging it in.

The word Amplify pops up on the backdrop and I step back in front of my screen, moving myself in the middle of the webcam.

When I'm finally centered, I glance over at Ethan, worried that I should have told him more about my presentation to prepare him for what he will hear right now. I turn back and give Dane a quick nod, telling him I'm ready and he hits the digital timer displayed on this desk.

I tap my keyboard, initiating the program, then step back in the center of the screen, exactly where I need to be so it can read my words and I begin to sign.

"Good Morning, my name is Hannah Parker and this is Amplify. Amplify is an AI code that's able to read ASL visually through this webcam and is programmed to speak on my behalf.

"I lost the ability to speak four years ago due to a car accident. Communicating the way I used to is no longer an option. For anyone that is unable to speak, they are limited in life, but the restrictions in the corporate world are massively debilitating. Amplify changes that."

I take my eyes away from the webcam to peer over at Dane, his brows are pinched together, his eyes bouncing between the screen and his panel. He's never been good at hiding his emotion but this one is a mix of things I can't read.

"Amplify is both a standalone program—so if you are nonverbal you can still present to one, two, or hundreds of people, and it's also built to integrate into systems for video calls so that instead of typing in a chat box you can use Amplify to speak, just as others are speaking."

I pause again, turning my gaze to Ethan. He's leaning on to his desk, his palms cover his nose and mouth, and his eyes are glossed over.

"It's programmed with forty different voices so each user can select the voice that best fits them. But even better, Amplify is built to not only speak but listen. For users like myself that may have just recently lost their speaking voice, you have the option of using your own just by uploading recordings or videos with sound bites of your voice into the program. Amplify will recreate that voice and utilize it as your own."

"Wait a minute. That's *your* voice?" Dane asks, standing abruptly. "You created this?" He circles his pointer finger at my laptop.

"I did." I sign proudly.

49

ETHAN

I was fully expecting a couple things today. For Dane and his colleagues to see how incredible and smart Hannah is. For them to fall in love with her program and to feel an unrelenting pride that she's been able to accomplish something so remarkable.

I was prepared for people to see how beneficial this will be for anyone who is nonverbal, because they will be able to use this personally, not just in the corporate world. For this to change everything for her, for them.

What I was not prepared for was to hear her angelic voice again. The tone is impeccable. It's exactly as I remember it. Soft and warm with a cheerful confidence only she ever mastered.

My eyes pool with tears. I look up and blink them away because that's fucking embarrassing but as I look over at Dane he's already appraising me, knowing I'm on the verge of completely losing it.

He's always been easy to read but as he's grown into his role as our professor he's been better about masking his feelings and not wearing his heart so blatantly on his sleeve. Right now though, it's taking everything he has to hold himself back from running over to me.

"This is solely yours?" Baker VanBuren stands, asking Hannah. She nods again and he and Christian share a look that only two businessmen know.

The same way people looked at Dane's code when he created it.

"Great job, everyone! You guys did a stellar job and it was truly an honor being your professor this semester." He'll be teaching a new group of students next semester and it's bitter-sweet for us. I love seeing him as my professor but the fact that he won't be ours directly is best considering how our relation-ship has grown.

"The panel will consult to grade your final presentations and post the results tomorrow. Have a great winter break!" Dane adds ending class quickly, which didn't look all that suspicious considering we already went over time.

Hannah begins to unplug her laptop when Baker VanBuren walks up to her. Dane and Christian are on his heels as he holds out his hand, introducing himself, "It's great to meet you Hannah. Do you know who I am?"

Her eyes flicker to Dane, then me and back to him as she nods with a confident smile.

"I'm incredibly interested to know more about your program."

50

DANE

This past week has been wild. Ever since Hannah's presentation she's been meeting with the VB Technologies team and they're fully vested in helping her bring it to life.

All of this is happening exactly like it did with me. The moment a company heard about it, they were adamant about working with me and staying in such close contact to make sure I wouldn't consider selling or licensing to anyone else. Which is funny to think about now because I was so naive at the time. I mean, I knew it was special but the severity of how much I was completely blind to.

Once I built it, I wanted to get it out in the world. I was fine with letting it go. It almost felt as if it was symbolic of what I needed for my college years. It helped me grieve. By the time it was perfected I was ready to sell it and move on. Like sharing it was the last step I needed to get past the heartache of losing Celeste.

It didn't.

I felt even more alone, traveling mindlessly around the world thinking about how different my life could be.

Hannah is different though. She didn't create this as a way

to get things off her mind. She created it to say more than she ever could. She isn't ready to let this go and I know that she needs to continue to be involved in its development.

Which is why this break couldn't have come at a better time. I've been able to go to the meetings she's had with Baker and his team at VB Technologies. Sure, they'd love to offer her more money than she could ever dream of having but that won't be fulfilling for her.

She needs to be involved.

Another reason why I insisted she not make a decision on this until after she finishes her MBA and is ready to take the next step. I trust Baker wholeheartedly, but I don't think she's ready to let this go yet and her priority should remain. Graduate with her Masters then decide what she wants to do. She completely agreed.

So we're finally winding down and getting ready to bring in the new year at the masquerade party at Afterburn. It's honestly the first time I've spent New Years with my friends and not traveling abroad somewhere. I've never looked forward to it more.

Not just the party but the symbolism of me standing still with my two favorite people by my side in a room full of my closest friends.

I step out of the shower, freshly clean, and wrap a towel around my waist. Walking through the doorway into the room, Ethan is zipping up the back of Hannah's dress as he presses a kiss on her shoulder.

"Oh wow, you look stunning." My words fall out of my mouth without a filter because she does that to me.

A shy smile tips at the corner of her mouth as she glances down at her dress. The thin, sheer satin is a deep purple and it floats over her body in waves. Her dark, thick hair is curled and draped around the purple mask that covers her eyes. There are lines of crystals that catch the light and twinkle with the barest of movement.

Ethan is dressed in a dark charcoal suit and satin tie that matches the color of Hannah's dress. He isn't wearing his mask yet so his face is still fully exposed and he's as sexy as the first time I remember seeing him.

There's something behind his eyes lately though. I think maybe I'm comparing it too much to when we were in Paris and we hardly carried a worry in the world. He was easy going back then—well as easy going as Ethan gets—but lately, there's a tiredness in his eyes that never manages to go away. It's more apparent as Friday approaches, after a long week of balancing the classes he's taking and the demands of his father.

Edward has reached out to me multiple times. He asked me to do everything under the sun. Dinner, breakfast, coffee, golf. You name it, he's probably invited me.

I've been able to keep my distance but I'm not sure how much longer that will last until I just have to completely turn him down, but I'm a little worried how that will affect Ethan considering how close we are.

He knows we've spent some time together but obviously doesn't know the extent.

Still, I want to make a good impression because for me, Ethan is going to be part of my future, and naturally, so will his father.

Ethan tips his chin in the direction of the closet; I crane my neck back to see a matching charcoal suit and shiny purple tie hanging waiting for me.

Instead of walking in that direction and getting dressed, I drop my towel.

Hannah's eyes widen from behind her mask while Ethan gives me the look he's famous for.

We don't have time because, well I'm already running late, and they're fully dressed for the New Year's Eve gala tonight but it's always fun to be a bit of a tease, especially when I get a reaction out of Ethan.

I run my hand over my hip and wrap my hand around my cock, giving myself a long pull as it grows thicker.

"Don't you dare," Ethan threatens.

"*Dane.*"

"Fine. Fine. Cockblockers," I say laughing, as I turn around and get dressed and I don't need to see them to know they're smiling, watching the globes of my beautiful ass as I walk away, so I give it a little shake before I turn the corner. "You know how much I love being on time and keeping a schedule." Everything I said is dripping with sarcasm, except for the love part.

Love is a complete understatement of how I feel for them.

51

ETHAN

Afterburn is exactly like I thought it would be but nothing like I expected.

Coming here last month after the World Series win was completely different now that it's opened and packed to the brim with other masked guests.

It's clean and classy but has that underground sensation that we're doing something we probably shouldn't be doing. Like the people here are all-in on the secret but once you step outside these walls no one can talk about it.

There are women and men, even couples performing on the stage with a crowd full of people watching from behind their beaded masks. The voyeur rooms are full and I could only imagine that there's a waitlist of people that are waiting to get in there, like it was last year's New Year's resolution and they only have a few short hours to make it happen.

The architecture is completely different from *Avec Plaisir* but the vibe is the same and everyone is here for the same reason.

Dane and I stand on either side of Hannah with a drink in each hand as we observe the performers on stage.

The stage is bare with only a large bed with black satin sheets. There are straps attached to the corners that can be connected with restraints, which currently, are in use.

Ironically it's a trio like us, except there are two females. One of which is straddling the man's face, while the other is alternating between sucking and stroking his fully erect cock. His groans are muffled, mixing with the moans of the woman riding him.

The room is completely engaged in their performance. All the eyes in the room taking in their writhing bodies, the echoes of slurping, slapping, and moaning which is only accentuated by the public display, in not only this room, but all the other ones.

It's all incredibly sensual, but I don't seem to care as much about the three of them as much as I care about the two next to me.

I can't take my eyes off Hannah as she shifts her stance, then signs as she peers up to me with fire in her eyes. She's turned on and the look behind those gorgeous blue eyes could literally drop me to my knees.

"I want to do that to you both."

My brows pinch together confused.

"Do what?"

"Tie you both up."

Okkayyy. I'm interested.

Dane watches her sign out of the corner of his eye then perks up and looks at me, silently begging.

"I'm on it." I step around them and head straight to the front of the lobby area where I can ask about the private rooms.

"Unfortunately we don't have any private rooms available. We do have a voyeur room open. It's available for the next hour since the previous couple ended early. Would you like to take it?"

I sigh, disappointed, but we could just go home instead or maybe waitlist our names for a private room.

Pulling out my phone, I shoot Dane a text.

> Me: They don't have any private rooms. Only one of the voyeur rooms.

> Dane: And?

> Me: The voyeur rooms are surrounded by glass windows and you know…voyeured.

> Dane: So.

> Dane: We're wearing masks.

That's such an annoyingly Dane thing to say. I don't necessarily love the idea of being the center of attention, knowing all eyes are on me. Normally I'm the one in the lead. Especially since Dane's been in our dynamic. But as I envision Dane and I tied to a bed with Hannah in that role, my cock stirs to life and not even a crowd of people or my logical brain can ignore the desire.

> Me: Ask Hannah.

> Dane: Oh, she's down. She's a feral cat crawling all over my body in need. Get the fucking room before she claws my eyes out.

I roll my eyes but can't help but chuckle. He's so dramatic.

I glance back up to the girl behind the desk, sucking in a deep breath. Are we really doing this?

She tilts her head as she awaits my answer.

"We'll take it."

52

DANE

"Are you sure you're okay with it?" I ask Hannah again as I pocket my phone.

She nods quickly, with more excitement than I expected. I mean, she's the more open minded one between the two of them, but being fully exposed in front of a group of people during any kind of sexual act is a different level of being *open* to things.

I bet Ethan is freaking the fuck out right now.

I'd go check on him but I refuse to leave Hannah's side. She's fucking stunning. Men and women alike would flock to her the moment she was alone by herself.

I pull out my phone, lifting my mask so it can scan my face, then type out a text to Ethan.

Me: You better not back down now, you bastard. I'm way too excited about this.

The trio just finished on the stage and the room has cleared out a little bit. There are still some people standing around, kissing, touching, watching others. Others have gone to another part of the club or the bar.

A man near the back of the room, opposite the stage, catches my attention. He has his phone in his hand, looking in our direction. His mask fully covers his face. The top portion of his face and even a majority of the bottom is mostly covered; there are long extended pieces of the mask that drape over the corners of his mouth like the design of an old style gladiator mask.

I squint to get a better view but he turns, exiting the viewing area as he heads to the bar.

Stepping forward, my eyes attempt to follow him but he gets lost in the crowd.

People recognize me often and I don't really care about whether or not I'm here, or what people see me doing, but I don't want the fact that I'm teaching now to be an issue.

My phone buzzes in my hand, stealing my attention.

Ethan: Voyeur Room 1. We have an hour.

Pressing my palm to the small of Hannah's back, I lead her in the direction of the voyeur rooms and the moment we get to the door Ethan is there.

He's stiff as a board, his usual demeanor, but there's a nervousness I'm also not used to seeing. It's adorable.

I usually let him take charge, especially when it comes to us sexually because he needs that in his bi-curious state. I just hope that when he finally accepts his bisexuality, he'll let me take over like he's letting Hannah.

We already don't have much time, so before his nerves get the best of him I usher them both into the room and lock the door behind us. We're hidden behind a small alcove in the corner of the room. I tap the panels on the wall and dim the lights just slightly, fogging out the glass so we can't see the faces of the spectators that will be watching.

One of my favorite features about these voyeur rooms are these windows that act almost like one-way mirrors, so that people can see in, but whoever is in the room can still feel like it's personal if that's what they need and I know Ethan needs that.

Not wanting to waste any time, I sign, *"Ready?"*

Hannah bites her lips and nods. I don't ask Ethan because I don't need him to overthink my one word question and I know he'll follow Hannah. Instead, I step toward him, adjust his mask to remind him it's there and take Hannah's hand, leading her to the bed.

Glancing over my shoulder, Ethan trails right behind us, peering out of the corner of his mask at the translucent windows. Hannah sits down softly at the edge of the bed and she gazes up at me with those bright, ocean blues and the most charming little smirk at the corner of her lips.

Meeting my gaze she pats the left side of her mattress and as Ethan steps up, she shifts her gaze to him and pats her right.

We share a look as we sit down beside her, our bodies are now facing the large floor to ceiling windows. The haze allows for some silhouettes to be seen from behind it but it just looks like blurred shadows with the glass being a shade darker than the top portion.

Dipping my chin, I lean in and kiss Hannah's scar. My touch is light as I trail my lips over her skin giving her a full body shiver as she tilts her head back. Ethan matches my movement on the other side and both of our hands move up her thigh and over her hips.

Our lips meet hers at the same time; she turns toward him, parting her lips as their tongues collide and he moans, squeezing his eyes shut.

I love how he loves her.

They've been together for years and he still kisses her like it's the first time.

Pulling away, she faces me, cups my jaw, and pulls me in for a kiss that rivals theirs. Her lips taste like her, laced with traces of him, and the mixture is my kryptonite.

It turns passionate and I lean harder into her, wanting more, needing more. My heart pounds in my chest, not from nerves, but from the sensation of them. Both of them. Here with me. It's everything I need.

She uses both her hands to cup my jaw and pulls back, that gorgeous smile adorns her face as she shakes her head.

"What?" I ask, confused.

Holding two fingers up on one hand, palm up on the other, she places the tips into her hand, signing for me to stand. She does the same to Ethan and it's amazing how demanding she is with so few words.

Or maybe it's just that she rules us in every way.

We both comply and stand, facing her with our backs to the window.

"*Undress each other.*"

My face splits into a mile wide grin while Ethan's eyes shoot up to his gorgeous thick hairline.

Oh, I fucking love bossy Hannah.

Turning toward him, I hold my hands out, giving him the lead. His eyes bounce between the two of us, his chest rises and falls behind that crisp, white button down shirt and I have really dirty thoughts of what I'm going to do with the purple satin tie I want to rip off his collar.

His hands unravel my tie and he tosses it on the bed next to Hannah, then my shirt and pants, and I'm now standing in just my matching purple boxer briefs—because I'm fancy like that —in front of my two favorite people.

I waste no time, as I step forward, removing his tie the same way, tossing it next to mine on the bed. I unbutton his shirt and push it over his large shoulders, using my fingertips to graze his soft skin, forcing his breath to hiss and I love how sensitive he is to my touch.

He's frozen, his shirt still stuck behind his back as if it traps his arms and I unbuckle his belt and unzip his pants, allowing them to drop to the floor. His black boxer briefs, snug tight around his dick, the bulge behind it just as undeniable as mine.

Hannah stands, her satin dress a perfect fit to her gorgeous body slithers with her steps. Everything about the movement and flow is soft with exception to the peaks of her nipples piercing through the fabric.

"*Lay down.*"

We easily comply again, each taking one side of the bed as we lay down beside each other.

"*Put your arms over your head.*"

My arms fly up. Ethan's more cautious as they slowly raise.

She walks around to my side of the bed, grabbing a pair of bondage cuffs, wrapping them around my wrists then hooking them to the strap at my corner of the bed.

Repeating the same to Ethan, it probably only took a minute but it feels like a lifetime that I've been riding this wave of anticipation.

She taps my hip as her eyes gaze in mine. My body listens to her command as I lift my hips but keep my eyes locked on hers. Pulling my boxers off, I groan as a cool breeze wraps around my cock. It bounces out of the tight fabric and rests on the base of my abs, a string of pre-cum linking it to my skin.

"Oh fuck," Ethan whispers next me, his eyes flicker at the window then back to my exposed cock with an undeniable shock that this is all really happening.

"*Your turn,*" Hannah signs as she steps toward him, I think as a warning, or maybe a question to make sure he's still okay.

His breath is heavy but he nods, lifting his hips, giving her permission and fuck, it's so goddamn sexy.

She strips the material down his legs and my mouth waters at the sight of his lean, tight body and jutting cock.

Hannah tosses his boxers somewhere, then opens the drawer next to the bed, grabbing a small bottle of lube. She walks slowly toward the end of the bed, kicks off her shoes, and pulls the satin fabric of her dress up over her knees, then kneels onto the mattress directly in between us.

"*The first one to come loses.*"

"What?" We overlap each other in response.

She squirts lube on both of our cocks then wraps her perfect fucking hands around each one and begins to stroke us rhythmically together.

"Oh fuck." My head drops back against the mattress.

Ethan's eyes roll back as his hips push up and we both moan in unison. Neither one of us will last long after the drawn out fucking strip tease and anticipation of this moment.

She continues her perfect goddamn cock massage, both of us completely on edge, then stops.

I hiss. Ethan groans.

Her fingertip grazes the backside until she reaches the tip, then she wraps her hand around our shafts and squeezes as she strokes again. I grow impossibly hard and I'm doing everything in my power to hold back, but she knows us both really fucking well and switches up the movement, keeping us both on edge.

This goes on for-fucking-ever. I'm dying. I need to come. I don't care if I lose. I mean, I don't want to lose but as I look over at Ethan's trembling abs as they contract with each tug of his cock I know he's right there with me.

"Don't come yet," I grit out.

"I'm not coming first," he spits out. His eyes squeezing shut like he says it as a mantra.

Competitive bastard.

"Together," I grunt out, holding back my orgasm.

His eyes shift to mine. I can tell how relieved he is by my suggestion.

"Yeah?"

"Fuck, yeah." I nod.

His needy gaze sears into me and the knowing sensation of my pending orgasm builds as my balls begin to tighten. His brows pitch together and he's so close.

Just then, she releases our cocks and we both whine, pumping our hips reaching for more.

"You want to be teammates? Then you can take care of each other."

"What? How? We're tied up, Hannah." Ethan's so mad and it's so fucking adorable.

That beautiful dimple appears on her chin as she smothers a smile and shrugs, glancing over at the clock.

"If you make each other come, you can have me anyway you want when we get home."

Our necks jerk toward each other.

"Five minutes left."

53

ETHAN

"Oh shit," Dane spits out, wrapping his leg against mine. He pulls me against his body, our dicks slapping together, just as he ruts his hips into mine.

"Dane. Fuck." I toss my head back and attempt to move my restrained arms.

I can feel every ridge as he rubs against me, the skin of our cocks straining against each other as his hips desperately pump.

My body has a mind of its own and I can't think of anything other than matching his pace.

"Fuck, yes." The words leave my mouth with so much need and it just fuels Dane more.

He thrusts into me and we're both so close but it's just not enough friction, not enough to get either one of us there.

I glance at the clock. Fucking hell. "Three minutes," I call out.

"The countdown is not helping."

"Need your hands?"

"Yes. Please, god, yes," I say urgently.

"I swear to god I'll buy you a goddamn country. Please," Dane begs.

Her finger taps her chin like the gorgeous tease she is as we both plead more, then she smiles, signing, *"Two minutes,"* as she unclasps Dane's restraints.

Pushing himself up, he reaches for the buckle on my wrist cuffs and unclips it. He pulls me up, placing me flush against his body and our cocks are reunited again as we kneel in front of each other.

He wraps his hand around both our lengths and pumps into his hand, my hips jutting forward with his, matching the tempo as an uncontrollable moan vibrates from my chest. It feels so goddamn good.

"I think your cock likes mine," Dane says with that stupid smirk I'll never admit I love. "It's dripping for me."

I glance down and, fuck, he's right. There's so much pre-cum leaking out of me we don't need any lube. He circles the tip, smearing it down our shafts as we frot into each other. My body shutters and the rising sensation at the base of my spine starts to tingle.

"Oh fuck," I hiss.

"You're going to coat my fucking cock with your cum, aren't you?" I squeeze my lips together because I don't want to say something needy and stupid. "Tell me, tell me how much you love my cock."

I know what he's doing. He needs me to admit how much I want him because I never tell him, not with words at least.

I grab the back of his neck and press our foreheads together.

"I love your cock. I love how hard it gets for us. I love that you always call out both our names before you come." I lean in closer to his ear, admitting something I never thought I would because Dane loves when I talk dirty to him. "I love how you taste when I suck your cock."

"Oh, fucking christ." His mouth falls open.

Using my other hand I pull Hannah into our circle. She kisses my shoulder, then his, the one permanently inked with her marks.

"I love everything about you," I confess, "We both do."

He might be pulling it out of me by sexual coercion but I still mean it all the same.

He pulls back, his eyes bouncing between mine before squeezing shut. His hands are steady in stroke but trembling as he pumps his hips, moaning through the most intense orgasm I've ever seen, spurring mine.

Thick ropes of white liquid shoot out of his cock, spraying my chest and arms. Cum leaks out of mine, coming in fierce waves of intense pleasure. It feels never-ending as he drains our cocks, squeezing the tip, milking us dry until we finally fall into each other on the bed.

The lights dim in the room making everything a shade darker, signaling it's time for us to vacate the room. Even with the timer countdown I completely forgot we were in a room where everyone could see everything we were doing but as I look at the two laying down next to me, as spent as I am, nothing else matters.

Pushing up on my elbow, I place a kiss on Hannah's temple and breathe in her addicting scent.

"Come on." I toss Dane's clothes over to him as I take Hannah's hand. "Let's go home and take care of our girl."

54

HANNAH

Ethan leads me out of the voyeur room with Dane right behind me. I'm sandwiched between my two favorite people and the sensation of both of them on each side of me is a comfort I never knew I needed.

Ethan told him we loved him.

Which we do. I'm not surprised by that.

I'm surprised it was with words and not some other cryptic way for Ethan to express himself.

Regardless, I smile knowing how far he's come even with the underlying stress from work and his father, he's found something with both of us that I could never provide.

Surprisingly it doesn't make me feel less than, it makes *us* feel complete.

I'm about to ask if we should tell the others we're leaving, although if they saw what happened in the voyeur room, they probably already know where we are headed.

A blush forms over my cheeks at the thought, even though I was fully dressed the entire time, my guys were completely exposed and I was in control. It was erotic and sensual and addicting.

"No, we're leaving now!" Seamus' voice echoes through the lobby with a power I've never heard.

He's got his arm around Mimi, shouting at Hudson.

"Are they okay?"

"Hey!" Dane screams, shifting into a jog as he treks over to them. "What's going on?"

"She's been having contractions and didn't tell anyone. Her water just broke and we should be at the hospital already," Seamus says, as he glares at her in the most annoyed but loving way I've ever seen.

"I'm two weeks early, I didn't think they were real contractions," Mimi bites back.

"I'll get the car." Ethan runs toward the exit.

"Hudson, grab the bag from my truck, we're going with Ethan."

Dane runs on the other side of Mimi and drapes her arm around his shoulder.

"Nothing like bringing in the New Year with a baby, huh Meems?"

<hr>

I've never seen Ethan drive so fast. Even before the accident he was an overly cautious driver but after it happened, he rarely wanted to drive and when he did he would always drive just under the speed limit and would be so uptight and fully aware of everything around us while we drove.

Seamus was able to stay with Mimi in the backseat even though I think he hated not being in the driver's seat. But it all worked out with impeccable timing, like the amazing miracle that childbirth is, and now I'm holding this beautiful soul in my arms.

"I told you it was going to be a girl," Dane says to Seamus as he stares at his little girl like she hung the moon, while cooing in my arms.

Seamus just rolls his eyes with a smirk. I think he knew too, but didn't want to admit it.

"Have you guys picked a name yet?" Dane asks.

"If it was a girl Mimi wanted to name her Stella," Seamus smiles as the name leaves his lips, "after my mom."

Dane pats his shoulder with a comfort I'm familiar with. She must mean something, or meant something to Seamus, and his eyes shine bright with pride as he shares a look with Dane.

"I'm going to check on Mimi," he tells me like he's entrusting me with his life. But I totally get it. I would be the same way.

I smile and nod, giving him a reassuring look.

He walks over to Mimi and I know we only have a few more minutes holding this beauty until we need to give her back to her mommy.

"She's beautiful," Dane says as he wiggles one of her teeny, tiny fingers.

"Do you want kids?" Ethan asks with a concerned curiosity.

Dane sucks air in through his teeth as I hold mine.

I want kids. So does Ethan.

For a moment it hits me how much this thing between us may not actually work. How would it work? What if Dane doesn't want kids? If he does, would he want something like that with us? Would Ethan even be okay sharing me so deeply?

I know I'm overthinking but I suppose these are things you have to think about when there are more than just two.

"I always thought I was just cool Uncle material. But lately..." he pauses, exhaling a deep breath, "yeah, I want kids."

I feel relieved by his answer. Although, I don't know if that means he would want that solely with one woman or whether he'd want to see what that looked like with us.

As I peer over at Ethan he seems relieved, too. Like Dane answered exactly like he wanted him to.

"It's getting late," Ethan says, glancing at his watch.

"I want to stay with Mimi."

I somehow manage to sign with Stella still in my arms.

"We should let them have some time together." That probably kills Ethan to say because he knows I'll be disappointed but he's right. "We'll come back for a visit tomorrow."

I nod as Seamus comes back and I gently transition Stella in his arms.

"Thank you for driving us here and staying. For everything," Seamus says before walking back over to Mimi and we finally make our way out of the hospital.

"She's so cute," I can't help but sign excitedly as we get in the car.

"I've never seen a just-born baby and I can't believe how small they are," Dane adds.

Ethan remains quiet as he checks his phone that just dinged with a notification.

It's six in the morning on New Year's day. I squint, confused as to who would be texting him at such an odd time.

His entire body tenses as his brows pinch together as his eyes oscillate over his screen.

"What's wrong?"

He drops his phone, clicking the screen dark then places it in his pocket.

"Nothing, it's just my dad. He wants me to meet him at the office in the morning." My eyes peer over to Dane in the backseat and we share the same thought. The same thing we've been telling Ethan since the beginning of the school year. His father is pushing him too hard, putting too many demands on him and I'm getting tired of how much he lets him run this life.

"As in this morning? It's a holiday. You don't need to do everything he wants."

"You don't understand," he spits back quickly.

As usual he ignores our concerned looks.

"Let's go home and get some sleep." His answer is curt and not assuring at all, even as he attempts a tight-lipped smile.

It takes fifteen minutes for us to get home from the hospital. Another ten minutes to strip down, ignoring any night time ritual of teeth brushing and face washing, and crawl into bed.

Dane runs his hands over my back, pulling me closer to him but I cup his face and shake my head with a silent gesture that he doesn't need to 'take care of me' like we planned after the club.

I'm beyond tired and we all need sleep. I see his compliance as he blinks slowly and smiles back.

Kissing me, he whispers over my lips, "Goodnight, Poe."

I look to my right as Ethan kisses my shoulder and I dip my forehead to meet his cheek. "Goodnight, my love."

And two hours later, when I roll over, his side of the bed is empty and cold, leaving Dane and I alone again without him while his dad continues to run him into the ground.

55

ETHAN

Getting a text at 6:00 a.m. from my father on New Years day, telling me I had to report to work that morning, wasn't on my wish list this year. Nor is it something I wanted to comply with. So, I texted him reminding him that it was a holiday, yet he didn't care and told me it was the only day we could use to catch up and work on our first quarter projections.

And what he means by that is, confirming his target list of clients and all the ways we need to kiss their ass this year to gain their business.

He's been pushing me harder and harder; even with the college courses he demands even more from me every passing week. Yet, there's no compensation for anything I do other than a base salary that hardly gets me by. Especially because he takes his 'cut' of what I *owe him* and still it seems like I never make a dent in it.

I don't regret it. I don't. Hannah got the care she needed and I'm so grateful. But I fucking hate how much control he has over everything in my life now.

I pull up in the empty parking lot of our office, parking in the front because the only other car that's here is my fathers pristine baby blue Lamborghini.

Didn't Lamborghini's go out of style in like 1989? I think to myself as I forcefully keep my hand clenched in my pocket to avoid keying it as a pass by.

The building is locked so I use my key card to access the main lobby doors and take the elevator up to the top floor where his office is located.

"It's about time," my father spits out as I glance at my watch a look of confusion on my face because I'm actually five minutes early.

"What are we doing here on a holiday anyway?" My tone drips with annoyance and he snaps a glare in my direction.

"You wouldn't be in the financial predicament you're in if you put in some extra effort. Your entitled generation has no idea what it's like to work hard. Do whatever it takes to get the job done."

...whatever it takes to get the job done... I internally mimic as he says the words because he's said that more times than I care to count.

"Right. So, what do you need me to work on?" I ask, ignoring him, something I've learned to become highly proficient at.

He's always been this way but over the past few months it's gotten worse. Probably because I'm forced to work so closely with him, but he also hasn't been able to get *in* with Christian or Dane, and I think his poor-sport attitude is rearing its ugly head.

I never really understood our relationship. I mean, we've never truly had one. Life has always been about work for him. His image. Even my mother couldn't take it anymore. Not only did he only care about work but he had multiple known affairs. She stayed married and miserable until I turned eighteen, then finally left—just a few months before the accident.

"You know, I debated bringing this sensitive matter to your attention but with your attitude this morning I don't think I care about your feelings or how it will affect you and Hannah."

I sit up, my spine ramrod straight, because he has my attention now. He never talks about Hannah unless it's to remind me of her medical expenses. Frankly speaking, I know he doesn't like her. He tolerates my relationship with her. Why? I'm not sure, but I never wanted to question him about it.

"What are you talking about?" I inquire, my words slow and calculated because his body language makes me feel completely on edge.

"I knew I didn't trust her. That she would betray you the moment she had the chance," he says, shaking his head as if disappointed.

But that's the thing. He's never worried about anyone but himself so his behavior is...weird.

"I was told Dane would be at Afterburn last night so I decided to go."

Oh fuck. Fuck. Fuck. Fuck.

He pulls out his phone, tapping on the screen then angles it in my direction. My eyes saucer out of my head as I hold my breath.

"He was there with your girlfriend. Hands all over her, kissing her." My fathers voice is oddly calm, almost kind. It sets me on edge even more. He's never kind, especially about my feelings.

"I snapped these pictures and left because I'd seen enough after that."

I peer down at his phone and the picture is of Dane and Hannah standing in the viewing area next to the stage. I must have left to check on the room already because my father swipes through and it's just the two of them.

Dane wrapping his arm around her waist, kissing her neck.

Swipe.

Dane using his fingers to tilt her chin so he can kiss her lips. *Swipe.*

Dane having his eyes only on my girl and taking care of her while I'm getting us a room.

He swipes again and this time it's Dane, his face exposed as he lifts his mask, peering down at his phone with a smirk as he texts me back. A glint of pure joy in his eyes as he responds and it takes everything in me not to smile.

"I didn't think anything of it, until I saw her hideous scar and I knew immediately who it was. He's fucking your girlfriend, Ethan. Stealing her from right under your nose."

I pause, trying to articulate words. How do I tell him? How do I tell him we're all involved? I want to spit out the words, *I'm bisexual.* They're there. *Right there.*

My heart rate picks up as my pulse pounds in my ears. I swallow thickly, taking in a deep breath. I need to tell him, there's no other way.

This is the first time he's shown any concern for me, for something that could affect me so dramatically. He seems worried about me, like he's on my side. I still feel skeptical though.

"It's not what you think," the words come out a whisper that he doesn't even hear.

"He's fucking one of his students. That's a huge problem for him." He pauses and I almost blurt out my secret. I open my mouth but he quickly spits out, "It's great for us."

"What?" I reply, confused.

"He's fucking a student. If that gets out it will destroy his reputation and credibility. Hannah will be ruined, she'll lose her course credits and will need to start over—if any other University will even let her in."

I'm stunned as I take in his words. He's not concerned for me or worried about Hannah. His words are sharp, confident. Intentional.

"I don't think he cares much about Hannah, but he sure as hell wouldn't want this getting out. We'll be using this to our advantage," he states, factually as if were part of a strategy in his first quarter projection report.

Jesus Christ. I knew my father was a horrible, disgusting man. I never knew he would go to these lengths, ruining everyone around him solely for his own benefit.

"You can't do that," are the only words I can manage to muster as my thought process explodes into a sea of confusion.

How do I stop this?

If I tell him the three of us are...What are we? A thing? Together? In love?

That will make it worse. He'll think Dane coerced me into being with him sexually. He'll attach whatever is owed on Hannah's medical expenses to her and I hate the stress that will put on her. If he does all this I won't have to work for him.

A brief moment of relief passes through me knowing I won't be stuck under my father's thumb, controlled by him. He won't be able to hang the money over my head but I hate how selfish that makes me feel.

That makes me just like him.

My scowl is unavoidable as he snaps his neck in my direction.

"I can do whatever the fuck I want!" Thankfully the office is empty, otherwise everyone in the building would have heard him. "I'm going to the Dean with this."

"Wait. Don't." I put my hands up. Everything Hannah worked on this semester, her perfect grade, diminished and everything she stands for, ruined. "I can get him to work with us...with you, without any of this."

A moment passes between us as he contemplates my words. A look of disgust passes over his face. "You're weak for her son. Women aren't worth it."

"Just let me take care of it. Give me a week."

He pauses again. Appraising me. He's right. I'm weak for Hannah. For Dane. I'm weak but not in the way he thinks. I just need time to figure out how to get out of this mess without anyone getting hurt. Specifically Hannah and Dane.

"Your classes start back up next week?" he asks.

I nod.

It's the last semester. We don't have Dane's class anymore, he's teaching the same course to a new group of students, but Hannah still has two more courses that she needs credits for. I have just one more.

"Get his accounts here with us in a week and I won't say anything about this. But that doesn't mean you should let this go. Once a cheater, always a cheater."

You would know.

"I'll get it done," I say with an undeniable confidence.

He smirks. "That's the spirit I've been looking for."

56

HANNAH

"Are you sure we shouldn't just go check on him? It's been two days," Dane asks me as he looks at the clock again.

It's past 9:00 p.m. and Dane's right. It's been two full days. Both days, he left before the sun came up and didn't come home until we're in bed.

He was gone again this morning, even though I set my alarm to try and catch him before he left.

Am I worried about Ethan? Yes, I am. More so than ever recently. He's been acting unusually strange lately and the stress he's carrying is something I've never seen.

But I also know that if you push him too early, he'll retreat further.

I've been through phases of time where it's exactly what he needs, time. But something about this is different. It's like his father is slowly draining the soul from his body.

"We already agreed. Give him three days. Don't say anything, just let him work through it for now."

"Well, I'm not a patient man. So I'm going to be a really big pain in your ass for the rest of the day. Then tomorrow I'll be a pain in his ass for putting us through this."

"Great. I have two pain-in-the-asses to deal with now."

"Hey, you take that back, woman." He plops down next to me on the couch and attempts to tickle my feet, but I pull them back, smacking his hands.

We laugh for a second but the laughter dies down quickly, as it's been lately because we know something is going on and we both know it's time to intervene with him.

I told Dane that I felt like there was something I was missing with Ethan. Before the accident our lives revolved around each other and baseball. There wasn't a lot of pressure from his dad. Don't get me wrong, he's always been a jerk and he never supported Ethan's love for the game.

I never understood why. Not only was he physically the best player on his team, he literally knew everything about baseball. He was every dad's dream.

Yet his father still berated him, telling him that baseball was for kids and not a real job, reminding him he had a family name to live up to. You would think Russo on the back of a jersey playing professional baseball would make him proud, but to Edward Russo it's always been about him and his company.

The worst part about the accident wasn't losing my voice. It was losing the man I loved and seeing his passion whither away to nothing.

I hate that he feels like his only option is his father but after this recent set of demands he's been pulling, I've had enough. I'd rather him work minimum wage doing something he loves than work for a man like him. Father or not, nobody should have to deal with what Ethan has been putting up with.

Dane's phone buzzes in his pocket and he sits up quickly as he slides it out. The corner of his lip ticks up and I know by the look on his gleeful face it's Ethan.

57

DANE

I can't express the happiness I feel when I get a text message from Ethan because this sexy-as-sin master grump doesn't really text anyone. Except Hannah of course.

He loves two things. Hannah and baseball. That much I know for certain. But lately, I feel a bit of that love, too.

Then I see the text and question all of my previous thoughts.

Ethan: Can I ask you a question?

Text messages like this set me on edge. Because lately, he's been so unpredictable. I suck in a deep breath and reply as nonchalantly as possible.

Me: Shoot.

Ethan: Would you ever work with my father?
Allow him to manage your portfolio?

I squint at my phone screen, rereading the words. That's an odd question. I've never said exactly how I feel about Edward to Ethan out of respect. But I think he knows how much I don't like him just by my natural response to him.

If I like someone, I'm all in. Things click into place and a friendship blooms easily and that's how I've met most of my friends who I consider family. None of that happened when I met Edward Russo and the most entertaining thing about that dinner we had with him, was how Ethan fell apart for me, coming in a napkin under the table while his father was none the wiser.

A favorite memory of mine, but not because of his dad.

In fact, I have nothing good to say about that man.

I glance over at Hannah and she's appraising me, worry laced behind those gorgeous blue eyes of hers.

"He's asking if I'd ever let his father manage my money."

"*That's weird.*"

"Yeah...." Very weird.

This is so unlike Ethan. He doesn't care about accounts or portfolios. Money isn't a driving factor. It never has been.

A wave of nausea hits me. Why didn't I see it before? I've been taken advantage of in the past, used for my money and connections. I never thought someone I cared about would be tempted into betrayal for the same reason.

I hate the idea of someone I love being put in a situation like that and my hatred for Edward Russo instantly skyrockets.

Then it hits me.

The man at Afterburn that ran off the moment I looked in his direction.

It was his father.

Shit.

I hate myself for not recognizing him sooner. I know to be more mindful of that kind of shit and I hate that I've brought them into this. I shouldn't have gotten involved with them again. My lack of willpower is putting him in this situation with his father and Hannah is risking everything she's been working so hard for.

So, I reply back with the only truth I have.

> Me: If you needed me to, I would.

Dots pop up as he types a reply, then they disappear. This repeats for a solid minute.

Fuck, this is excruciating.

Bubbles come up, then fade off.

I type out, *you good?* Then erase it. *What's up?* Delete. *Talk to me.* Delete.

"Ah, fuck it," I spit out, then lean down giving Hannah a kiss. "I'll be back."

58

ETHAN

I knew that would be his answer. I knew that if I just asked Dane he would bring his accounts to my father without any questions asked.

But I'm still speechless.

Not that I'm asking him. I would never allow him to give my father access to his money, but the confirmation that he would do it for me is all the assurance I need that I'm making the right decision.

I've worked endless hours every day since the meeting with my father. I've been waiting until I know they're sleeping before finally returning home. Then setting my alarm early, leaving for the office before they wake up. I told them I'm taking advantage of the time since we don't have classes until next week.

I'm partially avoiding them so I don't rope them into the mess I'm in, but really I've spent all my time digging deep into Russo and Company, finding everything my father doesn't want me to know.

And what I've found is enough to turn the tables of blackmail right back on him.

I've printed a stack of documents, proof of the money he's

skimming from his clients accounts and the past five years of tax returns that don't match his altered bank account statements and 1099 forms.

I've managed to locate locked files in our shared folders and found so much incriminating evidence of money laundering and tax evasion, it physically makes me sick.

Sure, I owe him money for Hannah's surgeries and I'll pay him back every penny. But, I'd rather do it with dignity. At this point, the hardest part will be telling Hannah I lied to her about her medical expenses and took them on without her knowing about it.

She'll be pissed that I didn't tell her. She'll be even more pissed that I indebted myself to him because she's always disliked him.

I second guess myself for a moment, knowing I'll be coming clean to her with a mountain of debt, no steps for my next plan, and unemployed.

The anxiety of the unknown laces through me and it's completely overwhelming. But, it's better than building my life around his terms.

I finish typing out my resignation letter and click 'Save', the company secured documents folder pops open and as I move my mouse over to the confirmation box, one of the subfolder titles catches my eye.

Ridgeway.

"Ridgeway...Ridgeway," I hum as I repeat the word out loud because it looks familiar. Clicking the folder open. It prompts for a password and I use the one my dad always uses: Ca$hMoney! A list of PDF icons appear, all named Parker—Hannah's last name—with a date in ascending order.

I hold CTRL-A and tap enter, opening all the documents at once, the most recent one stacked and visible on top.

It's a letter from the insurance company. Ridgeway was the

insurance company that my father said denied the claims for Hannah's care.

I skim through the document dated four years earlier, a few months after her last surgery.

The words *submission, claim*, and *granted* blind me like the light from a thousand suns.

"Holy shit." I tap through the other documents, skimming over all of them.

He lied about it all. He may have had to pay for her care initially, but the insurance company covered *everything*. All he ever showed me was bank statements showing all the debits from when he paid out the hospital bills and doctors offices. I never assumed it was covered because that's exactly what he told me.

And I fucking believed him. I scold myself wondering why I never thought to question him.

My father left for lunch a short while ago so I know I have at least thirty minutes before he returns.

I quickly click back into my email, type in my father's address, and before I can overthink anything, I hit send. Attaching my resignation letter along with zip drive folders with proof of all the illegal shit he's been doing.

I have no intention of using them against him, not right now at least. I just need to leave without a fight from him or any other repercussions.

Selecting all the documents, I print them all so I have copies for myself, then remove them from the base of the printer and tuck them in a folder inside my backpack.

Knock. Knock.

"Shit." I zip up my backpack and pop up from behind my desk.

"Come in," my voice is raspy as I call out. Because it could only be two people, my father—I really should have checked if he was still gone before sending that email—or Sarah, our receptionist.

Thankfully, Sarah pops her head through the opening of the door, announcing herself as she walks through it.

"Mr. Russo, Dane Campbell is here to see you. He insists you had an appointment but I don't see anything on the calendar."

I'm stunned because we didn't have an appointment. I know he's probably confused and curious about my last text message but I didn't expect him to show up here. My heart flutters at the idea that he cares enough to be here.

"No worries, send him in."

Sarah hardly has one foot out the door when I hear his voice; he must have been waiting just outside the door.

"Thank you, Sarah," Dane says, the velvet sound of his charming, professional voice runs through me like lava.

Standing, I walk around my desk and lean on the front of it, crossing my arms over my chest.

He shuts the door, and stares at the lock on the handle for a moment before turning around and making his way toward me.

"We didn't have an appointment," I say flatly.

"I know."

"So, what are you doing here?" I smother the smirk that wants to make an appearance because he looks adorable as he glances around my office. It's the first time he's been here and it's like he's taking in all the little details.

"I missed you."

That forces a chuckle out of me. His tone is factual. Certain. He just doesn't care if you don't like what he says or how he says it, he's going to say it anyway. I love that about him. I love a lot of things about him.

"We both miss you a lot, actually. I just came here to tell you that," he adds.

I've seen Hannah blush over his words, more times that I

can count. I've never been good with praise or compliments, but Dane's honesty has always flooded me with a warmth I've never understood.

Even from behind that damn glory hole wall, he went out of his way to make me feel comfortable. He's been doing that since the moment we met.

"So, did you make a bad investment?" he asks.

Pressing my lips into a flat line, I shake my head.

"Secretary run off with one of your employees and a large sum of money from a client's account?"

I smirk and shake my head no.

"Did your father discover something and he's holding it over your head unless I agree to work with him?"

My eyes snap to his and I freeze.

He doesn't have to say anything, he just nods. A slow, accepting up and down gesture with his neck as if he's dissecting my silent response.

"You got that all from one text?"

He shrugs.

"I am a genius, you know."

Smug bastard.

"He wouldn't be my first choice, but like I said, if *you* needed me to, I would."

Key word, *needed*, not wanted.

"Do you need me to?" he asks as he steps into my space, standing only an inch or two away.

His usual bright blue eyes are shadowed by concern. He knows something has been going on, but has respected me enough not to pry. Unlike his normal behavior of pushing on everything.

It's practically a silent declaration of love for Dane.

"I would never let you." I wrap my hand around the back of his neck and pull him into me, crashing my lips against his because I've avoided them for the past few days and I hate myself for it.

"Mmmm." A moan gets caught in his throat.

"Did Hannah tell you to come?" I ask, between kisses.

He nods. "Sort of. I was going to come on New Year's Day but she told me to give you space. She said three days. We compromised on two. Then I got your weird ass text and came right after."

I can't help but chuckle knowing they were negotiating the approach. I love how well they know me.

"I told her I would bring you home. She still owes us for New Years Eve, you know? She's probably naked on the bed waiting for us."

"She has a lot of faith in your negotiating skills."

"She should." This time he kisses me, palming my erection behind my black dress pants and I can't help but groan into this mouth.

He grips onto the front of my shirt, pulling me even closer. "Stop pushing us away."

"I know, but I already figured it out."

"Of course you did, you stubborn brute." He kisses me again. "What's the plan and do I need my attorney or my shovel?"

I laugh, a deep, hearty laugh as I throw my head back. "You don't own a fucking shovel."

"No, but I'll buy a gold plated one for the occasion if you want."

"I just quit." I spit out the words and it feels fucking liberating. His body stills, mid-kiss. "I have no idea what I'm going to do but I can't work for him anymore and now I have no reason to continue."

He pulls back, taking me in. His eyes bounce between mine then a slow, sexy smile spreads across his face.

"Need me to be your sugar daddy? Because that's my kind of investment."

"Oh, shut up." I roll my eyes and lean in to kiss him again.

"Fine, but will you tell me the reason why you *had* to work for him?"

He finishes just as my office door flies open, banging against the back wall.

"What the fuck is going on?" My fathers voice tears through us as we pull apart, both our necks whiplashing toward the door.

59

ETHAN

"Were you two just kissing?" my father asks incredulously with disgust, as he stands frozen in the doorway of my office.

"Is this the part where I get my shovel?" Dane whispers and somehow I manage to hide my amusement as I side-eye my father.

He's more frazzled than I expected him to be. His hair is unusually unkempt, his tie is crooked, and there's a mustard stain on his shirt. He's got a white knuckle grip on his phone and I imagine it's my resignation letter on the screen behind it.

I wasn't prepared to have this conversation face-to-face, especially with Dane here, but I suppose I should have expected it.

Nothing about what has happened since the accident has been in my favor. The healing process, physically and emotionally, losing everything baseball related and relearning how to communicate with Hannah. It was all so debilitating. Working for my father was the only option and, at least, it finally got him off my back.

"Is the only reason you wanted me to work for you purely

because it made you look better? Like you were some present, stand-up dad and family man?" I ask, ignoring his previous questions.

His lips curl up into a scowl. He's always hated when anyone talks back to him and my disobedience is skyrocketing him to another level of fury.

"If it weren't for me you would have nothing. You would *be* nothing. I won't be the father with the deadbeat, no-good son who does nothing but daydreams about playing a silly game with his useless life. I won't let you embarrass me and run the image of my name into the dirt."

"So instead of loving and supporting me through the most difficult time in my life, you lied about the medical expenses so I'd have no choice but to work for you. Just so I wouldn't make you look *bad*."

"If I didn't do what I did, you would already be a washed up baseball player with nothing but his memories of the MLB draft and his days in the pros. Baseball is not a career."

"It wasn't your fucking decision!" I scream. Never in my life have I yelled at my father.

"Hiring that driver to hit your car was the best decision I ever made for you." I flinch, as if his words are bricks launched at me with nothing but a paper shield to defend myself.

The room goes eerily silent as his eyes blow wide with his confession.

"What the fuck did you just say?" Dane asks, as he turns his gaze to him.

I'm trembling but stunned solid. It feels as if my soul has catapulted from my body and I'm living outside of myself.

He did that?

My mind speeds through memories of that night. The lights, the ear-splitting squealing of the rubber on asphalt that I still hear when I close my eyes. Hannah's last words, shrieking my name, as I held my hand out over her body in a last attempt to protect her, before the crunch of the metal and the airbags deployed.

A shard of the dashboard panel blew out in some once-in-a-lifetime, rare instance. It cut straight through my hand and into Hannah's neck.

The doctors said if it weren't for my hand taking part of the damage, she would have died on impact. My hand—and coincidingly losing my baseball career—saved her life.

I've lived with guilt my entire life. Wondering how I could have done things differently. How I could have avoided him. But it was inevitable. All because my father made a decision to make it so.

He couldn't control me or my decisions so he eliminated it the only way he knew how.

The structure and routine I have to have in my life, I know I get from him. The need to have a schedule and always be in control. I always viewed that as a good quality, but now I hate it. I hate that I'm rigid like him. I don't want to be anything like him.

I splay open my palm, the skin still tight and tender from the scar as I appraise my hand.

I have no regrets. I never have. But I can't say I'll be able to stop myself from killing my father right now.

"You don't see it now, but I saved you from a life of misery, son. A life of chasing a dream that most never achieve. They end up as drug addicts and homeless, sitting around a bonfire under a freeway talking about their glory days. That would have been you."

I clench my fist and step toward him.

Dane steps in front of me, blocking my view of my father and my anger gets the best of me.

As if it has a mind of its own, my arm cannons forward, my scarred hand cupping around his neck as I slam him against the wall.

"You touch him, you know what he'll do." His voice is hoarse from my grip.

"I'm not going to touch him, I'm going to kill him." My chest heaves and my breath is shaking. "He did this. He fucking did this! And Hannah..." I grind my teeth together, squeezing my hand tighter.

Years. For years my father has manipulated me, guilt tripped me, blackmailed me into an unavoidable life in an effort to control my every decision. He physically hurt me. Hannah. Hurdled me onto a path only he could steer. All because he cares so fucking much about his image. Everything is boiling over. I can feel the rage in my bones, all the emotions I've pushed down, the wall is finally breaking and the wrath is inevitable.

Dane's face reddens, the pink flush turns to a deeper shade of red bringing out the blue in his eyes that match Hannah's, and not just in color, but in the way he appraises me. The way the similar shade of cerulean gives me the comfort I've always needed.

He gazes at me without pity, without concern for himself but in pure admiration. Like he accepts every single part of me. The good, the bad, the scarred part of my physical body and soul.

His tight jaw slacks open, sucking in air as I soften my hold.

I lower my hand as my gaze drops to the ground, but he cups my face and he looks deeper into my eyes, pulling me back into the present. He always seems to know exactly what I need, how to get me centered. Just like Hannah.

The realization of how perfect they both are in balancing me out hits me square in the chest and suddenly I want nothing more than to do what's best for them. For us.

"If you hurt him, you know what that starts, you know what kind of man he is and what he'll try to do to you. I'm all in, whatever you decide...but think about Hannah."

I lost everything that night including the power and control over my own life. All my decisions were forced by my fathers deceit and manipulation. Finally getting a little bit of that back is wildly dangerous and I can't help but smile. It's wide and mischievous, odd for me considering I hardly ever smile.

Dane looks terrified by this fact. He pushes himself further into the wall, as if it will swallow him whole. But I yank him against me, pressing our bodies together and kiss him like it's the only thing that's going to stop me from losing myself in this mess.

It's all teeth and tongue and I love how he instantly melts into me. In his past relationships I know he's been the one to always take the lead and be in control. But he's always been mindful of my hesitation and curiosity. My uncertainty has set the dynamics in the relationship between the three of us and now all I can think about is giving him all of me, however he needs.

"Jesus fucking christ." My father shifts uncomfortably in his stance, repulsed by our actions and I love how much I'm setting him off.

"I'm done here," I tell Dane and he smiles back at me, turning back to my dad I give him a smug as hell look and it feels fucking freeing.

I round my desk, grab my bag, then tilt my head to Dane as we head toward the exit.

My father steps forward attempting to block my exit. "Where you do you think you're—"

Dane takes a large stride toward him, pulling back his fist, slamming it directly into my father's face. His grunt vibrates through the room as he hits the ground with a hard thud.

"You're lucky he didn't tell me to get my shovel," Dane says as he steps over him, then leans down and adds, "Oh, and don't try anything stupid. My attorney will fucking destroy you." He palms his face, patting his cheek in the most condescending gesture of dominance.

Fuck, that turns me on.

"Come on, lover," Dane says cheerfully like he's been waiting a lifetime to slap that title on me.

I glance down at my father one last time, because after this I'll never see him again. Not in person and not intentionally at least.

I crouch down next to him. He props himself up on his elbows, blood drips from his nose and over his lips. A piece of lint sits on the corner of his blood spattered tie and I pick it off, flicking it on the floor. "Did you see the files I sent to you?"

His scowl deepens. "Yes."

"You know what will happen if you ever come near me or Hannah or Dane, right?"

His Adam's apple bobs as he swallows thickly, taking in my question with the seriousness it deserves.

"Yes," he spits through his teeth, hating his words.

"Good." I stand, wiping myself off as if being so close to him could have rubbed off on me, leaving an invisible layer of filth.

"Oh, and you should know. I love cock. Specifically his." I point at Dane. "So, when your friends question you after seeing pictures of all of us together, know that not only is he *our* boyfriend, but tonight I'm going to bottom for him and love every single second of it."

If I wasn't dead to him before, I sure am now.

It's my turn to step over him as I walk out of the prison cell I've been living in and the invisible weighted vest I've been wearing for the past few years is instantly stripped off.

Even though I have no idea what I'm going to do, I'm met with the sensation of true freedom and an overwhelming amount of relief that I haven't felt in a long time.

Our strides are quick as we exit down the hall and into the

elevator. The moment the doors merge shut, Dane is on me, using his entire body to pin me against the wall.

"I'm so goddamn hard from that." His erection presses into me as his hips roll over mine. "I especially liked the part when you said you were going to bottom for me," he runs his lips against my five o'clock shadow, hovering over my ear, "But, my cock isn't going anywhere near your sexy ass until you're good and ready and begging me for it."

60

HANNAH

"I still can't believe we're here," Ethan says with the excitement of a toddler on Christmas morning, his eyes gleaming with joy as he takes in the Seattle Smashers spring training field. Dane and I share a look and a smile because the last month has been an adjustment for him as he's navigated through the fallout with his father and his newfound freedom.

It was inevitable in my opinion. Even though we had no idea his father was behind the accident nor did I ever think he was capable of such a thing, Ethan couldn't go on living like he was.

The constant demands and control over everything was unbearable. The day they came home together and he told me everything, it was like a long overdue therapy session. Over the last couple years we had talked about the accident here and there, but more than anything we avoided that topic. He finally opened up in a way he never had before.

I hated that he took on the burden of my so-called medical expenses. He was the driver, it was his insurance, I never questioned anything. He told me he was taking care of it and he did because he always has. Even though I hate that he hid every-thing from me, I know why he did.

Now, I glance between the two men that have my whole heart and I can't help but feel so much love I might actually explode. They both take care of me—and each other—in different ways and everything about us just works.

"Hudson!" Dane calls out, getting Hudson Byrnes' attention as he jogs past us on the field. He slows as his head turns in our direction, smiles, then walks toward us.

"Hey! I'm so glad you guys made it." Hudson and Dane slap palms and Dane leans over the barrier giving him a sort of bro hug.

Both Dane and Ethan are tall, but Hudson feels like he towers over them both. I swear he looks like some type of juggernaut decked out in his catcher's gear.

"Thanks for the invite. We snuck out of class to be here." Dane wiggles his eyebrows at us like we're playing hooky in junior high, but really we're on a planned absence.

We went to the Dean when school returned to session and told him we were all dating. Dane offered to quit but the Dean refused, knowing how impactful Dane was the first semester.

We explained everything to him, even how we met in Paris and I think he may have had some type of minor heart attack when we tried to define our unique relationship, but he composed himself enough to figure out how to get through the last semester without the school board getting on our case.

All my assignments were assigned to three different profes-sors and re-graded. I also had to retake the final so that they felt comfortable with allowing my full credit for the class.

After the reevaluation of everything, I ended up with an even higher grade.

Can't say I didn't gloat about that for a few days.

Ethan didn't have to do any of it because he dropped his last class and decided to not go for his masters. He could have continued but I think that was a final *fuck you* to his father and I supported whatever he felt like he needed to do.

I wanted him to focus on what he wanted for himself. It was the first time he's had a choice and I'm grateful that he's taking the chance on himself. He's applied to different accounting and financial jobs that I think he feels is the right thing to do for us, but I'm not sold that it's something he really wants.

It's comfortable and something he knows how to do, but it doesn't set his soul on fire. That's what I want for him.

We know we're staying in Seattle because Baker VanBuren has offered me a position at VB Technologies after I graduate. I'm going to lead the project with my ASL platform and I couldn't be happier with the outcome. I get to continue to work on my code, building the platform and utilizing the resources of one of the biggest tech companies in the world.

Win-win for me and more than I could have ever dreamed of.

Hudson steps toward Ethan, giving him the same palm slap and chest bump over the railing between the field and the stands.

"We're warming up for the exhibition game against the Dust Devils and they've got some young hot catcher from their minor league playing today. Jett James. Have you heard of him?" he asks Ethan.

"Jett James is...here?" Ethan glances around the field. "His speed, power, and arm strength is unmatched. He even had a higher RBI than you did when you were in the minors and outranked—"

"Okay, okay, that's enough of that. Come on. Jump over the railing. You're coming to the dugout," Hudson says, waving him over, already heading that direction.

Ethan eyes blow wide as he looks at both of us in shock, then swings two legs over the railing as he jumps onto the field.

He breathes out a stuttered breath as he looks down at his

feet, rubbing the souls into the dirt, then back at us with a boyish expression. "It's been a long time since I've been on a field."

"*GO,*" I sign with a smile as I tip my chin up at Hudson who's already half way to the dugout.

"Love you guys," he screams back as he jogs forward to Hudson. I watch the way his body moves and I'm met with the flashback of seeing him on the field like when I used to watch his games.

He doesn't have a uniform on but he looks just as good. It's the way his jeans hug every part of his thick legs and the back muscles that peek through, even under the dense fabric of his Smasher's jersey. Then, when I think he can't get any sexier, he grabs the rim of his hat, turning it backwards as he always would the moment he dips into the shade of the dugout.

Old habits die hard I suppose.

"Ethan on a baseball field might be my new favorite sight," Dane says, his eyes glued to his ass before he rounds the corner into the dugout. "I bet we'll get to see more of it." He winks, like he's up to no good. But before I can ask, he grabs my waist, hoisting me closer to him and we plop down on the seat with me in his lap.

He gently grips my chin, pulling my eyes to his and I feel so grateful for how far we've come and what he's done for us. Just by being him.

I press my lips to his and he moans, as he usually does when we kiss. He always says how much he loves my sounds, but I crave his just as much.

When it's both him band Ethan, well that's a melody I'll never be able to live without.

He deepens the kiss, pulling me closer to him and I feel so alive, so fulfilled in every aspect of my life. Because I might be silent, but with these two, I feel so heard.

I pull away, giving him a curious look.

"So...what's going on?"

"Nothing."

But the smug look on his face as he avoids my eye contact tells me he's a big fat liar.

61

ETHAN

The sensation of being back in a dugout, players squeezing by, patting each other on the ass or fist-bumping as they walk by brings back core memories that leave nothing but a smile on my face and the entirety of my soul full.

I never got the chance to come to spring training, as a player or spectator, so all of this is overwhelming in the best way.

But as I walk toward the head coach of the Seattle Smash-ers, a step behind Hudson, my throat constricts and it feels more like sandpaper than an esophagus.

He's known to be a complete hardass. Tough on his players but will fight harder than anyone for each and every one of them.

"Don't let him intimidate you, he's a straight shooter but a big softie." I don't have time to respond before Hudson is calling for his attention. "Coach Raymer, this is Ethan Russo, the guy I told you about."

Holy shit, Hudson Byrnes has talked about *me*...to the head Coach of the Smashers.

My blood pressure goes through the roof and I can feel my heart beating behind my eyeballs. How I manage to hold out my hand and give him a normal shake, as I tell him it's great to meet him, is beyond me.

"Hudson tells me you're a baseball encyclopedia?" he asks, I think, but I'm not sure I'm supposed to answer.

"I—I—"

For being referenced as an encyclopedia I sure have a lack of vocabulary.

"He's a wealth of knowledge, knows more than anyone I've ever met. I think John should give him a run." Hudson speaks for me.

What's a run? What the hell does that mean?

"My Head Analyst just told me he's retiring next year. I've had a few people in mind for his replacement but," he places his hands on his hips like he's trying to make his point clear, "I took a chance on Hudson here and he says I should take a chance on you."

My jaw drops as my head swivels toward Hudson. Is he serious? Was that another question or do I just keep my mouth shut. Hudson's lopsided grin and raised eyebrows as he nods, silently urging me to reply tells me he's not joking.

Is this really happening? I run my hand over the back of my neck and grip hard. Jesus, this is a dream. This has to be a dream.

"I—" I'm cut off by Coach again but I don't care, it's better he talks than me because I have no idea what nonsense will fly out of my mouth.

"If you're open to it, you'll shadow him for ninety days. We'll hire you as our Assistant Analyst this year and if John gives you the green light, you'll replace him as Head Analyst next year."

"Yes, sir. Of course, I'm more than up for it," I reply with more confidence than I feel.

"Great." He pats me on the shoulder with his left hand and holds out his right for a gentleman's shake.

I slide my scarred hand into his and he peers down at it, turning our shake to the side as he inspects the top of my hand.

"I read up on you, even saw some old clips of when you played. It's a shame what happened. You had a bright future." I give him a tight-lipped smile because he's right. I did. But something tells me this new one might be even better.

62

DANE

"Hey Dandelion." My voice is shaky, a mix of restrained tears and nerves bubbling up in my throat.

I crouch down, picking off stray pieces of grass as I wipe my hand over the top of the grey headstone clearing off the excess grime.

It's been a long time, too long, since I've visited. Not because I haven't wanted to or don't think about Celeste. Being tied down with a job for an entire school year and the addition of Hannah and Ethan moving in with me, life has been busy. Absolutely amazing, but busier.

"I've been thinking about you a lot." My squat turns into a seat as I plop down in the grass next to the front of her tombstone.

The last time I visited was before the school year started, but after Paris. I was still confused about my feelings on Ethan and Hannah then. I felt more heartbreak than happiness at the time with how they left and, frankly speaking, I never thought I'd see them again.

So the last thing I told Celeste was that I met two phenomenal people in Paris that I couldn't stop thinking about. A dumbed down version of the truth at the time.

This time. I tell her everything.

The anonymous meeting at the glory hole—I chuckle because she would get a kick out of that. Then the fortuitous way we chose the same hostel. The days in Paris that were some of my favorite of all-time. How they left because of a really big misunderstanding, or the fact that they thought I was a complete lunatic by buying out the hostel.

Not far from the truth.

I share everything with her, just like I always did.

"I miss you." My words are nothing but a whisper. I squeeze my eyes tightly and swallow thickly. "Is it normal to feel guilty about finding love again?" I toss my head back and forth. "I suppose it is or I suppose nothing is normal. But, they're amazing. I'm so in love with both of them and I feel so goddamn lucky because I never thought I'd find one person to love again, much less two."

I smile, knowing she'd be smiling back.

I glance over my shoulder, Hannah and Ethan lean on the rental car that we got at the airport. We flew here only for the day since it was Ethan's only non game day in weeks. I've been wanting to do this for a long time.

I wave them over and they immediately push themselves off the back of the car and head toward me.

Hannah kneels down in the grass next me while Ethan places his hand on my shoulder standing on the other side of me.

"Guys, this is Celeste. Celeste, meet Hannah and Ethan." Those are all the words I can muster—the worst introduction of all time—but Hannah starts signing to her, smiling like she's talking to someone that can read ASL.

She's animated and giddy, recapping how we met. Telling her everything I already shared with her but her version is even better and it's the most beautiful thing I've ever witnessed.

Ethan squats down next me, smiling and he's been doing so much more of that lately it makes me feel so goddamn happy.

I never thought I'd be here, like this, happy. Especially in front of the headstone of the person I thought was my only chance at love.

"Celeste." Ethan clears his throat as he looks at his watch.

Old habits die hard I guess.

"We don't have as much time as we'd like but we promise we'll come back and visit again soon." There's a brief pause as he looks between us, and then down at the stone. "A legal marriage might not be in the cards for us, but we're committed to each other like we are, and I promise you we'll always look out for him."

Well, fuck.

Tears well up at the bottom of my eyelids and I blink them away, turning my head away from the two people that have stolen every ounce of what was left of my heart in the most astonishing way.

As my vision clears, a couple walks in the distance, a little blonde girl at their side stops and looks our way. She must be five or six, the same age I met Celeste and it instantly brings me back, and I can't help the smile that spreads across my face.

Apparently that was like an invitation for her because the little girl beelines in our direction leaving, who I assume are her parents, behind and walks directly up to me.

Her smile is so big her gums are showing and her eyes squint as if she's purposely trying to make it even bigger. Then, she lifts her hand, a yellow bloomed dandelion between her two little fingers. It flops over in my direction and my stomach jumps to my heart at the serendipitous gesture.

"Holy shit," I whisper out as Hannah covers her jaw-slacked mouth with her hand.

The little girl gasps, "You said a bad word. Don't worry I won't tell."

I'm too fucking stunned to say anything. I should be apologizing because that's probably going to be her new favorite word she says on repeat.

"Bridget! Bridget," her parents come running up in a frantic mess. "Oh my god, I'm so sorry."

Ethan stands and waves, nodding with a smile, telling them it was no problem.

Bridget pushes the flower closer to me and I take it between my fingers. "Thank you." She smiles again, then turns back away to walk with her parents.

I glance over at a stupefied Hannah and Ethan as we watch them leave, then down at Celeste's name engraved in the granite stone.

"Well, Dandelion, it looks like I'm due for another tattoo." I twirl the flower between my fingers and glance between the three loves of my life, knowing the bloomed dandelion will be a perfect addition to the other side of my back.

EPILOGUE
DANE

"What do you get the guy that has everything?" Ethan says as he hands me a small gift wrapped box with a tiny ribbon that decorates the top.

"Did Hannah wrap this?" I ask because it looks way too pristine and matchy.

"I did, asshole." He tosses the box in my lap and takes the seat next to me. "I'm actually really good at wrapping," he adds, offended.

"I'm impressed. If it doesn't work out with the Smashers, you could definitely work full time as a professional gift wrapper."

But we all know it's going to work out just fine for him because in the short few weeks he's proven to be a huge asset with everything he knows and even assists the batting coach some days. He's been the happiest I've ever seen. It's a stark contrast compared to when he was working for his father, trapped in that prison of an office.

I can relate. I couldn't work a regular nine to five either and never plan to, nor can I stay in one place too long. Which is why I'll be figuring out what sounds exciting to dive into next after my teaching stint is over.

Ethan rolls his gorgeous dark eyes at me, a typical response no matter how deep we get into our relationship because, apparently, I just bring that out in him. But I love every bit of that eye roll. Hannah sits down beside me and gestures to me to open the box.

Okay, they're both anxious for me to open it.

Picking up the box, I hold it to my ear and shake it as I side-eye a look at Hannah.

"Hmmmm, what could it be?" I shake it some more and their impatience is showing as I weigh between my fingers and sniff the box.

"Just open it already."

"Okay, fine...fine." I raise my arms up in surrender.

There's a tiny card tied in between the ribbon, roped through a small hole in the corner. I spread the paper apart and read it.

"Do you remember what you said in Paris?" I whisper out loud.

Okay, I said a lot of things in Paris. I glance between them as I tear open the wrapping blindly then pop open the plain black box.

"A bottle of lube?" I state questioningly.

Then my eyebrows raise in realization. "Oh! A bottle of luuube," I state with more gusto. Then lower my voice and repeat what I said in Paris.

"He who holds the lube, gets to top."

"Does this mean what I think it means?" I ask Ethan, as I actually hold the lube.

Avoiding my gaze he shifts in his chair and I sit up closer.

"I told you I wouldn't until you were good and ready. Begging me for it," I remind him because I don't want him to do this because I want it. I want him to do it because he wants it.

"I want it," he says quickly, with more breath than words and almost inaudible.

"Say what?" I tilt my neck to the side, cupping my hand around my ear.

"*Dane,*" Hannah signs as a warning, but I just wink at her because I know he'll never *beg*. But I'm damn well going to get him flustered enough to demand it.

"I'm ready." His voice is tight, like that adonis fucking jawline of his that I immediately fell in love with.

"Mmmmm," I squeak out, "I don't know, doesn't really seem like it."

"I swear to god." Ethan presses into his heels and without even fully standing, he's hovering over me. He palms my chest, sinking me further into the soft cushions of the couch. He seems massive in this state, but I smile and wave the lube in front of his face, reminding him.

"You better fuck me, I'm tired of you making me wait. Fucking do it already." His lips are close to mine and I smile, the thin skin brushing over his with the movement.

"That's more like it," I reply, slipping around him to stand, as I make a beeline for the bedroom. We need to be in a comfortable space and now I'm anxious to get started.

They both follow quickly behind me and as I turn through the doorway, I kick off my shoes while I strip off my shirt, leaving me barefoot in just my joggers.

My thick bulge is easily noticeable behind the grey fabric and I make no point to hide it.

I know it's going to take a while to get him ready, so when they walk into the room, I tilt my chin toward the bed and tell them exactly what I want. "Take care of our girl." My voice is husky and deep. "I want to watch you two before I prep you."

Her eyes connect with mine and she strips her clothes off slowly, seductively. Like she's the one in full control. Who am I kidding? She's always in control when it comes to the two of us.

Ethan shares a look with me that tells me he's thinking the same exact thing, especially as she bends forward, the fabric of her panties trailing down the sides of her legs, before she crawls onto the edge of the bed.

We both have the perfect view of her gorgeous ass, her arousal shines over her folds and I can't help moan at the sight.

On all fours, she crawls forward then flips over on her back.

Ethan wastes no time, ripping the buttons off his shirt as he shrugs it off his shoulders, then pushes his pants down. He presses into the mattress, crawling toward her just as seductively and I take a moment to just watch.

They're so fucking sexy together and I thank my lucky fucking stars they opened up their relationship in a way that makes me feel like it's a fully shaped triangle and not some lopsided third wheel.

She brings me balance and security.

He allows for my unpredictable side that still needs that high, that chase. He's the yin to my yang and I think he needs me as much as I need him.

"Spread your legs for me, baby. I want to see everything while I devour this pretty pussy of yours."

Oh, well isn't he talkative tonight.

The tone of his words send molten hot lava through my bloodstream and my hand reaches for my cock without another thought.

My jaw is slacked and my breath is labored as I stroke myself, base to tip, circling over the crown as he licks and laps at her center. He stops to suck on her clit, using his tongue behind his pursed lips, just to stop again and repeat the process until she's writhing underneath him. She's gripping on to sheets so fucking hard, the whites of her knuckles are glowing against her skin.

I flip open the cap, sure to make as much noise as possible. Ethan looks at me through the corner of his eye, still not stopping that perfect tempo and sequence he's performing. The desire blazing behind his eyes sets me in motion.

He wants this.

He may not beg me with words but his eyes tell me everything.

I line myself up behind him, coating my fingers with the cool liquid and rub between his cheeks.

He hums, his back rounding as he tucks his pelvis.

Leaning forward, my chest lines up against his back, as the underside of my cock rests in the crevice between his cheeks.

"Don't run away from me. It might be a little uncomfortable but I promise you it won't hurt." I lean closer, lowering my voice, "I want to make you feel good," repeating the same statement I whispered through the glory hole wall because I know he trusts me.

Wordlessly, he relaxes, arches his back and the friction of his skin on mine is fucking divine.

I groan, rolling my hips into him before pulling back and pressing my finger to his puckered hole.

He doesn't repel away, instead he pushes back, giving me more, giving me all of him. It makes me feel powerful and trusted, and when he looks back at me with a fire licking behind his pupils I know he's ready.

I press in past my knuckle. His eyes blow wide as his jaw drops. "Oh, fuck, that's good," he groans, turning back to devouring Hannah as if he needs the distraction.

My cock grows impatient and deliciously hard watching her squirm under him as he writhes under me.

I press two fingers in, using the same pace moving in and out before adding a third, using my middle finger to press down toward his belly to find his prostate. Finding the polished tissue, I flick my fingertips deeper and—

"Oh my god, Fuck!" Ethan shouts as he grumbles and he pants heavily into Hannah's thigh, his eyes squeezed tight.

I lean over, looking underneath him and see a strip of cum that decorates the bedsheets.

"Did you just come? I barely touched you," I add, but I know the exact feeling he's experiencing.

"I don't know what happened, it just fucking shot out." I can still hear the surprised tone behind his labored breath.

The first time Celeste touched my prostate it was like a fucking firework exploded inside me and the only exit was through the tip of my cock. She was stroking me at the time though.

I see a hands free orgasm in my man's future and I'm feral at the thought.

He wraps his lips back around Hannah, she grips tightly on his head rolling her hips as she chases her orgasm and, fuck, I want them falling apart at the same time.

I pull out, add even more lube, then press back in finding the same magical spot.

He moans, this time controlling any release but I push in a little deeper and massage the tender spot as I spread my fingers, feeding him so much pleasure the discomfort isn't even a second thought.

"Mmm," he hums, as Hannah tosses her head back, her orgasm slamming into her and the moment she starts to come down, I change my angle.

"Fuuuuuuuuccccckkkkkkk." His cocks spurts underneath him, spraying the white liquid over the dark, satin sheets. He grips his cock, squeezing the shaft hard in an attempt to stop his orgasm. "Fucking Christ. Fuck, Dane. Stop that."

My cock throbs; it always does whenever he calls out my name.

"I need you, need you now," I confess, pulling my fingers out of him as I push him on his side, away from the mess he made and he turns on his back.

His eyes are wide but needy. I can hardly see the rich brown color of his irises, only the pupils blown wide and curious.

I press my knee into the mattress, placing myself between his legs.

"You ready?"

Ethan

Dane's current energy resonates as more of a lion than a man.

His hair—that's grown out quite a bit since the beginning of the year—is wild, mirroring the feral look behind his eyes.

He's desperate, but confident and I don't need him to tell me with words how much he wants me. He's been waiting for this moment and not for the sense of dominance or control but the sense of possession.

Like this is the final act that solidifies our relationship.

"Tap my thigh if you need me to stop," he says, as he presses the head of his cock at my backhole.

Hannah comes to my side, wrapping her hand around my half hard cock, that's partially spent and partially asking for more. I glance down at the stain I made on the sheet and I'm still shocked by my body's reaction when he hit my G-spot.

It was as easy as pressing a button and my cock pulsed with each thrust. I had no control and my mind was just as confused as my body.

The odd sensation of coming without the build up of the orgasm is what makes me feel only half satisfied. So, naturally my cock hardens quickly and easily, as Hannah wraps her lips around the tip and pushes the length down her throat.

It's fucking distracting and it feels like there are a thousand hands all over my body.

Dane groans, then wraps his hands around my hips, changing the angle yet again and his cock slides through the ring of muscle as he slowly presses into me all the way to the hilt.

"You look so good taking my cock. I love taking you in a way no one else has," he says like a confession, claiming me.

I growl, a mix of pleasure and pain, grunting because I've never been good at being quiet. "Fucking fuck." Other profanities my brain can't register fall out of my lips as he pistons in and out and Hannah bobs up and down. The way they're both taking me, the way they're claiming me, is more than I can handle.

I'm sitting at a constant state of the peak of my orgasm, and with every pass Dane's cock makes over my prostate, it creates trust issues with myself.

I won't be able to hold back.

I have zero faith in my dick. Dane's fingers obliterated every ounce of my confidence.

They both hold the control that I've always needed and I hold my head up to look between the two of them.

There's a carnal look behind Dane's eyes and I know he's hanging on by a thread. His sharp jaw slacked, brows furrowed, abs flexing, all signs of how he's teetering on the edge. His hands grip my legs hard as he moans and I love the sounds of his desperation.

Hannah looks up at me, her mouth full of my cock with those gorgeous crystal blue eyes swimming with lust and I'm no longer a man. I'm only part of a soul that needs these two to survive, to make me feel whole.

I have no idea what the hell to do with my hands; I reach down, slipping my finger between Hannah's wet lips. Still swollen from when I feasted on her.

My finger moves quickly over her clit and the vibration of her throat around my cock is all I need to send me over the edge.

Reaching up, I take a hold of the side of Dane's head, his

hair interlacing between my fingers, needing some kind of control.

Hannah's lips pop off my cock and she replaces it with her hand, the shaft thick and wet, pulsing underneath her perfect grip.

"Fuck, I'm close," My teeth grind together as Dane's cock begins to pulse in my ass.

"Fuck," he groans as he throws his head back then dips his gaze back to mine. "I'm coming and you're going to take every drop of my cum." He leans forward, our chests slap together and he tucks his face into the crook of my neck, gritting through his orgasm.

His teeth sink into the flesh of my collarbone and he grunts loud, emptying himself inside me, and I lose it.

My ass clenches, tightening around Dane's cock and I know the moment he feels it because his mouth falls open and he shouts, "Fuuuuuckkkk."

His cock pistons harder, forcing more cum out of my cock. It sprays out in waves between us, landing on Hannah's hand, my stomach, and his glistening abs, layered with a sweat and now my cum.

It feels like a never-ending high and one I never want to come down from.

"That was out of this fucking world."

I hardly heard what he said with the whooshing of my racing heartbeat in my ears.

A comfortable silence passes between all of us, until of course Dane breaks it.

"We're so fucking doing that again. Every day, twice a day is acceptable, I think."

Hannah's body vibrates with laughter and I manage to chuckle out an exhausted breath.

"Is that right?"

"Did you like it?" I ask Hannah, running my hands through her hair.

"Loved it. So much."

"Hannah approves, it's settled," Dane quips before I can say anything.

"You bit me." I crane my chin trying to look at the red, flared mark, somewhere between my neck and shoulder.

Dane glances over his shoulder, looking at the one I gave him months ago.

"Couldn't help myself." He smiles. "But I know exactly what to do with that."

I whiplash my head in his direction. Shaking my head. "No, nope. Not gonna happen."

Hannah lifts her head, gazing up at me with those gorgeous ocean eyes and fucking hell, I already know I've lost.

Two hours later, I'm leaving the tattoo parlor, inked with Dane's bite mark on my neck and my two favorite people on each side of me and I'm loving what our future looks like.

"Hey you guys, Kobi's calling!" I call out toward the hall as I finish plating our omelets.

Yes, I'm cooking if you can believe it. I hardly believe it myself considering I haven't even had a permanent residence with a kitchen for as long as I can remember.

Cooking breakfast for my favorite people is absolutely my new favorite hobby. And frankly speaking, pancakes and eggs are my jam and mine are fucking delicious.

Picking up the kitchen towel, I wipe off my hands and pick up my buzzing phone accepting the video call.

Kobi's face comes into view just as Hannah and Ethan sit down at the kitchen island.

Well, Ethan sits on the stool. Hannah, presses her arms into the countertop and props up on it and it's my favorite place for her ass to sit.

Other than on my—

"Hey, Kobi!" Ethan says, excitedly. It's night and day different compared to how he used to greet, well, everyone. But that's his new normal. Waking up excited to go to the field, craving the game like he used to.

Plus Hannah and Ethan have joined me on my weekly catch up calls with Kobi so they've gotten to know each other pretty well, even with the ocean between us.

Hannah waves into the phone as I hold it high and far to get us all on the screen.

"Hey guys." Kobi gives us a two finger wave and his demeanor is a bit more serious than usual.

"Everything okay?" I ask, immediately sensing something is off.

"Oh, yeah, yeah. Everything's fine. I just wanted to find out what your plans were for the summer because I've got something that's come up here. It's…putting quite a wrench in things."

I suppose being the right hand man and translator to the Japanese Prime Minister will have some *wrenches*.

"Actually," I say, "we're staying in Seattle for the summer because Ethan's schedule follows the Smashers and they'll play through October—if they make the playoffs. We're planning to spend the holidays in Europe instead."

Looking at their faces in the tiny video box, both are smiling because Ethan's got time off between the season, before he starts as Head Analyst for the team and Hannah has a six week sabbatical anytime she chooses to use it between November and January from VB Tech.

Kismet if I don't say so myself.

I'm consulting for VB Technologies as well and working daily with Hannah is by far the my favorite job I've ever had.

"Oh, nice. That works out well then," Kobi says, "I—" He glances over his shoulder at no one. "I'll be in the states for the summer."

I'm excited about this unexpected news because I can easily visit him wherever he might be, but I furrow my brows as I appraise his facial expression that looks more concerned than delighted.

He normally loves coming home and spending an extended amount of time here.

"That's great news!" When he doesn't react, I add, "Right?"

Hannah senses it as well, tilting her head to get a better look at him.

"Yeah, no. It's great. It's just, it's for work. We're doing another US Tour."

I nod, a long, slow nod. That's not unusual either. "With the Prime Minister, I assume?" I chuckle at how coy and awkward he's being.

He pinches his brow, squeezing his eyes shut, then looks back at us huffing out a long breath.

"No... with the Prime Minister's daughter."

THE END

Balance of Power
Book 5
Kobi's book

Coming soon....

THANK YOU FOR READING!!
I am a self-published author. If you loved this book, please
consider taking the time to leave a review as it helps me
tremendously!

www.berlinwick.com
Please sign up for my newsletter to keep up to date on my
upcoming releases and receive exclusive content!

ACKNOWLEDGEMENTS

I'm writing this on January 1st, 2026. So, I just spent the last week reminiscing on the successes and failures of 2025. I had many of both, but 2025 brought me so much love for this authoring journey.

I met so many amazing readers and friends this year with the same love for reading and writing that I have and I realized having that type of community is truly a blessing.

If you're reading this book, it's more than likely because you found me through some sort of social media platform or referred by another one of your reading cohorts and I can't tell you how thankful I am for each and every single reader that picks up my book.
Thank you. Thank you. Thank you. I am beyond grateful!

I need to acknowledge my fabulous beta readers: Kelly, Susan and Tyleigh. I can't express my gratitude for the time and energy you put in for me and I am so thankful for that. You're kind, honest and loving and I am so lucky!!

My amazing proofreaders; Taylor, Elysia, Shae, Michelle S., Inge, Jessica, Michelle M., Danielle and Becca. You ladies are gems!! Thank you for helping me perfect Dane's story.

I hired a PA this year! I'm beyond blessed that I'm at a point in my authoring career to feel like I needed this and met someone so wonderful who fits with me perfectly. Jamie… this book is out sooner than expected because of everything you've taken off my plate. You are a genius and I adore you so much.

To the anonymous individual who let me pick your brain about glory holes. Couldn't have written that chapter without you! I have such a wonderful support system in my world. Not only from my author group with my twin souls in authoring, but my friends and family who provide me the patience, love and judgment-free zone I need to spend time with my fictional characters. I can't express in words how fortunate I am to have that kind of support because I know some people don't.

I have written down a laundry list of goals for 2026… some of them completely delusional! I hit a couple of delusional goals in 2025 and completely missed the mark on others, but hey, manifesting and trying to keep your goals in front of you will help challenge you in more ways that you could ever imagine. I wish for all of you to surpass one of your delulu goals this year!

For anyone that listened to me talk about this book, or just authoring in general. To those that have supported me on socials or in person. To my husband who shows me more love than I could ever dream of. To my boys who bring me so much laughter and joy. I am so grateful for you and your support.

And finally, for Gina Celeste. I think you'd be proud of me, bestie.

XOXO,
Berlin

OTHER BOOKS BY BERLIN WICK

<u>BALANCE OF POWER SERIES</u>

The Secrets We Hide
Jake, Elena and Christian's Story
An MFM Voyeur Husband Billionaire Romance

The Promises We Break
Hudson and Ember's Story
A drunken Vegas wedding turned marriage of convenience.

The Games We Play
Seamus and Mimi's story
A neighbors-to-lovers, second chance romance

<u>STANDALONE</u>

LETTUCE TURNIP THE BEET
An MMFM Firefighter Reverse Harem

Truth or Dare?
Truth.
Have you ever played Guess Who while blindfolded with three irresistible firemen?
Not yet...

ABOUT THE AUTHOR

Berlin was raised in a tiny town in North Idaho who moved to the Bay Area, California, at the age of eighteen. She now resides in San Diego with her husband, two boys and her massive Cane Corso named Blu! Her bucket list items include skydiving, attending the Oscars, becoming a New York Times best-selling author, and cruising the world for retirement. She loves writing and reading, ANY and ALL kinds of romance novels, and loves engaging in the booksta community. You can find her most active on Instagram!